The Society of Sin

To see was not to believe. You would only be witnessing a gathering of ladies who, to the untrained eye, expressed all the gentle virtuous qualities so beloved of their gentler sex. But, were you to creep a little closer, were you able to listen and to feel, to touch and to taste and to inhale you, too, would have succumbed to intoxication and the subversive spirit fermented within. Here were fear and danger, wrapped tightly for their own safekeeping and folded neatly like starched Sunday best. Nobody would have suspected.

What they had in common was a desire to prise open their own Pandora's box even though they were all aware that once the lid had been unlocked it could never, ever be slammed shut. Some had come only to observe, some to satisfy their curiosity but others were willing to totally immerse themselves in passion and desire.

The Society of Sin
Sian Lacey Taylder

BLACK LACE

Black Lace books contain sexual fantasies.
In real life, always practise safe sex.

First published in 2006 by
Black Lace
Thames Wharf Studios
Rainville Road
London W6 9HA

SetSystems Ltd, Saffron Walden, Essex
Printed and bound by Mackays of Chatham PLC

ISBN 0 352 34080 0
ISBN 978 0 352 34080 1

Prologue

I am trying hard not to apportion blame and, at the same time, trying hard to assuage my own guilt. I am perfectly aware that she and she alone should bear responsibility for the events of the summer but I cannot bring myself to condemn her outright; I will not be the one to cast the first stone. The letter arrived yesterday; I knew immediately who it was from and realised that, for my own safety, it had to be hidden so it lay unopened under my pillow until darkness provided the protection I needed to break the seal. She asked, once more, for forgiveness but that was quite impossible; to forgive would have been an admission of wrongdoing on both our parts.

My trembling fingers ripped the envelope apart. I turned the lamp low and began to read:

Chilcombe Lacey
Wednesday, 12 September 1876

My dear Charlotte
As I have received no reply to any of my previous letters I have little hope in hearing from you again. But you know me! 'A woman of persistence', is that not how I was once memorably described? By the vicar, I think, though I don't suppose he meant it as a compliment.

The village feels empty without you; I seem to spend most of my waking days wandering through the valley, always looking for you, even though I know you are not there. Emma tells me I sleep too much, she has even offered to fetch the doctor but what potion can he possibly prescribe to cure me of lovesickness? No, it is more than mere heartbreak. I'm suffering from a madness, dear Charlotte; the madness of desire. You are my obsession; you inhabit my dreams and walk into my nightmares. I smell your sweat on the morning dew and everywhere, everywhere, I sense the darkness of your eyes and the soft sheen of your flesh. I am, even now, looking out the window to see the contours of your body carved into the valley and hills.

They have all gone, all except Emma; pursued and dispersed. Even you have forsaken me but I understand that I have only myself to blame. You were the special one, my purest disciple. The others I can live without but not you; without you I only exist.

Forgive me, please, my dear Charlotte. You know where I am; come to me, come to me before I am lost in the labyrinths of lovelessness.

Your ever-loving fellow scholar

P

1

It had not always been thus. Indeed, at the very genesis of our relationship it was quite the other way round. I can still remember when I first caught sight of her, a month after arriving to spend the summer with my father in Chilcombe Bredy. Having passed the winter months in more agreeable Mediterranean climes, the prospect of a wet English summer was beginning to depress me. Indeed, I was already planning a return passage and concocting an excuse for my father. At the time I was naive enough to consider it nothing more than fate; I learnt later that she'd been watching me for days and that, once she had baited her honeytrap, I would, sooner or later, be devoured.

When the weather finally let up I took advantage of the sunshine to take leave of the company of my father's housekeeper who had been entertaining me with the local gossip. I'd been sitting at the table, watching her prepare lunch and listening to rain pounding hard on the window. I was lacing up my boots, expressing a wish to explore my new surroundings when she turned on her heels, eyes blazing at me.

'You might be a headstrong young lady, Miss Crowsettle, and I daresay you will have had your fill of danger but let me warn you, here and now, that there are places, even in this valley, where a woman ought not to roam.'

My ears pricked; there is nothing I like more than indulging myself in that which has specifically been proscribed. 'What on earth do you mean, Mrs Bexington? Surely Chilcombe Bredy is one of the safest places on Earth?'

'Well may you mock me, miss, but you take heed of my words and keep well away from Chilcombe Lacey estate. There are strange goings-on there and the "lady of the house" – well, she is no "lady", make no mistake. Only a year ago she had a mother, a father and two brothers; within months they were dead. All of them. I am not one to spread rumours, Miss Charlotte, but what happens there – well, 'tis not right; 'tis not natural. The place is cursed.'

I dismissed Mrs Bexington's warning as idle chitchat; when I related her advice to my father he burst out laughing. 'My dear Charlotte, you of all people should know that there's nothing so vacillating as the mind of the English peasant; they're terrified of change, especially when it comes in the form of a woman. I'm sure the new occupant of Chilcombe Lacey is a charming lady, though I have yet to make her acquaintance.'

'Then how do you account for the deaths of her parents and brothers? Mere coincidence? Perhaps Mrs Bexington was right, Chilcombe Lacey is cursed.'

My father, Sir Napier Crowsettle, smiled; however much I sought to challenge received opinion, I was still, in his eyes, very much a child. 'That, Charlotte, is hardly a rational explanation. It is the kind of uninformed opinion I would expect from our neighbours, not an intelligent young woman like you. Coincidence? I would imagine so. The deaths were investigated by my good friend Inspector Lefebure; nothing untoward was found. Fate, my dear, is a cruel mistress, as I am sure you will learn one day.'

I knew I was being patronised and I liked it not one bit. He was, of course, right; I considered myself a product of the Age of Reason and despised those who succumbed to superstition. But I also liked nothing better than a good mystery, so I told myself there was no smoke without fire and, as the sun emerged from the clouds, set off in the direction of Chilcombe Lacey.

The River Bride was in full flow, its clear chalk waters winding their way through the village to the sea and, here and there, spilling over on to the thick green pasture. The Chase rose above, dark and brooding in the haze. Mrs Bexington had reluctantly given me directions but geography has never been my forte and I was soon toiling, hopelessly lost, knee deep in mud. I failed to notice her until she was directly in front of me, towering above my supplicant form; to the unknowing observer I might well have been a devotee genuflecting at the feet of my very own personal goddess.

For that is how she first appeared to me: an apparition emerging from the ether, a phantasmal figure concocted from hot sun and moist air. It was only when she spoke that I recognised her as a living, breathing human being, my sight stolen by her lips, blood red as poppies in late summer. There was a flash of light, for a split second the Earth spun off its axis and inverted natural law, that eternal conflict between good and evil which, for the most part, governs our lives. I was immediately, irretrievably addicted, standing before her, head bowed, like a docile mute.

'I do believe you are trespassing, Miss Crowsettle. Have they not told you how I deal with intruders?'

She was smiling, but it was a thin and dangerous smile. Her voice was like the crack of a whip cutting through the heat; authority oozed from each and every pore and embraced me like a mist rolling in from the damp declivities of the Atlantic Ocean.

'Come along, my child. Have you not got a tongue

in your head? I've heard an awful lot about you, I do hope you're not going to disappoint.'

It wasn't the first time I'd encountered power; it had manifested itself in numerous guises in a constant attempt to consume or subjugate me. I am proud to say that I never gave in, that I had always held out against the sweetest temptation, for I'd always seen through its ambiguity. Until now; Lady P descended into my life like an angel from heaven, smothered me with affection until she considered me ripe.

And when I was ripe she plucked me.

13 June 1876
Chilcombe Bredy

Dear Diary
Do you believe in God? I have never professed to but I think I now understand what is meant by divine revelation. I think I also understand the nature of perfection because, this morning, it appeared before me.

You must think me crazy; I have never talked like this before, have I? That is because I have never felt like this before, I have never allowed myself to feel this way before and I'm not sure I can cope with it. It is, I am sure, unnatural. Should that concern me or should I throw caution to the wind and let the emotions sweep me away.

I dreamt of her last night. Imagine that! I have known her less than 24 hours and already she has invaded my most intimate territories – not that I am complaining.

I dreamt of her this morning, too. She had me by the wrists but what she was doing to my poor body I cannot for the life of me remember. No! That is not true. Much as I wanted to turn my head and shut

*my eyes blind shut, I was drawn to what should have
remained unseen; a fatal attraction.*

*Is this where madness begins? Do you think they
will lock me up? If I tell them I could not help myself,
would they forgive me? But it is not as though I do
not want it to happen. Far from fighting against it, I
am inviting it in.*

But it was only a dream, dear diary.

Only a dream?

Attired in a riding habit that represented the epitome
of cultivated elegance, she cut a fine figure in her
tailored costume of deepest emerald and silk top hat. I
am used to continental haute couture but her lean,
understated, almost masculine simplicity was a fashion I had never set eyes on before. The severe cut of
her jacket, the full flow of her skirts and the riding
crop she brandished in her left hand all combined to
give her the appearance of being, at one and the same
time, both martinet and benign dictator. She was one
of those women for whom the description 'handsome'
was particularly apt; tall and slender (had she been
poorer I would have called her 'scrawny'), she was
blessed (some might say cursed) with looks that were
distinctly non-Anglo-Saxon. From her uncovered face
her skin radiated a Mediterranean hue that, framed by
a cascade of curled black tresses, seemed to suck in the
light surrounding her. Her angular physique might
have made her appear clumsy had she not carried
herself with a self-reverent dignity that warranted
unconditional respect.

It was only when she leant forwards and proffered
me her hand that I finally summoned the wherewithal
to respond, albeit in a nervous stammer. For some
reason it seemed appropriate to curtsey.

'Please forgive me ... madam ... I am new to the village ... and ... I appear to be lost ... I had no intention of straying on to your property ... I am truly sorry for any damage I've done ... I'm sure my father will compensate you ...'

Though clearly taking great pleasure in my discomfort, she had become accustomed to both men and women falling for her charm; her frown crumbled as she took pity on me. 'Yes, yes, yes. I know full well who you are, Miss Crowsettle. My spies have been abroad and I have been doing my research. You have just returned from Spain where you were governess to the Duchess of Crewkerne.' She tilted her head to one side, her smile took on a more ominous form. 'Very impressive, Miss Crowsettle. Now, I hear you are fluent in both Spanish and French, two languages I would very much like to learn. Perhaps you could teach me; you must lack sophisticated company as much as I.'

'I would consider it a great honour, madam.'

'And so would I, Miss Crowsettle. But please, much as I appreciate your subservience I do not really think it becomes you. I have heard that you are quite the upstart. So, are you a rebel tamed or a rebel without a cause? No! Don't tell me. I would very much like to find out myself. You have heard of me?'

'Forgive me, madam, but are you not the owner of Chilcombe Lacey? Whom the villagers sometimes call "Lady P"?'

'"Lady P"!' She laughed. 'Well, I ought to inform you, Miss Crowsettle, that I have been called much worse.' She paused for a second, ruminating. 'Much, much worse. Insults I am sure that even you have never heard, let alone would comprehend. Remind me to tell you one day. A woman of your substance should really understand the fine art of abuse. But I suspect the inhabitants are too simple to utter anything more obscene, unless it's in the secrecy of their own hearts and minds. I made sure I put the fear of God into them the moment I set foot in the valley. Lady P to them, Lady Persephone de Mortehoe to members of respectable society, Percy to my friends, who largely aren't – members of respectable society, that is. But you are, Miss Crowsettle; so I shall have to mind my Ps and Qs.'

She used her words like a cat uses its claws, amusing herself with her victim's discomfort, not allowing it the assured certainty of either pain or pleasure. I cared not; she could maltreat me as much as she wished. She was a woman I aspired to. I wanted her to teach me no matter how much it might hurt.

'Lady Persephone . . .'

'Come, come, Miss Crowsettle. Intransigence is a wonderful virtue but, by the same token, friends should know when to lower their defences. I do not seek a companion; Emma entertains me whenever I am bored. You have chosen me as much as I have chosen you. We will address one another as "Percy" and "Charlotte", no matter how impertinent that might seem to others.'

With her gloved hand she reached out and grabbed my wrist, drawing me firmly towards her. I flinched; no woman (or indeed man) had ever touched me with such tactile vigour but I allowed her to manhandle me from the filthy puddle which had dirtied my skirts to the relative safety of green grass and dry land. Gesturing towards her trap, she gently entwined her arm within mine.

'I daresay Mrs Bexington has already been counselling against me. What do you think, Charlotte? Am I the ogress she described? But you're not like them, are you? You are an intelligent young woman; you are capable of coming to your own conclusions without listening to hearsay.'

'I barely know Mrs Bexington, Lady Persephone ... I mean, Percy. But then again, having only just made your acquaintance, I barely know you.'

'And your father? What was his response to his housekeeper's half-truths? He took a more rational view, I would imagine.'

'Indeed he does. he more or less told me to ignore them.'

'I am sure your father is a shrewd judge of character. He is, after all, one of the few members of society to have earned his status on merit rather than breeding.' She eased me up into the carriage and, as I sat there in the full glare of the sun, I watched her shadow leap out from behind her and disappear into the ether. There were two sides to Lady P, the kind and the malevolent, and I never learnt to recognise which was in the ascendance. She could switch from one to the other, swivel between alarming degrees of intensity, all within the passage of a single second.

'Now, I am sure both your father and Mrs Bexington would rather I took you home; all the paths are under water. If you wait a few days I will accompany you on a tour of the valley and the Chase. I shall ask Emma to make us a picnic; she might even like to come herself.'

Lady P carefully straightened the minute, barely noticeable creases in her long black velvet gloves. She was a perfectionist – is still a perfectionist – who would not be seen with a single lock of hair deviating from its allocated position. I watched as the whip descended on the rear of the piebald mare who immediately understood its authority. And that's what it was – an assertion of power; a light blow that the animal would have barely felt but therein lay the enigma of her superiority. Lady P had done little more than flick her wrist but even this casual act was carried out with supreme grace and refinement. The midday sun was stiflingly warm; the gentle roll of the carriage lulled me into a sweet daze, the content of which would have unnerved me had I not been sitting right next to its source. I was wondering how it might feel, trying to imagine exposing my naked flesh to the elegant cruelty of the whip; in Lady P's hands it seemed more an instrument of pleasure than pain. My reverie was disturbed, perhaps fortunately, as the trap shuddered to a halt outside my father's cottage.

'Whoa, Tully!' she called out to her horse. 'We had better return Miss Crowsettle home before her dreams turn to nightmares.' She turned to me. 'Did you sleep well, Charlotte? Perhaps you should take more heed of Mrs Bexington's advice; Ashley Chase is no place for a woman to wander alone but the dangers are in her own head, of her own imagination. There is, after all, no smoke without fire. Farewell, my sweet. You will come, I hope, at my request.'

My eyes were still half-closed but I could feel the sweetness of her breath, laced with garlands of flowers, as she reached over to kiss my cheeks. I must have blushed for she laughed and, in a moment of pure mischief, placed her lips over mine and puckered up.

Even at that relatively tender age I had, on my travels, seen more than my fair share of scandal and shame. I was, in short, no innocent but even the experienced have their limits. Whatever her intentions, Lady P's advances were too much for my poor little heart and I fled, in tears, from the trap. I could hear her laughter even as I dragged my muddy skirts up the stairs, could still hear it when darkness fell and I slipped into reverie.

I wondered, for the remainder of the day, why Lady P had referred to Mrs Bexington's gossip as half-truths and had not bothered to refute them. 'No smoke without fire,' she had said; 'no smoke without fire'. All evening I dwelt upon her words, trying to unravel their significance. I've never believed in the gift of hindsight, much in the same way that, until recently, I've never felt the need to regret but in retrospect it seems clear to me that I was in blissful self-denial.

The subconscious had assumed control. Mrs Bexington looked on with a self-righteous concern she would have communicated to my father had he not, thank goodness, departed for Exeter to spend the weekend with his friend and mentor, Professor Samuel Walditch. I suppose, had he been there that afternoon, had he not spent so much of the following weeks in the company of the professor, I might never have fallen under her influence with such gusto. For all my 22 years I was still impressionable, some would say vulnerable. Mrs Bexington was not the first to question the lack of discipline that characterised my motherless childhood and on more than one occasion she reached instinctively for the wooden ladle which served no purpose other than that for which it was designed. She knew full well that, however much my father valued her, if she so much as raised her voice to me she would be dismissed.

Exhausted by emotion, I retired as soon as a cool evening breeze, blowing down from the Chase, had overpowered the heat of the day but if I had hoped to find respite between the starched cotton sheets I was very much mistaken. Perhaps I should have kept the casement locked tight, sealed myself in against the nameless dangers of the night. I could have sworn that is exactly what I did but, at some point, as the last midnight chime rang around the surrounding hills, my waiflike figure arose and unlatched the window. When I was woken by Mrs Bexington rapping frantically on my bedroom door the sun was streaming in through billowing curtains.

'Miss Charlotte! Miss Charlotte! Are you in there? Are you ill? Open up! Please . . .'

Down in the village the clock was striking eleven, drowning out her anxious cries. I barely heard them, anyway, crawling from the bed in a semi-comatose trance and dropping like a stone to the floor. From that morning onwards I ceased to exist in a wholly lucid world; I had transgressed into a distorted reality where the sacred and the profane were gloriously subverted and decadence held sway. Lying there on the floor, I felt myself fading once more into the half-light.

I was back in the world of my childhood. A balmy summer's evening in the garden from where, unsupervised by my father, I was wont to stray. I waded through the thick grasses and high bracken, allowing them to induce within me a lethargy that seeped like an elixir into each and every limb. I had the whole valley to myself. I lay down amongst the poppies and ferns to daydream. All was still, perfectly, sumptuously still; the hot sun beat down, pollen drifted down from the surrounding foliage, the baking scent of young bracken wafted over from the thick hedgerow and I was lulled deliciously into a deep sleep.

I dreamt of nectar, of wandering into the thickest of forests and drinking from fragrant, fast-flowing streams. The aroma went straight to my head and I danced to a tune created by the rustle of the leaves in a light breeze, a wild, inharmonious waltz that dragged me into the bushes from where I emerged ambrosial, covered with blossom. As I whirled around like a dervish something began to arouse deep inside of me, not, this time, the pit of my stomach where guilt curdles but a gentle stirring between my legs that swelled as my gyrations increased. Suddenly, the globe ceased to spin beneath my feet and silence plunged over the trees. My head spun and I came to. The rays of sun breaking through the eaves spread themselves out luxuriously over my body and danced over bare flesh. I lay hot and dishevelled, panting, clothes wrapped around my sweat-soaked body. Something moist oozed out from within, a warm, viscous lake of molten lava whose source I was unaware of. Had I known it was a sin I would have cared not a jot. I was vaguely conscious of having encountered the forbidden but I never quite managed to comprehend the exact nature of my misdemeanour and I certainly had no idea of its position in the grand progression of depravity.

With an impressive display of strength, Mrs Bexington burst through the door and found me draped over the couch, my knickers cast aside, the skirts of my nightdress hoisted up to my waist to reveal a patch of damp, discoloured cotton twisted around my thighs. No longer pure white, the stain might be removed but my soul was irretrievably despoiled. Poor Mrs Bexington. She was not an overtly pious woman and knew more about life than she let on but this vision was too much for her delicate constitution. She was carrying, in one hand, an envelope which she tore in two and let float to the floor before turning on her heels and fleeing, never to be seen again. I later heard that she spent the remainder of the week within the virtuous seclusion of the vicarage, waiting for my father to return to lecture him on my moral deficiencies. I do wonder what might have happened had he not been so engrossed in his volume of local geology, which had so impressed Professor Walditch that he hoped his university might publish it. As a child I had valued his long periods of absence; they fostered within me a spirit of independence I am sure my father approved of. Now, whilst my contemporaries were contemplating the prospect of a lifetime imprisoned in marriage, I was blossoming into something quite resplendently different. Some would have called me a she-devil, the very likeness of Eve herself. I, on the other hand, considered myself an angel devoted to the expression of liberty but liberty, like desire, was a word I worshipped without really understanding its consequences.

Mrs Bexington's distress was infectious. I scrabbled around frantically, gathering together the various torn pieces and placing them lovingly together. It was, as I expected, a communication from Lady P; a letter I had been both anticipating and dreading.

Chilcombe Lacey
13 June 1876

Dear Charlotte
I would be delighted to have the pleasure of your company for tea this afternoon at four o'clock. My maidservant, Emma, will call at a quarter to four; please oblige me by accompanying her.

Yours
Percy

Short, concise and to the point; its ominous inference in words that were unwritten. She left me no option but to comply, did not even offer me the opportunity to decline though I already feared the consequences had I possessed the temerity to do so. I made absolutely certain that by the appointed time I was standing at the door, scrubbed and clothed in my best frock.

To be perfectly honest I did not possess a best frock. A mere governess rarely has the opportunity let alone the financial wherewithal to take an interest in fashion and for me, free from the tyranny of organised religion, each day of the week was much the same as the others. The day had turned warm and sunny once again and from my limited wardrobe I selected an outfit that seemed appropriate: white and, perhaps subconsciously, innocent. When Emma appeared at the gate I could immediately sense her disdain. She raised her nose as if to 'tut-tut' then appeared to think better of it. It was most unusual behaviour for a servant and, even though I had always opposed the hierarchical status quo, it ill-behoved a maid to act above her station.

It took me a while to understand that Emma was a 'servant' in name only. It was a role she played in accordance with her mistress's desires and her own inclinations. Indeed, her very voice and demeanour suggested that she was born of better stock than myself and might not have looked out of place at Lady P's side rather than at her feet.

Her 'uniform', for a start, seemed quite inappropriate, more coachman than chambermaid. It was the first time I had ever set eyes upon a woman dressed in trousers. I ought to have approved but I was, even then, suffering the first stirrings of a counter revolution. She did at least manage a semblance of a bow although it might as well have been an act of mockery, Emma was a woman whose respect had to be earned, not blithely assumed.

'Miss Crowsettle? Miss Charlotte Crowsettle? I have

been sent to collect you. Would you care to come with me?'

A legitimate member of the serving classes would have stood aside and followed in my wake. Emma barely hesitated before striding out boldly before me, as well she might in her smart black breeches. My dainty boots – a pathetic attempt at femininity – permitted me only to hobble along behind her and, as she opened the door for me to climb aboard the trap, I was acutely aware of my vulnerability.

14 June 1876
Chilcombe Bredy

Dear Diary
What time is it? I can barely bring myself to look at the clock; the midnight chime sounded more like the toll of bells at a wake but that, I think, was many hours ago. Does Lady P have the power even to slow the passage of the night to drag out its most secret pleasures?

I would not put it past her.

For a woman who claimed no prior knowledge of language she picked her way through a series of Spanish, French and Italian texts with great aplomb. She denied any previous experience, pretending to have acquired a smattering of Latin and Greek when studying science. She was too smart to allow an uncharacteristic slip of the tongue; I'm sure she erred deliberately when casually admitting to a word-for-word familiarity with the Catechism of the Roman Catholic Church immediately after denying any dalliance with the Christian faith. That is exactly how she weaves her subversive spells, creating an aura of mystery by constantly contradicting herself.

My grasp of Mediterranean wines impressed her, we had sampled several bottles by the time the sun sat like a glowing orb over the woods of Ashley Chase but as the shadows set we turned to the gin. I had only once flirted with inebriation, at the farewell party my father threw for me the previous summer. Now, heady with the scent of freshly mown grass, the intoxication was absolute. We had, in turn, discussed politics, philosophy and science, or rather, Lady P lectured me on their fundamentals whilst I nodded as and when appropriate.

What else? What else? I am trying so hard to piece together the events of the night, the early morning, the very rich hours. I can remember little, just the moment when time slipped away between us. Under the soft glow of the dim lights in the warm darkness the glowing embers of her eyes reached deep into me and discovered some hitherto unknown interior that, beyond hard, high mountains and waterless deserts, might well be lush and fertile.

She was sepulchral and grand, a tabernacle wherein dwelt all that was unholy and all that was divine. Whenever she moved a riot of scarlet rose into the space around her and flickered in dancing moonbeams, as if she were standing by a roaring fire. Her curls, blacker than any abyss I have passed through, attracted every particle of light in the vicinity and banished darkness to the extent that a halo seemed to glow around her. She put her arm around me, ruffled my hair and placed her lips on mine.

What I have I done? Where has she left me? Stuck fast halfway between love and desire? She tapped into my veins, exploited my weakness with tart words. The eyes, the splendid grin of cold steel.

But it was not her arms I woke in. Of that much I am, at least, certain.

2

I can remember that night quite clearly, recall almost every changing shadow as the sun vanished behind a bank of thick cloud. Black and full of woe.

The rain. It was the last of the summer or rather the last of my own private summer that came shuddering to a halt in a similar cloudburst. The lightning flashed across our faces, lit up her eyes before the guilt came, pounding hard on my soft little soul.

In the absence of a housekeeper the letter lay undisturbed. Indeed, it had slid under the doormat and, had I not slipped precariously on Mrs Bexington's immaculately polished floor, I might not have come across it for days.

Would that I had not. What might and might not have come to pass – no, I can't bear thinking about it, either.

The envelope was dry, crisp but perfumed. The scent I vaguely recognised; I'm sure the Condesa Dolores de Orgaz had been wearing something similar when I was introduced to her at the Lenten Ball in Cartagena. It was barely three months ago but, her beauty being as overpowering as her scent, I could remember it still. Until that moment I had steadfastly refused to subjugate myself to my so-called superiors but the Condesa exuded an elegance I had never previously encountered and, I assumed (and perhaps hoped), had long since ceased to exist. In Cartagena I left behind the drab décor of English society and caught a glimpse of the decadence that

I simultaneously despised and desired. I fell into a deep curtsey and she graciously acknowledged her triumph.

It was only a glimpse. Lady P offered the whole glorious vision in a riot of colour, safe in the knowledge that I was unable to resist temptation.

Chilcombe Lacey
14 June 1876

My dear Charlotte
What delightful company you were last night. I confess to being utterly charmed by your mere presence, let alone your exquisite wit and repartee. Emma tells me you are very much your father's child and I trust her judgement of character above all others – with the obvious exception of myself.

Oh, how time drags. I am awaiting the arrival of another dear friend who, it appears, has been delayed on the Weymouth train. Perhaps you are acquainted with her work? The famous poetess Samantha Poorton?

Are you free this evening? I do not want to monopolise your friendship but one night in your presence was quite insufficient and I cannot wait to see you again. Furthermore, I would very much like you to meet Miss Poorton. We will be dining at eight. I shall despatch Emma to collect you at six. I understand that your father is away on business and Mrs Bexington, God bless her soul, has unexpectedly taken leave of her duties so it seems fate has, for once, conspired in our favour. Samantha and I talk long into the night, more often than not until the very break of dawn so I shall not have to worry about incurring your guardians' wrath.

Until tonight, my sweet
Percy

I read the letter over and over again, focusing, once more, not on what she had written but what she had, by omission, tacitly implied. Her handwriting was, in itself, a work of fine art I would have framed and hung alongside Velasquez in El Prado. Despite the absence of my father and Mrs Bexington I secreted the letter in my wardrobe trying, perhaps, to keep it a secret even from myself.

A desultory sun cast its prying eye over the Chase and into every corner of the valley revealing in its wake the vices of the guilty and the virtues of the innocent. All that had been hitherto hidden was now laid bare; what is, what was to be and what might have been had cruel circumstance not sought fit to intervene.

I wandered aimlessly from room to room but wherever I went the stultifying heat followed. The past, they say, is another country threatening to invade and colonise the present. The truth was baying for blood, crying out for revelation. I opened my diary and gave it a voice.

14 June 1876
Chilcombe Bredy

Dear Diary
His name was Mario, or so he told me. I never doubted him, not even when the innkeeper let slip a sly smile and addressed him as 'Don Rogelio'. It was not that I implicitly trusted him; rather that I tried hard to convince myself that his intentions were honourable when it was blatantly obvious that they were anything but. Yes, I was naive but naivety is no excuse. I had seen enough to know the difference between right and wrong. Until that night I remained an innocent but I was far from being free

from sin. What does it say in the Good Book? 'If your eye should cause you to sin, tear it out; it is better for you to enter into the kingdom of God with one eye than to have two eyes and be thrown into hell.' My body was chaste but only for the want of opportunity; if my hands were clean, my roving eyes were already stained with wicked blasphemies.

He spoke not a word of English, at least that is what he told me and I suppose I was grateful for that; it made the whole messy business a lot less complicated. He spoke not a word of English yet I could swear he cried out 'Rebecca' in his moment of ecstasis. It was the scream of the devil birds mating over the rooftops of Cartagena. From the moment I set eyes upon him I was aware that love was not his motivation, that I was the latest in a long line of conquests. Perhaps, when the truth finally dawned upon me, when he had breached every barrier of trust I had placed in his way, I should have turned my back and refused to take any further part in our sordid encounter but I cannot even make the excuse of succumbing to force.

He had been spinning yarns that were becoming every more grandiose and improbable but I am a fool for romance and, cradled in his arms, watching his fingers encroaching upon my virgin territory, I would have believed him the very conquistador himself. In the space of a mere ten minutes he had promoted himself from cabin boy on a Catalan freighter to one of Admiral Pasqual Cervera's most loyal captains.

With the only Anglican service in Cartagena commencing at three in the afternoon and lasting a good two hours, I was still in my Sunday frock. My employer (some would say 'mistress' but I deferred to her in nothing) had been invited to spend the evening with the ladies of the English-speaking community so I relinquished authority of her children to the junior governess and awarded myself an evening of leisure although the duchess added the strict proviso that I should return by nine at which hour the door would be locked from within.

I lay back and closed my eyes, lost in hope and trepidation, flinching at every touch of his clammy hands. Within minutes I was beginning to regret my decision for he was neither rough nor gentle but merely uncouth; a fraudulent knave dressed in false finery with a silken tongue that very nearly deceived me.

Mario, Don Rogelio. I can, with very little effort, forget him but I have never felt the urge to forgive. You are thinking how he wronged me, how he abused the trust of a naive English governess who had never set eyes on a naked man. You have, I suspect, already guessed that I failed to return home before the appointed time and was unceremoniously dismissed the following morning. Dear Diary, you really don't know the half of it. Do you imagine that I really cared?

I told you he very nearly deceived me; you must cast aside your prejudices and preconceived ideas and allow me to conclude my story.

He had my skirts around my waist, rummaging like a snotty-nosed ragamuffin through layers of lace and taffeta. His quest for his holy grail had consumed him. I opened my eyes, watched him licking his lips and observed a dribbling rivulet of saliva rolling down his unshaven chin. It was my first encounter with the irrational fury that descends upon all men once in the close proximity of their *glittering prize. He had taken leave of his senses and, in a split second of weakness, allowed the impossible to become reality.*

I seized one of his long locks of tangled black hair, so drenched in sweat that it slid through my fingers. Determination had taken hold; I grabbed another strand, wrapped it around my fingers and pulled hard then muffled his scream in my petti-coats. He was utterly lost in a world turned upside down, couldn't possibly imagine what spells a woman possessed might unleash upon him. He was unprepared, how could he have foreseen my delir-ium? What happened next I have tried so very hard to erase from my mind, not because I am ashamed but because I fear it signals the beginning of insanity.

And here the pen paused as I rose from my seat and stood gazing from the window for even though the valley was stuck fast in its mid-morning languor I could feel the undercurrents of disorder rumbling through the strata below. They say that long before an earthquake wreaks its havoc upon the globe nature senses the impending disaster and falls silent in antici-pation. So, in a not dissimilar way, I felt the rumbling of Lady P's carriage long before it burst over the hori-zon like Boudicca's chariot. She was not alone; at her side was the poetess, her chestnut hair flowing in the wind and a wide smile upon her face. They looked up and waved. I turned, tried to remove myself from their line of sight but they had seen me and were, even now, awaiting my arrival.

I have long since managed to convince myself that there was no coercion on either part. He wanted more, they always do, but having satiated myself on his own avariciousness I was in no mood to grant him any further concessions. Taking his head in both my hands, I eased it down until I felt his breath upon my navel and his stubble on my stomach. He might have been there a dozen times before but never, I am sure, on any terms other than his own. As his lips descended further still and began, with a little 'encouragement' on my part, to delve deeper into the acquiescent concavities of my body, the first stirrings of an inevitable revolution assumed control. With every thrust of his greedy tongue another barricade fell and another portal presented itself for his exploration. I wrapped my legs so tightly around him that every time he paused or allowed himself to come up for air I squeezed his skull hard between my bare thighs until he wanted for breath.

It came unlooked for, at first a trickle then a thick and sticky flow such that, for a split second, I thought it blood from a wound he had opened inside of me. He had, of course, done nothing of the sort and, although I should have thanked him for being the catalyst, I was furious with him for being part of the conspiracy. Nothing, no one had ever prepared me for this, for an implosion of euphoria that had been proscribed as being beyond the bounds of human experience. They had all lied to me, all the ministers of religion who had tried to inculcate me with their two-faced morality, the priest and the pastor, the bishop, the very pope himself and, although I had vowed never to believe them, I had spent five long years in search of temptation. And was this all there was to it?

It was not enough; he was insufficient, inadequate for my purposes. He might have had the nous to entice me into what was little more than a squalid little bordello but that, I figured, was the limit of his *intelligence. I desired more; I demanded it and he gave — generously if not, perhaps, altogether freely.*

I let my arms drop to my side, allowed my body to lay limp and supine. It was a trap too subtle for him to comprehend; to be the hunter I would have to play the hunted. Now his jagged contours rose and enveloped me in a sweaty embrace I would not have permitted had I not had an eye on the greater glory.

Innocence had already ceded to experience. By means of some bodily osmosis I already knew what to do, what my role as his passive victim should have been and how I planned to subvert it. His buttoned fly I prised open with consummate ease, with the bold audacity of the most dextrous pickpocket. His cherry-red helmet oscillated in nervous anticipation, his hands slipped between my legs searching for the thin and fragile chord that held my purity intact. Purity? What was the worth in preserving it as such? What possible value might it possess that could possibly equal the pleasure its despoilment promised.

Mario's quivering little dragon might never have located its treasure had I not taken its fleshy form in my hands and guided it in the appropriate direction. Under my tactile jurisdiction it suddenly sprung into life and stood erect like a proud infantryman. I should confess that despite my detailed research this particular functioning of the male anatomy took me so entirely by surprise that I was almost distracted from the task in hand.

More coiled serpent than expectant Eve I seized his cullions and squeezed them until he writhed in sweet agony. Only then, whilst he was still distracted, did I facilitate his penetration on my own terms. He had boasted of riding me like a stallion but the truth is that he fucked like a mule and arrived at his climax so soon that I had barely sufficient time to raise a sweat, let alone repeat the delicious experience his earlier perlustrations had provoked.

They say Hell hath no fury like a woman scorned but the devil and myself only know the rage she suffers when deprived of the bodily bliss I considered, quid pro quo, to be rightfully mine. Whether or not he cried out 'Rebecca' is irrelevant, he had denied me. He was about to slump into narcosis when I threw him to the floor and, while he was still cowering in disbelief, surreptitiously removed his wallet from his trouser pocket. In lieu of what he conspicuously failed to deliver.

It was just as well that the respected governess turned thief for it was nigh on midnight when I tried my key and found the door barred to me, as promised. I left the service of the Duchess of Crewkerne in unpardonable disgrace but with a long and lingering kiss from her loyal handmaid, Leticia, who forged me a letter on her mistress's behalf extolling the virtues of my character. With Mario's money safe in my purse I had no intention of returning home until it was all frittered away. That night I put the past behind me and recreated myself as the wronged and innocent Miss Charlotte Crowsettle. I had almost managed to convince myself, until this afternoon but, as only you and I, dear diary, are witnesses to the truth, I would very much like it to remain that way.

And then came the rain, great swathes of silver rods tearing down from the heavens, beating hard upon the windows and the dry, dry earth. So engrossed had I become in telling myself my own story I had neglected, in the absence of Mrs Bexington, to address my wardrobe. I remained in a state of loose déshabillé, draped over my escritoire in a camisole and petticoat watching the torment unfold, mesmerised by its intoxicating ferocity. Compounded by guilt and compromised by shame I saw, in the tempest, an opportunity to cleanse myself, for the downpour seemed to bring with it a purging energy in which I merely had to douse myself to make contrition. The gods themselves were stirring above, demanding my sacrifice, a soul to placate them.

I ran out into the torrent just as it reached its greatest intensity. The sweet refreshing water flowed into and over me, drenching my loose attire, which stuck, transparently, to each and every protruding angle of my body. In that diamond-studded cloudburst I made myself a water nymph set free from the shadows, running from raindrop to raindrop lest one falling pearl of precious water be needlessly spilt until the rising tides of the flood cradled me in their arms. A dream or a nightmare or a conspiracy on the part of reality? The rain ran down my back, found its way into all my dark declivities and, though my soul considered it punishment, my body welcomed it as a sublime reward. My mind, however, had relinquished the capacity to distinguish between the two; pain and pleasure were fast becoming synonymous.

Arriving some time before the arranged hour, Emma found me lying in a muddy pool, coiled around the trunk of a great oak, murmuring to myself as if in the beginnings of a fever even though I was fully conscious. The late-afternoon sun, slanting through the dripping leaves, cast its mottled shafts of light upon her, creating a golden halo around her head. But I saw no angel before me and when she reached out her hand to lift me up I flinched and made a vain attempt to shrink into the shadows. She would have none of it, moved faster than me, seized my arms then my waist and carried me unceremoniously back to the house. There, she deposited me in front of the fireplace which, in the space of ten minutes, was filled with flame and poured forth warmth into the chilled room. Wafts of steam rose from my still sodden apparel as Emma fussed around me, searching for blankets.

'I will not have you catching your death of cold. For a start, my life would not be worth living if you had to take to your bed for a week. Not that I would object to nursing you, Miss Crowsettle, but I do not want you to get any such notions in your pretty little head, you understand that, do you not? It is just that Lady Persephone was so looking forward to seeing you this evening, asked me to call earlier and bring you something a little more pretty to wear. Not that she's been casting aspersions on your fashion sense, Miss Charlotte, it's just that she has a wardrobe of frocks and gowns she rarely sets eyes upon, let alone sees fit to wear. She asked me to choose a couple for you. I spent all afternoon selecting the ones I thought might suit you best. Never mind, there'll be another time, though I know not what my mistress will have to say when I return empty handed.'

I tried to protest, to explain that once I'd warmed up and had a bowl of broth I'd be in a fit condition to accompany her back to Chilcombe Lacey but she would have none of it.

'I would never be forgiven for bringing you home in that state. You look as white as a sheet, Miss Charlotte, as if you had just bumped into your own ghost.'

Something in the way she delivered that final phrase. It might not have been a ghost that crossed my path but something supernatural had passed my way and left me looking like a woman possessed. Emma took the mirror from the bathroom and set it before me. She was right, my face was so translucently pale that my cheekbones stood out like the snow-covered ridges of the Sierra Nevada and my eyes, normally as marine blue as the summer Mediterranean, had lost their lustre to become a faded grey. My very life juices, it seemed, were ebbing away.

'Come along,' she said. 'I shall put you to bed. Perhaps you might feel better after a good night's rest.' She plumped up a couple of pillows and laid them carefully on the chaise longue, but the sheet she had retrieved from the laundry was creased. 'I'll have no charge of mine sleeping under unpressed linen. Where does Mrs Bexington keep the iron?'

I had no idea. I had become as dependent upon servants as the landed gentry and without Emma's assistance I would have been impotent. She raised her eyes to heaven as if to say, with an air of authority, 'I have seen it all before.' As anyone with an ounce of domestic knowledge could have informed her, the iron was in the scullery. She placed it in the direct heat of the fire and, whilst it warmed, directed her attention towards me.

My reluctance to disrobe in her presence appeared to amuse her, all the more so when I looked vainly for some corner of the room that might have offered some privacy. She addressed me not as was customary for a woman of her social standing but with a self-assurance that hinted at a more exotic but clearly noble upbringing. Her features – the thick eyebrows with barely a break in the middle, the dark eyes and the long aquiline nose – reminded me of the gypsy girls who descended from the hills every Sunday to attend mass at the Church of Our Lady, Star of the Sea, on the quayside in Cartagena. Suitably absolved, they spent the rest of the day drinking, dancing and dodging the attempts of the constabulary to detain them. The local boys were their preferred prey but I remember one of them, more woman than child, who sat alone and for a full quarter of an hour never took her eyes from me. No matter how hard I looked in the opposite direction my gaze was always drawn back to her but, the moment I plucked up the courage to approach her, my employer and her darling children appeared to save me. To save me? I know not what from but although I was initially relieved to be spirited away there grew within me a gnawing sense of unease, that I had spurned an opportunity I might live to regret. I turned around but she was gone.

What might I have learnt from her? At least how to evade the likes of Emma who, kneeling at my back, had encircled my neck with her broad hands. She had already unhooked my silver necklace and was gently unfastening the buttons on my camisole before I sensed her presence and instinctively cowered beneath her touch.

'My, my, Miss Charlotte. What on earth's the matter? Anyone would think I was strangling the life from you. Undress yourself if you so wish, I was only trying to help.'

I saw her reflection in the mirror; she was smiling, the corners of her thin lips lifting in a gesture I might have been recognised as being either tender or tyrannical had I acquired the knowledge and experience to distinguish like from like. She drew near me once more and placed her hand upon mine. I recoiled again, rose to my feet and scurried towards the corner like a mouse. Still smirking but now, apparently, sensitive to my predicament, she erected the folding screen and suggested that, if I really was so protective of my modesty, I might disrobe behind it. She, in the meantime, turned her back on me, folded the sheet carefully on the ironing board then stoked the fire, leaving within its the rising flames the iron poker.

Now, wrapped comfortably in my white nightgown, and with the warmth from the hearth emanating around the room, the chill subsided and I perched myself on the chaise longue, fascinated by Emma's every move.

She had removed her jacket and hung it over the back of a chair but such was the heat that she was obliged to divest herself of her crisp ivory blouse and continue to work in what was little more than her corset cover. It was, I suppose, quite improper but so much did she fascinate me that I suddenly cared little for convention and her bustling manner rendered her quite oblivious to my enrapt attention. Taking a rag from the kitchen she bound it around her hand, withdrew the poker from the flames and then, like Arthur with Excalibur, held the incandescent rod before her, gazing lovingly at its white-hot tip.

I feared for her then, much in the same way that several weeks later I would fear for my own safety, as she stood, quite motionless for a good two minutes until her wand cooled to a faint pink glowing. 'I think,' she said, apparently to herself, 'that will suffice.' Satisfied, she took the iron that had been sitting within the embers and proceeded to press the sheets. This required some considerable dexterity on her part for neither my father nor Mrs Bexington would stint on quality and all the bedlinen had been purchased from Gould's of Dorchester. In addition, it was clear that, even though Emma and Mrs Bexington were poles apart in matters pertaining to polite society, they were both equally circumspect in their devotion to duty. She replaced the iron by the fire to reheat and manoeuvred the fabric so that the unpressed fabric was uppermost on the board. To achieve this she had to twist her upper torso through one hundred and eighty degrees and, in doing so, exposed the upper part of her left arm which had hitherto been hidden from my view.

Perhaps she had assumed that I was still preoccupied with my privacy and had not yet emerged from behind the screen. Either that or she cared little what I saw or, indeed, quite wished that for some reason or other I should observe it. The angry-looking wound, raised and of about inch and a half in diameter, was several days old but not so fully healed that I was unable to make out its unusual yet quite distinct shape: SoS.

She caught my head turning like an axle burning. A slim volume of the world's history might have summed up her smile – 'I have seen it all before, there is nothing new under the sun'.

I could not be sure whether it was the precise creases of the starched linen or the draught that Emma had concocted from the bottles in my father's drinks cupboard that lulled me into a welcome and gentle sleep. She forced me to swallow the cocktail in one gulp, refusing to take her leave until I had done so, and, when I lay back, she began to sing, a soft lullaby in a tongue I could not understand and had never, in all my travels on the continent, come across. Whatever its source, it did the trick; my last memory was of her hand running through my hair, a kiss on my lips before darkness descended.

Would that Emma had prepared for me something more potent or greater in volume for when I woke it was clear from the moon's elevation that the night was still young and, as I struggled in vain to regain my slumbers, I heard the clock strike nine then a quarter and half past the hour. Unless, on the other hand, the heady brew was so powerful that I must have passed from pleasant sleep to waking dreams for I find it difficult to account for my subsequent actions.

With the echo of the final chime I surrendered and rose from my virtuous couch, lighting the lamps and flooding the cottage with light for the shadows disturbed me, as if a faint sense of paranoia had settled upon my soul. Thanks to Mrs Bexington's unexpected departure the cupboard was bare leaving me no option but to dine on a hunk of stale bread and a mug of flat cider. It wasn't the alcohol that went straight to my head; I have imbibed all the fine wines that Europe has to offer and not once have I let slip my dignity but the cider was coarse and loaded with sediment. It was brewed on the Chase from apples which, according to local gossip, are direct descendants from those on the Tree of Knowledge in the Garden of Eden, still bearing Eve's guilty fingerprints, or so they say.

Sitting in the gloom at the empty table, pouring mug after mug of cider until my head spun, it was inevitable that my thoughts should drift down the valley to Chilcombe Lacey where they were welcomed by bright lights and laughter. And braised pheasant, venison, woodcock pie and the numerous bottles of Chateau Grand Puy Ducasse, one of which we had already enjoyed together. Perhaps, if I could just look and not touch . . .

I followed the road as far as the Dower House where, notwithstanding my innocent intentions, I decided to take Park Lane, circle the village and approach the house from the opposite direction. There were prying eyes everywhere, not least the rectory, and, observing a group of shadows gathered beside the bridge, I considered discretion the better part of valour. Despite the mud I decided to take to the paths and lifted my skirts to hurdle the stile and cross the fields. They were, in all probability, nothing more than cattle whose silhouettes, carved like ghosts by the waxing moon, had taken on the shapes of lurking giants but I was not prepared to take the risk of being watched. What on earth was I doing that could possibly be construed as iniquitous?

And there lay the rub. I was, by my own reckoning, being slowly drawn into a cleverly constructed web the like of which could only manifest itself to the curious and the indolent. Had, for example, the vicar's dear fiancée, Miss Grace Fitzpiers, passed this way, an innocent Red Riding Hood oblivious to the existence of wolves, she would have come to no harm. Quite simply, to put oneself in the path of danger one has not only to believe in its existence but also consciously seek it out at every opportunity until life becomes a thankless existence, leaving its willing victims with the red-embered eyes of burnt-out stars. Miss Fitzpiers might have walked into the baited trap without ever feeling its steel jaws biting into her flesh and bone whereas I would scour the woods in search of a snare to snag myself in. Sweet Miss Fitzpiers, secure in her faith and fidelity; poor little Charlotte, addicted to all that she held profane and wallowing in the guilt it inspired.

I crept into the grounds of Chilcombe Lacey through the small copse that forms its eastern perimeter. Here the infant River Bride spreads wide its shallow waters and trickles into the waterlogged sump they call the Rookery Bog where yellow flag and marsh mallow thrive. I had been there only once; yesterday, in broad daylight. With a coy smile she had parted the willows to reveal a string of stepping stones that guaranteed the well-informed intruder a dry passage across the watercourse. Had I trusted only to instinct and moonlight I might have come to a watery end but you can rest assured that other forces were guiding my footsteps that night. What I might do once standing before the great doors of the house I could not have said, only that, once discovered (and I fully intended to allow myself to be apprehended, preferably by force), I would be caught like a person transfixed by the sight of a fast-approaching carriage. As it transpired, I was never offered the opportunity to find out.

The yard gates opened and from within emerged an elegant landau hauled by two of the most handsome stallions I had seen north of the English Channel and raising clouds of dust that sparkled in streaks of silver moonbeams. I would have been caught in open country had I not paused by a statue of Diana, goddess of the hunt, to admire her graven beauty. And there I ought to have remained, crouched behind the plinth, to maintain the barrier that separated Lady P's world from mine. 'Ignorance is bliss', they would tell me, over and over again until it had become an unwritten rule that governed the lives of my fellow pupils, but I was always a doubting Thomas, even at that tender age of eight I refused to believe without seeing or feeling the matter of dogma. I should also admit that a streak of jealousy had made itself known. Who, if not I, was enjoying the company of Lady Persephone in my absence? Crawling forwards, hoping that the gloom cast by the poplars would conceal my lengthening shadow, I managed to make out the dim outlines of the three figures occupying the carriage: the driver, in a smart uniform of vermillion and polished brass, and, behind him, two gentlemen sharing a cigar.

Gentlemen! Without thinking, without stopping to consider the possibilities, I stole forwards – a step too far. As the landau gathered speed and hurtled past, there came from within impatient cries, bidding the coachman full haste lest, and I am certain this is what the taller of the two cried, 'The finest whores will be taken and we shall be left with the detritus.' The voice and the body whence it came seemed curiously incompatible, especially when it added, 'Show them the whip, my dear Emerson; show them the whip.' His companion turned to admonish him, exposing his face to the revealing light that I, too, had crept into. He raised his hat and mouthed a greeting, his lips spelling out my name, a hex that left me rooted to the spot, divested me of clothing, exposed my soul and all its wicked intentions. I am no expert on the mind or the matter of the stronger sex, for me they continue to remain a peculiar and not entirely pleasant enigma. But even before the events of that summer I knew enough of women to distinguish them in both sound and vision. 'Emerson' indeed! And yet she made a handsome lad, a touch of the rogue about her, although I rather preferred Lady Persephone in more traditional attire.

I watched the glow of the lights ebb and fade as they turned up the hill for the Weymouth road. And then they disappeared into the murk, the 'gentlemen' of the night.

3

It was the day the swifts returned, diving around the eaves, bombarding the air with their long loud shrieks. They were, I thought, a little late that season, a symbol of portent, of some meddling with Mother Nature that would set the globe awry.

The devil birds dived and soared, emitting their blood-curdling cries, their spine-chilling screams of grief. The devil birds were once women like me, until, consumed by the unbearable grief of their proscribed existence they made a deal with the Dark Lord. He took possession of our souls and, in return, granted us a lifetime of licence to behave in whatever manner we saw fit. But a lifetime is nothing in the passage of eternity in which we are condemned to perpetual indulgence. Pleasure, on its own, without the balancing virtues of love and devotion, is naught but a burden. All drugs are sweet with the first intoxication but familiarity breeds contempt and addiction destroys even the most resilient. I thought I had a countenance of steel; my flimsy frontier was too easily breached.

I was waiting for the letter, crouched in the hallway, behind the hatstand, within sight of the letterbox but out of sight of any potential visitor. Given the events of the previous evening – which were so lucid that even after the deepest of slumbers my mind could never mistake them for mere dreams – I had no doubt that Lady P would contact me to offer some form of illumination. The fashion for charades was of continental origin that had not, I imagined, even travelled as far as London let alone the bashful provinces but what other honest explanation could there possibly be?

There arrived not one but three envelopes, two directed to myself, one stamped, addressed and post-marked 'Exeter', the other in the unmistakeable flowing hand of Lady Persephone.

Chilcombe Lacey
15 June 1876

My dear Charlotte
You cannot possibly imagine my distress when Emma returned alone yesterday evening. Both Samantha and I had been waiting patiently for your arrival, gazing out along the drive with weary eyes until the gathering dusk rendered the task futile. We had been in the drawing room only a minute or two before Emma knocked and entered without you. Poor girl, how often has she born the brunt of my unwarranted anger – and how often have I had to plead for her forgiveness. But I make it a rule not to castigate my dear servant in front of guests so my interrogation was, you can be assured, just and gentle.

We passed a pleasant evening together but your absence wore us both to the very core and in our tedium we contrived to find alternative diversions. They do say that necessity is the mother of invention; Samantha's imagination knows very few bounds and she devised an entertaining, if unorthodox little game to keep ourselves occupied. What sport we enjoyed! I fully intend to invite you to participate next time we indulge ourselves but in the meantime we shall be dining again tonight, this time in the company of my good friend Yseult Tredinnick who has agreed to grace us with her presence. She has finally managed to find a publisher brave enough to print her latest findings but has promised Samantha and myself a sneak preview. As a devout (and, dare I say, virulent) atheist I am sure that what she has to say will interest you enormously. You did tell me you had seen enough of Roman Catholicism in Spain to deter you for life but I detected an innate Protestant obstinacy that doesn't fit well with the enquiring mind. The manner in which you blushed when I mentioned the convent of Our Lady of Consolation in Cartagena made me desirous to probe a little further. Has experience, perhaps, got the better of you? I thought it better not to pursue the matter at the time for fear of sounding like the Inquisition but, mark my words, I will tease the truth from you one way or the other! I am not at all convinced by that veneer of innocence you have wrapped around yourself. Your little white lies might well have fooled the Duchess of Crewkerne but both Emma and myself have an eye for the scoundrel and our research has been thorough.

Emma tells me your fever was temporary and expects you to be as right as rain today (if you'll forgive my little pun). I will accept no excuses, Miss Crowsettle, only a life-threatening disease will suffice!

Until this evening, then
Your dearest Percy

Her letters were becoming longer and more loaded with intrigue. Each exposed another aspect of her intoxicating character and hinted at more interesting revelations to come, should I choose to put my faith in her. And there, in that last paragraph, hidden within the flattery, was a subtle, unwritten warning: 'I hope you are not out of your depth, Charlotte Crowsettle, because once you are in there is no turning back.'

My father's chaotic handwriting was as distinctive as Lady P's, slanting hard to the right and barely legible. In style he was as short and perfunctory as she was elusive, he had his eye on his geology, words were superfluous.

Heavitree House
Exeter
13 June 1876

My dear daughter
Please forgive my brevity, Professor Walditch and I have been busy on my proofs. He's delighted with my work but says my style is still that of an amateur which, in the world of academia, will never do. Not a bit like the army, I'm afraid, though at least you see a little more of me these days.

The professor has asked me to stay on a while longer, no more than a week and much as I protested he refused to take 'no' for an answer. You know how he is, Charlotte, more friend than mentor and I didn't have the heart to turn him down.

I trust Mrs Bexington is looking after you without resorting to her usual severity. I have tried to assuage my guilt with the hope that Lady Persephone de Mortehoe might have befriended you. Whatever they say about her in the village, you will not find a finer friend and ally this side of Weymouth.

I will return next Tuesday, at the latest.
Your ever loving father

The third letter was addressed to him in all his official glory, 'Sir Napier Crowsettle GCMG, FRCS', in an envelope of poor quality which immediately raised my curiosity. Father was proud of his military career but rarely discussed it with those outside his immediate circle and even then I often had to ply him with whisky to lubricate his memory. He was, I think, aware of the conflicting nature of his calling: a surgeon dedicated to saving lives but within an institution – the British Army – dedicated to destroying them. The few who knew of his bravery were not the sort to insult their friends by communicating by means of such second-rate shoddy stationery. Using his absence as an excuse, I was sorely tempted to break my father's confidence and open the letter – there was, after all, no seal – but I thought better of it and propped it up on the mantelpiece.

I spent the entire afternoon scrubbing my body with an intense vigour, cleansing myself both without and within as if my behaviour of the previous night had in some way contaminated me. I stood naked before the mirror and examined my body more closely than I had ever done before. It was not, after all, the done thing and despite my liberal upbringing I could not remove from my thinking the notion that a woman's body is an entity of which I ought to be ashamed. Were we not, each and every one of us, an Eve? We were the Devil's gateway, the first deserters of divine law, which, however much I protested my refusal to confirm, still held me in its thrall.

The meagre portions of uninspiring food that Mrs Bexington had placed in front of me had taken their toll and since she departed I had barely touched a morsel. The fine wines of the Mediterranean, not to mention the sublime seafood for which Cartagena was justifiably famous, had filled out my contours to the extent that the Spanish considered me one of their own. But the figure that now appeared before me had a lean and hungry look, its slender frame suggesting the complacency of my previous existence had been banished. It was no longer welcoming or compliant. Its sinews were wiry and almost devoid of flesh but the muscles showed through and the image was not in the least repellent. It drew me closer and closer until the reflection and the reflected were almost touching. I might not have been born into great beauty but I possessed enough vanity to fall in love with myself and, when that had been exhausted, seek it elsewhere. I smiled at myself, the cruel carnivorous smile of a woman who refused to relinquish her inner child.

Hunter or hunted? Whatever suited my purpose, I had yet to make up my mind.

The proof of the pudding revealed itself in Emma's reaction. I had layered myself in what few scents I owned and dressed myself, with immense care and attention, in the military, navy-blue and white frock she had left for me yesterday. She had selected it and must have had some inkling that its vertical stripes would accentuate and enhance, for whose benefit had she contrived this scenario? Not mine, I was sure. I stood stock still, tall and proud whilst she circled me, silently inspecting the creation for which she was, in part, responsible.

'Well, well, well. Who would have thought it? What would your father say? His little girl transformed into a grown woman just like that.' She snapped her fingers. 'I do not think he would entirely approve, do you? And, as for Mrs Bexington, is it not fortunate that we managed to remove her from the equation?'

'What do you mean? She left of her own accord. I might have upset her but it had nothing to do with you. I'm sure she will return to the fold when my father has spoken to her.'

'I admire your self-conviction, Charlotte, even if it sounds a little hollow to the likes of me. You're beginning to acquire a reputation that some might not care for. Dancing half-naked in the rain, creeping through the fields in the dead of night and, dare I add, spying?'

Her accusations should not have taken me by surprise. She had, after all, been witness to at least two of the events and might well have observed the third. I was beginning to grow fond of Emma. I was grateful to her for taking care of me the previous day and for providing the link between myself and Lady P but she was, even to my progressive mind, a servant and should not therefore have addressed me as 'Charlotte'. To her it was only a game; she played along with the boundaries of social convention because she knew how to flout them. And how had she learnt how to flout them? Through experience – the machinations, the intrigues, the unwritten rules and codes of behaviour required by what was, to all intents and purposes, an antediluvian society. Those of us who raged against it would never understand. We saw life only in monochrome – that which was not black could only be white – whereas the likes of Emma had discovered the silver shining in between. She might well have been Lady P's maid but she was very much her own woman and when I tried to rebuke her she turned on me with the panache that was indicative of her pedigree.

'I do beg your pardon, *Mistress* Charlotte Crowsettle, I know not what came over me. Far be it from me to take on the airs and graces of my betters when I have barely a Christian bone in my body. Why, if I were you I'd show me the back of your hand and send me to sleep in the scullery.'

She threw back her thick mane of hair and proffered her cheek. How close did I come, God help me, to raising my arm and bringing my open palm down upon her face. I was so tempted, so sorely tempted, but I knew that were I to strike her it would have to be with full force, anything less would meet with her contempt and lower me further still in her estimation. Her eyes flickered but not a nerve flinched. She was taunting me, testing my mettle but I knew perfectly well that whatever choice I made I would lose. I have to confess that for the first time in my entire life I was caught between loathing and lust, unable to distinguish one from the other. The moment I let my arm fall my lips, as if part of a Newtonian equal and opposite reaction, parted and edged themselves towards hers until I could have stretched out my tongue and entwined it around hers. But I could no more kiss her than I could beat her so I turned away in a gesture of defeat, effectively conceding to her superiority. She curtseyed and held her head in mock shame but made no effort to hide her smirk as she glanced at herself in the mirror. She never could resist giving herself a self-congratulatory smile.

For the time being, at least, our little contretemps was forgotten and Emma reverted to type, taking my wrist and hauling me into the waiting trap. She was dressed in the breeches of a footman but with a jacket gathered at the waist and a shirt unbuttoned to reveal the long fluting bones of her neckline descending into a mass of ruffled white cotton. With her boyish good looks and her angular frame she cut a dashing figure, one that almost neutralised her femininity. Almost: she played the rogue male with disconcerting aplomb, handled me with a tender vulgarity and, while manoeuvring me into my seat, allowed her hands to rest in places a gentleman would consider uncharted, if not forbidden territory. She knew full well how much the tight-fitting bodice of my evening gown limited any sudden or unplanned movement and took great delight in striding around the carriage, at liberty to manoeuvre at will whilst I was confined to the pedestal upon which she had placed me.

The evening was bright and balmy. Above us the verdant canopy of Ashley Chase unfolded its limbs to allow the last sparks of the setting sun to illuminate its deep-ridden, comely folds. Emma steered the carriage with little sense of haste and its gentle motion put me at ease until we rounded the corner and entered the drive of Chilcombe Lacey. The moment I set eyes upon three figures waiting upon the front steps panic set in. How should I respond if challenged? How should I explain my presence in the grounds last night? Should I attempt a subtle hint or pretend it never happened? Nobody had ever taught me how to take care of events that should remain unacknowledged, that is, swept neatly under the carpet with barely a word spoken. The society in which I grew up knew instinctively when a wrong had been committed but as long as the error was never mentioned in public it was deemed forever forgotten. But those of us who overheard – or even witnessed – the punishment meted out in private decided that subterfuge was preferable to relying on honesty.

We learnt to tell tales, we learnt the fine art of fabricating reality, that although minor falsehoods were scarcely believed one could dine out for months on the most improbable of well-spun narratives. 'Stoke every deceit with hyperbole' might have been my motto and as such I spent many hours concocting an elaborate cocktail of lies to hide the unpalatable truth that lay behind my dismissal from the duchess's employment, my flight from Cartagena and subsequent unannounced arrival in Weymouth. My father took it as gospel; the rest, including Mrs Bexington, I steadfastly ignored. What business was it of theirs that I'd spread my legs for a Spaniard and fled, with his purse, from the wrath of the noblesse? More pertinently, how did they ever get to know?

I need not have worried. Lady P belonged to neither school; rather, she waited for a moment she considered appropriate then confessed. Not to just one misdemeanour, you must understand, and not just her own. Her cavalier attitude to the truth initiated all manner of confessions for which she could never be held responsible but for which she longed to accept the blame. 'Mea culpa,' she would cry, raising her glass to the heavens. But while most of her peers thought it a joke, by then I was privy to her innermost thoughts. Tired of Anglican mendacity she had carefully cultivated her Roman Catholic guilt complex until it became a Charybdis into which all trespasses would be harmlessly lured, freeing those who committed them from eternal damnation. But there was method in her madness: she considered it her mission to bear the guilt of all women upon her shoulders. She was that rarest of jewels, an independent educated woman who had succeeded by means of intellectual prowess rather than the tradition that had abandoned her two brothers. She had studied her martyrs: Perpetua and Felicitas especially, but while she admired their courage and was fascinated by their suffering she found their wit somewhat lacking. Rather, she modelled herself on Eve who, defying authority, chose knowledge over ignorance. But unlike Eve, she refused to be banished from her own paradise.

To her allies a messiah, to all others a pariah.

'At last, my dear Charlotte. Absence has indeed

made my heart grow fonder, if not doting. We missed you sorely last night but we shall more than make up for it this evening.'

Lady P had bounded down the long flight of steps and stood beside the carriage, almost twitching with anticipation. The two others followed with more dignity and, dare I say it, trepidation. Samantha Poorton, the poetess, I had briefly set eyes on and even in more conventional attire I recognised her unassuming figure, her petite, conventionally feminine frame. She suffered from a comparison with her hostess but, then, what earthly creature would not? The woman at her side towered over her and seemed to share her reluctance in coming forwards. I could not blame her. I was, after all, a mere governess whose reputation had undoubtedly been grossly exaggerated by Lady P. What on earth did she see in me? Why on earth did she crave my friendship so? I could feel scholarship and wisdom emanating from every pore of their bodies, their finest European scents, wafting over in the warm air, heavy with culture acquired from a lifetime dedicated to the pursuit of learning. And what was I? A shadow slinking away from their overpowering magnitude, not fit to raise my eyes to theirs. I didn't even belong with Emma in the kitchen. Perhaps Mr Darwin was right, after all. It was all a question of breeding. A clique from which I was automatically excluded.

Emma was in her element, parading me around like a cat toying with its prey. She unlatched the carriage door. I allowed her to take my hand and she eased me down on to the drive. Very well, if she was playing her role, I would play mine. It was, after all, only a game.

'Thank you, Emma,' I said, adopting my most dismissive and patronising tone, one that I had picked up from the Duchess of Crewkerne and mimicked to great effect in front of the downstairs staff. 'That will be all, now.'

She still had my hand in hers and pressed it firmly when I spoke to her. I did likewise but twisted her fingers until I could feel pain manifesting itself in the tensed sinews of her forearm which was locked into mine. It was time she was taught a lesson, that I was worthy of at least a modicum of my respect. I might well lack her history, her sublime ability to manipulate the laws of society and nature but she needed to understand that I was no innocent.

I turned the screw, applied more pressure. In Lady P's company alone she might have reacted but with guests present she knew she had no option but to do as she was told. 'You will show some respect and bow, you little hussy,' I whispered hard into her ear, with just enough volume for Lady P to hear. 'And mind you do it properly. I will not be ridiculed again, is that quite clear?'

She folded herself into the most perfect act of sub-servience, bending low with her free hand tucked into her abdomen. I released her hand and she backed away. It was a definitive moment in my relationship with both her and Lady P who enjoyed the spectacle immensely, adding her own flourish.

'Come along, girl, you heard Miss Crowsettle, don't overstay your welcome. Away with you now. There's dinner to cook and serve.'

Lady P's clipped consonants and fluting vowels floated up into the skies like a lark ascending. I had always thought cruelty harsh and oppressive yet in her it was quite beautiful, an act of such wonder that to question its authority would be tantamount to blasphemy.

She placed her arm within mine and we walked

towards her friends. 'You do surprise me, Charlotte. But then again you do not. Although I must confess to having entertained some doubts. You are one of those ladies within whom the whole is hidden and I am one of those whose sole *modus vivendi* is to locate that treasure and exploit it for our mutual benefit. I am not saying, my dear Charlotte, that you are yet the finished version but I can see that my faith in your potential was not misplaced. You are learning already, that is plain to see, and even the uneducated would admire your treatment of the errant young Emma. She is a wilful knave, she seeks out mischief for its own sake but I do not have the heart to tame her. One could never tame a girl like her but that does not excuse her from either discipline or duty. Perhaps you can impress the importance of each upon her.

'Now, come, allow me to introduce you to Miss Samantha Poorton and Miss Yseult Tredinnick. We will, I am sure, all get along famously but let us decamp to the walled garden to enjoy our wine in warm seclusion.' She turned to me. 'Charlotte, you are an excellent connoisseur of all that is Mediterranean. I have purchased some fine whites from La Mancha, in your honour. What do you recommend? A Verdejo, perhaps?'

Much to the amusement of all three women, I blushed profusely. I was not used to praise, certainly not praise so effusively delivered. And yet I had her confidence, I had begun to live up to her exacting standards and, though still little more than a child, my experience would shame a woman twice my age. Lady P's philosophy was slowly emerging but remained beyond my comprehension. Experience, I'm afraid, does not nullify naivety, nor does it make one worldly wise.

We shared a bottle of Verdejo and then a succession of dry fruity whites from Tarragona. Emma had excelled herself in the kitchen and presently emerged with a dish of venison steak covered in a thick garlic sauce and accompanied by delicately sautéed potatoes. I tried to keep quiet, confining my conversation to brief replies to an onslaught of questions until my companions began to tire and talked amongst themselves. After a while they became oblivious to my presence, unaware that I was listening intently, ears pricked.

'So, ladies. You have both had time to consider my proposal, as have the others I spoke of earlier. What do you say? Samantha, you were with me when we dreamt up the idea. Are you still game?'

Lady P pushed her plate to one side and took a long sip from her glass before refilling ours. She gave me a quizzing, conspiratorial look before returning to her theme.

'Well?'

Yseult was the first to speak. She was a tall woman, draped in the black of eternal mourning, a dark silhouette in a shadowless night. She was neither young nor old but belonged to an ageless era where time was a minor irrelevance. She had been introduced to me as a historian of some renown, a student of the Holy Grail, but it seemed to me that she had immersed herself so deeply in her chosen field of study that she had ceased to be an academic and had become a part of the myth she loved so dearly. Her voice was deep and formal; I was immediately in awe of her.

'Dear Percy, if I didn't know you any better I'd suggest you had finally taken leave of your senses.' She smiled, a warm inviting smile that melted any antipathy I might have felt towards her. 'Only you could have concocted a scheme so wild, so impossible and so deliciously dangerous. I have told you many times before, I will follow you to the ends of the Earth even if that is the catalyst that brings about my very own oblivion.'

She stretched out, placed her arm upon Lady P's thigh and began to stroke it gently, with feline dexterity. She was, indeed, a colossus who had, over the years, defeated a constant procession of critics who considered it their duty, as men, to belittle her, a mere woman. She fought them tooth and nail until, sensing victory, they chose to ignore her. It was still possible to sense the poor woman's fury. Anyone of a weaker constitution would have conceded and conformed but she was a pugilist and had learnt to fight her corner. She dropped her guard and passion oozed forth.

'The trap is set; the bait is primed. I am utterly given over to your ridiculous scheme, to abandon it now would be an admission of defeat. No, Percy, I am from hereon your most devoted disciple – and I will challenge Samantha for the privilege if she dares.'

The poetess stared hard at her, examining every defining feature as if they were portals to her soul. The moonlight flickered through the beeches and engulfed us all in a dappled silence. There was tension in the air, a static that crackled and fizzled. Samantha had removed her velvet Zouave jacket but there were still beads of sweat on her forehead as the night was warm and breathless. Her blouse was almost transparent, a thin, cream silk, laced but of a simple design such that all attention was drawn to the budding curvature of her body. Slowly, she unbuttoned the cuffs and rolled up her sleeve as far as her elbow where she paused. Her eyes were upon Yseult but she turned them suddenly to me and then, with a swift vicissitude, to Lady P, who, acknowledging her concern, nodded solemnly.

'Yes, yes.' Lady P sighed, as if immediately relieved of some unsolvable conundrum. 'I have been giving the matter my utmost consideration and I will own to you now that until last night I was reluctant.' She was staring at me, indeed all three were subjecting me to intense scrutiny the like of which I had never experienced since the night the duchess dismissed me. She was easily deceived; my present companions were more sophisticated and would see through any charade. Whilst the inquisitors confided, I sat back in my chair, clinging to its arms as if my dear life depended upon it.

'I would have deferred,' continued Lady P. 'She is a young lady, some would say no more than a girl, but fortune has already favoured her. Her youth lies in her looks and not her experience. Believe me, my dearest dark angels, there is more to Miss Charlotte Crowsettle than meets the eye. Much, much more.'

Samantha's fingers were still on her sleeve, she seemed impatient to complete her task. 'Are you saying, Percy, that we should welcome her only because she knows too much? Surely that would defeat the object? We have all dedicated ourselves to embrace risk and danger in pursuit of the forbidden. When we are apprehended, as we surely shall be, they will seize upon any excuse to bring us to what they deem to be justice. Miss Crowsettle already knows too much, but not yet enough to betray us.'

'There will be a Judas, Sam. If we are bound together by temptation then temptation must ultimately tear us apart. There seems little point in contemplating the whys and the wherefores when we are all resigned to our fate.' Lady P paused, ruminating deeply with folded brow. 'Indeed,' she continued, 'it would seem more in keeping with our doctrine if, rather than prevaricating, we acknowledged betrayal and invited it in with open arms. Having scorned polite society we must pursue its enemies with vigour: impropriety, impertinence and excess, these are the objects of our insatiable desire. I ask you, is it not better to burn brightly but briefly like an exploding star rather than fade away into ashes and dust?'

It was an impassioned speech, delivered in a gentle voice that belied the intensity of her emotions. Her fists were clenched tight; her eyes looked out into an infinity that neither Samantha, Yseult nor myself could hope to comprehend. There was a prolonged silence that was finally interrupted by Yseult's low, almost inaudible tones. She leant forwards and the black silk of her dress rippled over her breasts.

'You are right, Percy. You always are. I am beginning to understand your philosophy and I think that, as it requires us to put ourselves in peril, we must place our very existence on the line. Friend or foe, Charlotte has walked into our web. She may be the sacrifice, she may be the heroine who inspires us all but she is not, I suspect, an unwilling victim.'

'Very well. Samantha, you may continue.' Lady P raised her hand and Samantha rolled her sleeve to the very top of her left arm. I was suddenly overcome with a sense of déjà vu, I knew exactly what she would reveal, what mark had been indelibly inscribed into her warm, pink flesh. It was more scar than wound, less angry perhaps, but time had not healed it; rather, it had conferred upon it an even greater potency. The letters 'SoS' had already left an imprint on my mind. It occurred to me that, like Emma and Samantha as well as, almost certainly, Lady P herself, its presence would eventually become as physical as it was symbolic.

Yseult watched her intensely. When she saw the

burnt skin her jaw dropped and her eyes blazed like diamonds in the dew. Samantha, in turn, had her stare fixed firmly on me, examining me for an untoward reaction. Perhaps, if I had not already witnessed Emma's wound, shock might have got the better of me but I was already becoming immune. For several moments Yseult seemed to move her mouth without any words coming forth until her voice finally emerged.

'I see I have been usurped. I suppose I have no one to blame but myself for neglecting you. I shall pay my penance and you, Samantha, shall be my confessor. Whatever forfeit you see fit I swear to undertake. I understand what it means to fail, that I will be ostracised and forbidden from enjoying your company ever again. It is a prospect almost too terrible to contemplate but far, far preferable to my exclusion from your elite for the eternity of my lifetime, and beyond.'

Sinking to her knees she crouched at Lady P's feet like a supplicant, hands twisted together as if in prayer. 'My dearest Lady Persephone, my sovereign mistress, I offer you my heart and my soul and, in return, ask only that you grant me the opportunity to prove myself worthy of your faith.'

'Do you understand what that means, Yseult? Do you genuinely understand the consequences? That to succeed might, in all probability will, lead to damnation in this life if not the next. True, if you fail you will be excommunicated from our sorority but you will at least be spared its incessant calls and commands. Succeed and you will never be free from my authority, you will be always in my thrall.'

Yseult lowered her headed and nodded meekly. She took Lady P's hand and kissed it. 'I agree,' she whispered. 'I have no choice.'

'*Sic erat in fatis*,' replied Lady P. 'So it was fated. On Saturday, at midnight, we shall convene on the Chase, in the Chapel of St Luke, and you shall be put to the test. Charlotte, you will be our guest of honour; Samantha, Emma and myself will be your judges. There will, I suspect, be more witnesses present; the curious can never resist the cry of the unknown. We shall have them yet, shall we not, Samantha? The Society of Sin never rejects her own.'

4

Chilcombe Lacey
19 September 1876

My dear Charlotte
You know me well enough to realise that I never give
up, that I will never admit defeat. And, even if I
wanted to, Emma would never let me. Do not fool
yourself, child. You might think you are beyond my
sphere of influence but you can never be free of my
spell.

They tell you are being well cared for, that you
have almost recovered from the events of the sum-
mer and that the peace and quiet has quite restored
your sanity. I doubt it very much indeed; care is not
what you need, is it? It isn't what you crave. You
cannot ignore your base instincts forever.

I shall have my revenge, dear Charlotte, and you
shall be part of it. You have not seen the last of me;
I will come when I am least looked for.

Your ever loving, dearest

I should have torn the letter in two, I should have torn
them all into tiny little pieces, opened the window and
cast them out into the wind and the rain but instead I
opened my drawer and placed it under my clothes,
along with the others. Unlike Inspector Lefebvre I was
convinced of her guilt not least because she had told
me herself. Not face to face but in one of the long
autobiographical ramblings that now accompanied her

letters. She had told me the whole story, how her parents had been poisoned by a fortuitously incompetent Italian cook. How her two younger brothers had both come to grief in equally unfortunate circumstances allowing her to take possession of Chilcombe Lacey. It was what she wanted, it was what she deserved. Who was she, a mere woman, to take arms against destiny?

How could she have been sure I wouldn't go straight to the police? Because the truth was that she was quite right, I was still utterly under her spell.

There was a letter within the letter, another envelope bulging at its seams with several leaves of foolscap. The paper was pure white, the ink and the content quite utterly black.

Chilcombe Lacey
September 1876

My dear Charlotte
You will want to know how it all began. I must have promised to tell you a hundred times but the summer gathered a momentum of its own and I never seemed able to find the time to do so.

I am sitting at my desk, looking out at grey sheets of rain draping themselves over the slopes of Ashley Chase, watching the wind pick up the piles of ruddy leaves and blowing them around the garden. I think of the rain and the wind and I think of you; of your dew-drenched lips implanted upon mine, of your cold fingers somehow finding their way through layers of taffeta, lifting my skirts and slipping into the moist before I dowse them in a wave of uncontrolled pleasure. Did this ever happen? Is it a dream? You must tell me, Charlotte, or I swear I will turn insane with insatiable lust.

Listen, lie down on your bed, loosen your attire

and breathe deep. Imagine I am there at your side, on you and in you, invading every part of your body. Listen, I will whisper it. Can you not hear my voice? Am I not a siren singing softly in your ear? Can you not feel my breathing; my breasts falling and rising, like a tide poised to overwhelm you, the rhythmic perfumed waves of my exhaling and inhaling. My words are falling from my lips, a deluge raining hard on you from above. Listen, this is how it all began.

We had arrived separately: myself alone in a hansom cab, Samantha in a landau accompanied by her fiancé, Algernon Mawkwood. We had never set eyes on one other before, were never aware of each other's existence. Yet we left together, arm in arm, with that pathetic creature in tow.

I had been observing her all evening. She fascinated me, though for what reason I cannot now recall. The Samantha Poorton I solicited that evening was not then the woman you came to know at Chilcombe Lacey. She lacked a lady's refinement and grace. Nobody could even imagine her the primal matter from which might be hewn such a fair effigy. A thing of beauty is a joy that lasts forever, but first one has to gild it.

It was, I think, at that moment she suffered her own Damascene conversion, the earth spinning from its axis and inverting natural law. While her head cried out for reason her soul was already making its way, lost in a maze of opulent, diamond-studded lust that wrapped itself around her like a silken shroud. She was oblivious to her surroundings, unaware of her fiancé's cries as he watched her disappear into a veiled mist that had materialised the moment I turned to her and our eyes met. I was desire and I stood before her, draped in black and, like a beckoning finger, led her on.

She slipped in beside me and whenever our carriage negotiated a corner or pothole I allowed my body to cushion hers. She was static at first but the more I rubbed my booted ankles against her calves, the more I allowed my glove-clad forearms to lollop clumsily into her lap, the more I could feel the rising floods that filled her skin. It was ever thus, a rite through which we all must pass, the eternal war waged by curiosity on circumspection. Each juddering jolt brought us closer together until she finally allowed herself to abandon herself into my grasp.

We were both consumed by a heady cocktail of opium, anticipation and fear creating within us a barely tolerable sensation of intense self-awareness. Lust, like a drug, reverberated through our bodies, curdled our blood until we saw in each other's eyes angels and demons, the sacred and the profane.

It was I who broke the spell, the silence in which we both had been suspended whilst contemplating the inevitable. I was as swift as I was savage, sealing on the unsuspecting Samantha's lips a kiss so severe that it threatened to suck her lifeblood away. I set about my task like a woman possessed, any vestige of rational thought subjugated by desire. Like a hurricane I swept away every obstacle she laid in my wake until she was safely enveloped in the soft black silk of my skirts. Samantha had to learn what I had already studied with painful dedication – that to savour the elixir of true love one has also to taste fear and danger in all their malevolent façades.

By the time I laid a finger on Samantha's trembling flesh, expectation had already got the better of her. Guided only by the light of the fire and an instinctive knowledge of female geography, my painted nails dug into Samantha's inner thigh before releasing their grip and, just when my prey expected another surge of pain, sweeping up to her labia like a warm, moist breeze. The torment was over. Samantha was in the eye of the storm, drowning in waves of a pleasure so powerful that they broke over her body and sought out each and every declivity. And there she might have lain for all eternity had I not finally brought her to a delirious, shuddering halt.

I suppose it was her screams that brought Algernon to the correct window. He must have followed our carriage as far as the street corner but I made sure we entered unseen through the fog. He did not, of course, recognise the cry as belonging to his fiancée who would no more raise her voice than raise her eyes to meet his. Neither would he have recognised the naked body that lay straddled beneath my petticoats; it was only when he saw her face distorted in the shadows of flickering flames that the true horror of the vision revealed itself. After pausing to cast my lascivious eyes over Samantha's, I caught his petrified reflection in the mirror. I sneered and tossed back my head to make sure he understood it was directed at him. You must remember that these were the earliest days of my crusade and I was still uncertain as to how far I was prepared to push the limits. Seduction, even of one of my own sex, was but a minor peccadillo; to glory in the act under the prying eyes of a spectator was quite another vice altogether, one that had not previously crossed my mind. And the beauty of the scene lay in his impotence. He was powerless to put an end to the proceedings, not because he lacked the means – he would only have to call for assistance to condemn us both to a life of eternal shame – but because he was mesmerised by what he saw, just as you were. By all means condemn him as a hypocrite and voyeur but then read on; ask yourself, 'What wouldn't I have given to be in Algernon Mawkwood's stout and sensible shoes?'

While Samantha writhed before the hearth, consumed in the bittersweet juices of her own pleasure, I was consumed by the equally bittersweet emotion of envy. That I had, on more than one previous occasion, been where Sam was now did nothing to diminish my zeal. On the contrary, experience had only fuelled my greed. I had become an addict who needed her fix but, like an addict, each fix required a greater intensity and, in turn, a greater risk. I acted, as always, on impulse and seized upon the first implement I set my hungry eyes upon.

The iron poker lay in the fire, its pulsating red tip nestling suggestively in the embers. I wondered why on earth it had never occurred to me before and cursed myself for being such a prude. With great reverence I withdrew the poker from the hearth and lifted it high in the air. In the half-light and shadows I became a warrior with a sword I would present to my serf to knight me with. Even as I loosened my bodice Samantha knew what task she would be obliged – compelled – to carry out. Her protestations were as imagined as they were mute. She merely mouthed them without having the conviction to give them voice. I had uncovered her shoulders and now let her chemise fall to the floor to reveal the dark orbs of her modest but perfectly formed breasts.

Who was the more shocked? Samantha Poorton who, save in her own mirror, had never seen the naked body of a woman; or Algernon Mawkwood who had seen plenty in the brothels of the East End? But not even he, in all his depravity, had witnessed a scene as salacious as this. His sense of adventure got the better of his self-righteousness and he raised himself to the tips of his toes to gain a better vantage point. But his eyes had more appetite than his distended belly. He had never before allowed reality to encroach on his squalid little fantasies and the uncensored sight of our infernal machinations proved too much even for him and he vomited loudly on to the pavement before taking to his heels. I was so engaged in the act that I barely heard him and cared not a jot. I was whispering into Samantha's ear, urging her to strike while the iron was white hot and using my formidable powers of persuasion to undermine her reluctance. I brought her, once again, right to the brink, took her to the point of no return from which, once breached, there is no retreat. Samantha had no option but to acquiesce, pressed the poker firmly into the naked flesh of my upper arm and then, almost instantaneously, returned it to the fire.

There was only a single scream but it was sufficient to send all the watching choirs of holy angels fleeing for cover. It had its source in the depths of hell but found its resonance high in heaven; it was simultaneously driven by all that is evil but led by all that is good; it was pain and pleasure to such an excruciating degree that even I might have collapsed in paroxysms of delight had not Samantha passed the rod to me and requested the very same torment.

That night, as the fog lifted and soft moonbeams filtered through the window, Samantha and I lay together, sharing the dreams of the just and the nightmares of the wicked. In the hour before dawn I awoke, brushed away my curls and ran my hands through Samantha's hair. The poor girl needed sleep, so did I but now was not the time to take it. I cupped my lips and nibbled gently at Samantha's breasts *until she began to moan. We had known one other only a matter of hours but what we had created together had transformed our lives and rendered them forever inseparable.*

Our bodies fused, our eyes glazed, we stroked each other's wound for without that physical evidence neither of us would have been able to believe what we had committed ourselves to. Desperation was already setting in, the scars would heal and what would we have left but memories? My tongue circled the sweat-soaked lips of Samantha's vulva, then gently began to probe as if each exploration would open up new Edens and other unearthly delights. My pursuit had already begun. It would devour me, it would devour Samantha, leave us both with blood-shot eyes, like supernovae expelled from the confines of the galaxy. It was an immaculate conception – the Society of Sin, forged in flesh and flame, had sown its seed and secreted itself within the warmth of our coupled hands. Like us it was vulnerable but like us, given nurture and sustenance, it would flower and bear fruit, demanding from all its disciples both discipline and decadence. It thrived on hedonism, would wither and die if exposed to any form of moderation. In forming with its host a symbiotic relationship it embarked on a conquest of the mind as well as the body, a spirit that was willing and flesh that was rapacious in its unceasing quest for a temptation to submit to. And therein lay the secret of its success, for temptation is an insatiable mistress whose sylphlike figure disguises a voracious appetite for the sins of the flesh. In short, once was never enough.

Her writing was as elegant as her diction. In the same way that I would lie at her feet, hanging on her every consonant and vowel and gaze up lovingly at her face, so I ran each word lovingly over my tongue until I could almost feel her elixir merging with mine. The long slow pleasure had outrun the afternoon and the gathering gloom had penetrated my room. The evening spread itself out before me; the hours that had previously dragged in the company and instruction of my betters now oozed with potential. I lit only one candle lest an excess of light should break her spell. I stoked the fire and lay down on the rug before it. She might well have been there, next to me.

The letter lay at my side whilst I mulled over her tale. Much of it I had deduced. She had alluded on more than one occasion as to the beginnings of her – our – clique and the bizarre and painful way in which membership was conferred. As the last and youngest member it was my duty to preserve its history. 'We are only in exile,' she had told me as we parted in tears. 'I was only the prophetess; you are the messiah who will resurrect our dream. The Society of Sin might wither but it cannot die. When we meet again, as we surely must, you, my dear Charlotte, will have crowned yourself our new sovereign and I will be supplicant at your feet.'

She had, and indeed still, possessed sufficient wealth and influence to minimise any scandal our activities might have generated. Her prosperity was her protection. Whatever the poison spread by wagging tongues, she remained immune whereas I, though hardly a pauper, was now made subject to the rules I had transgressed. Algernon Mawkwood was easily bought off; the Poorton family accepted a modest gift of land for they were, in all truth, glad to be rid of their recalcitrant daughter.

Lady P's existence had hitherto been lonely and

proscribed. Though constantly wooed by the great and the good as well as the handsome and wealthy, she spurned them all. She had, during her travels, been offered a myriad of riches none of which had particularly appealed to her. The jewels and the clothes she had kept, not from a desire to please her hosts but with a view to selling them on her return home. The men were another matter. She found the younger ones, most of whom were little more than boys, pleasing on the eye but lacking in the fine arts required to satiate a women of her age and experience. The more mature specimens she found so uninviting that it was only after several draughts of wine that she could bring herself to sidle up to them. They tried. They poured the sum of all their strengths into attempts to please her but each left her frigid and frustrated. She began to believe the gibberish they had tried to drill into her during her brief sojourn at the convent: that pleasure was the sole preserve of the male species and women should console themselves to a life of duty and obedience. A staunch Roman Catholic, Lady P might have been prepared to accept this if her own experience had not exposed it as a blatant and dangerous untruth.

On returning to England she had managed to establish herself in comfortable lodgings in a respectable quarter of North London where she turned to her own advantage the imagination and ingenuity that polite society feared in a woman of her standing. Tired of playing the gracious hostess and frustrated by the plethora of rules which confined her and the numerous other women who had gravitated into her company, she decided that discretion would have to be the better part of valour. She accepted a proposal of marriage from the son of the Bishop of Bath and Wells but, on

the eve of their engagement, took flight for the continent with a considerable sum of money she had
managed to purloin from him. In truth she had already
earned enough to keep her in the luxury to which she
had become accustomed but Lady P's one great weakness was beginning to reveal itself: she despised the
mediocre and the banal, craved adventure and courted
danger. And yet, even a dozen days and nights in the
bordellos of Seville had failed to dampen her addiction.
It wasn't until that evening, when, in the unremark-
able countenance of the previously innocent Samantha
Poorton, Lady Persephone de Mortehoe had a vision of
the future – to drain the cup of concupiscence to its
sweetest dregs.

Tired of playing victim she decided to turn predator
and Samantha Poorton was her first prey.

I looked into the flames and saw her figure emerge;
she was mouthing the words I was following on the
page. She continued in her own mellifluous tones.

*I was so thrilled by my conquest that for the first –
and only – time in my life I acted in an uncharacter-
istically lackadaisical manner. I had, over the years,
developed a façade so unyielding that nobody has
yet managed to penetrate it. Every move I make,
every step I take is executed with a tender caution. I
am a mistress of disguise, I can assume whatever
role I fancy. Until that evening I had moved, almost
exclusively, in a masculine world, not, you should
understand, because I preferred their company nor
because I considered the fairer sex unworthy of my
attention. Indeed, nothing could have been further
from the truth. I found the gentleman with whom I
was forced to associate boorish and banal and
longed for discourse with another woman. But,*

denied access to the education I desired and the money I deserved – unless I yielded to one of my many suitors – I had no option but to become the ruler of my own destiny.

Had it selected me, Lady Persephone de Mortehoe, as its chosen host, or had I, in the dark crevices of my mind, dreamt up an ideal and, in paroxysms of pain, given birth to it? Whatever the manner of its genesis, ensconced in the arms of my first devotee I was already considering who next might have the courage to submit herself to the rite of passage that Samantha and I had created and, in doing so, prove herself worthy of the Society of Sin.

5

I gawped with undisguised fascination as a steady procession of carriages rolled up the drive and emptied their contents before the imposing façade of Chilcombe Lacey where Emma was waiting to greet them. Was there no end to the girl's talents? She had become, amongst many other roles, my maidservant, chaperone and trusted friend. I never quite knew which role she was playing; I never really knew where I stood with her. The contradictory nature of our relationship should have unsettled even a liberal such as myself but instead it merely added to the frisson.

It had been decided – or rather suggested by Emma and wholeheartedly endorsed by Lady P – that I should take up temporary residence at Chilcombe Lacey whilst my father was away. 'I fear for her safety should Mrs Bexington return,' Emma had told her mistress. 'Besides which, she is barely able to look after herself. She needs someone at her constant beck and call.'

It was only half a joke, she gave me only half a smile. She had unfinished business to attend to.

I had been allocated accommodation in the west wing overlooking the gardens, a palatial room almost half the size of my father's cottage which was, in itself, one of the village's more substantial dwellings. Emma fussed around until I felt myself at home then excused herself. She came back later that afternoon, after I had bathed, to assist with my wardrobe. I had not set eyes on Lady P since early that morning when I greeted her at the breakfast table. She was dressed in her riding habit and disappeared to the stables with some urgency once we had exchanged pleasantries. It was almost dark when the clatter of hooves echoed around the yard and drew me to the window. She had departed with the swift, haughty elegance of a fairy-tale princess, proud and self-assured; she returned spattered in mud, hair tangled with twigs and leaves, face flushed. Her costume was drenched in sweat, beads of dark liquid bulbed upon her forehead but the moment she dismounted her dignity was restored. Even amongst the golden pleats of dying sunlight her aura shone bright.

Never before, not even on the quayside in Cartagena, had I witnessed such a motley collection of distinguished but disparate womanhood. Femininity oozed from every pore, fecundity seeped into the balmy night air, perfumed it with a pungent, unhinging desire. It was as if, with every arrival, the continents were shifting beneath our delicately laced feet. Had you been there, looking on, from between the briars and the birches, the truth would have eluded you. To see was not to believe. You would only be witnessing a gathering of ladies who, to the untrained eye, expressed all the virtuous qualities so beloved of their gentler sex. But, were you to creep a little closer, were you able to listen and to feel, to touch and to taste and to inhale, you, too, would have succumbed to intoxication and the subversive spirit fermented within. Here were fear and danger, wrapped tightly for their own safekeeping and folded neatly like starched Sunday best. Nobody, but nobody, would have suspected.

What they had in common was a desire to prise open their own Pandora's box even though they were all aware that once the lid had been unlocked it could never, ever be slammed shut. Some had come only to observe, some to satisfy their curiosity but others were willing to totally immerse themselves in passion and desire.

First to arrive was Hildebrand von Bingen, a German theologian who had made a name for herself dissecting the esoteric writings of the Christian mystics. She was followed by the botanist Olivia Bar-le-Duc, a profession that did not normally lend itself to controversy but that Miss Bar-le-Duc had exploited to turn herself into a minor celebrity attacked with some frequency in the letters pages of *The Times*. The final carriages contained Miss Leticia Vauchurch, writer and philosopher, and Liberty Belle, sometime pirate of the Spanish seas. It was the last who caught my attention. I had seen women of her race and colour in the harbour-side barrios of Cartagena, although they, as second-rate citizens, servants or even slaves, lacked her nobility. Liberty Belle was every inch the aristocrat turned rebel. She dressed in male attire not through any desire to be identified as a man – with her long black dreadlocks gathered together in a black silk ribbon that would have been quite impossible – but because it afforded her the ease of movement her profession required. Not that she bore any resemblance to a salty old seadog, scoured by the wind and the rain. All that she wore shone with a luminous splendour that contrasted magnificently with her smooth obsidian skin. Her navy silk waistcoat was casually unbuttoned, her billowing white sleeves were slashed to the wrists and she had tied around her neck a scarlet cravat. All she lacked was a cutlass and a shipful of men to rule over. But, then again, she had us.

She bowed with a full over-elaborate sweep and

grazed her fingertips on the gravel. 'Captain Liberty Belle, angel of the high seas, protector of the poor and the unloved, at your service, Miss Crowsettle. It is I who right the world's wrongs. If anyone has done you a disfavour, I will gladly avenge it.'

I giggled like a silly child, bowled over by her flattery. She brought a blush to my cheeks and a rush of blood to my head. That disconcerting combination of raw masculine puissance and elegant feminine charm; the best of both worlds, like the Earth before its creation. She took my arm and led me into the throng.

The dancing had begun; the wine was flowing, served by Emma who made sure my glass was never empty. Each and every female taboo was being broken: cigars and cheroots, draughts of ale and, in a corner but barely concealed, Lady P and Samantha were sharing an opium bowl. From heaven knows where Lady P had engaged the services of a quartet who filled the ballroom with a string of melodies, which would turn increasingly discordant as the night progressed and a more sinister mood descended upon the house and grounds of Chilcombe Lacey.

The alcohol and the narcotics were, for me, at least, superfluous. I touched neither until we returned, like a pack of satiated wolves, from that night's nefarious activities. Then I needed the wine, sitting in front of the fire with Lady P to my left and Liberty Belle to my right, becoming fully cognisant of what we had done, trying hard not to remember. It was impossible; which of us could not forget the look on his face, those wild eyes, wide open with fear and sheer incomprehension, the terror that stretched his mouth in anguish? True, he came to no harm, but how was he to know that? When we released him, when our baying cries signalled the onset of the hunt, he must have feared for

his life. He was French but; he would not have understood a word even had we spoken in an intelligible
tongue but the awful truth is that our antediluvian
esurience reduced us to nothing more than snarls.

17 June 1876
Chilcombe Bredy

Dear Diary
*Why have I never been able to tell the difference
between right and wrong? Am I inherently evil? Was
I born into it? Have I already condemned myself to
eternal damnation?*
  Do I really care?
  What in heaven's name am I saying?
  *It was Yseult's night. It was Yseult's one and only
opportunity to prove herself worthy of her company.
Lady P had called for order and the ballroom had
immediately fallen silent. She stood upon the table
and let her voice ring clear around the room. I can
remember her clarion cry word for word: 'Remember,
ladies,* audere est facere *– to dare is to do.'*

The Chapel of St Luke lies in the heart of Ashley Chase,
surrounded by coppiced oak and, in late spring, a thick
carpet of bluebells, a million tiny amethysts dancing
in the glades. It had, many, many years ago, belonged
to the Cistercians and in that, I think, lay its attraction
for Lady P. She was, still is, a devout Catholic; the only
family tradition that she hadn't discarded. How did
she manage to square her faith with her philosophy?
Being a woman of no faith whatsoever, it is a question
I asked myself over and over again. I admired her all
the more for her contradictions.

On dissolution the monastery soon fell into decay
but the Chapel of St Luke survived for some time,

falling into disrepair but offering a sanctuary for the recusants that made the Chase notorious. It was only recently that their existence became public knowledge; it had been kept secret for three centuries by its benevolent protectors, the de Mortehoe family. Despite Mrs Bexington's warnings, which usually aroused my curiosity, I had never ventured that far up the valley, that deep into the woods, though I had spent several afternoons wondering what possible evidence she might have been able to produce to persuade me. It had tantalised me for ages; now, at last, I was about to enter its deepest declivities. I could hardly wait.

We marched by the light of the moon and the single torch carried by Lady P, who lead us through the fields to the long lane that wound its way up to the chase. I was by her side. She was holding my hand and so was aware of how much I was trembling. She spoke softly to reassure me. Behind us were Samantha and Yseult Tredinnick, and between them the French sailor who, having realised that his captors were only women and that his life was not, therefore, in immediate danger, had relaxed. He was still perplexed, but his perplexity bore a wry smile. I knew it would not be long before Yseult wiped it from his face.

As we entered the woods I finally plucked up the courage to ask Lady P what was to become of him, although I had already hazarded a guess that I knew would not be far from the truth. She clutched my hand tighter still and answered me with a question.

'Are you afraid, Charlotte?'

There was no point in attempting to hide it; fear was pulsing through my veins. 'Yes, I am.'

'And are you uncomfortable?'

'No.'

I surprised myself. It was quite true. Had she offered

me a way out, asked Emma to accompany me back to Chilcombe Lacey and thence to my cottage where my dear father might be waiting for me by the hearth, I would have refused her. I could imagine no intoxicant as potent as fear, no sensation so thrilling. I cared not for the consequences, to hell with them and all their implications.

Lady P continued, 'And do you realise that you have passed the point of no return? We are all beyond redemption now. You have told me much but I still feel I barely know the half of you. I wish to learn a great deal more. I will have it, my dear Charlotte. I shall have the knowledge from you, whether you consent or not. You are almost one of us now. We will have no secrets amongst us.'

The mob moved like possessed demons, silent and stern in the sweltering night. Rabbits fled from our approach, even the owl was silenced in her vigil. Their eyes were only on the prize whose fate became clear the moment we entered the ruins of the chapel.

It was an appropriate stage for the act that was to follow. The sacred would be profaned upon the very altar where bread and wine became body and blood. Even an agnostic could not fail to see the resonance. Through the Frenchman's sacrifice Yseult would metamorphose from mere mortal to join the ranks of the divine beings who numbered among them Lady P, Samantha Poorton and Emma, the honoured members of the Society of Sin. Each of them bore its badge; I had seen them all with my own eyes. The crude logo burnt into their flesh; it would never heal, they would never forget.

Our footsteps stammered through the undergrowth, brambles and briars tore at our expensive gowns and tangled in our hair. Tendrils of ivy gripped and crammed into the rotting limestone, piles of fallen masonry were lost under clumps of chest-high nettles that stung my naked arms. The pain was momentary; it soon passed into a pleasant warm glow, brought blood to the skin and fire to the brimstone. We gathered around the encircling flames, watched the swirling sparks leaping out of its midst like copulating demons. The spell had been cast, the world was changed; church to temple in wrecked piety. Mother Nature, for the time being, was distracted and with her prying eyes elsewhere we had licence to do as we pleased. But make no mistake, once she became aware of her mistake, that her laws had been broken, her retribution would be merciless and severe.

Yseult was kneeling before Lady P; the Frenchman had been shackled to the wall, his back to us. I could see now, in the clear and pure moonlight, that he was a handsome man, a sailor whose ocean adventures had tanned his skin and made rugged his countenance. Mario had destroyed my faith in love, turned me into a cynic and a servant of my own lusts. I cared not what others desired, to my mind the purpose of love was only to satisfy my own selfish cravings, to recreate love in my own graven image. I wanted to expunge Mario's memory. I could still feel his filthy presence within my body, his bloated body upon mine, his clammy hands crawling under my skirts. In the Frenchman's lithe frame I saw the chance of reparation.

The others' attention was elsewhere, fixed upon Yseult, even the omnipresent Emma was transfixed. I couldn't take my eyes off him, his torso struggling within the chains, knowing without seeing. Possession took a greater hold of me. He had been chosen not for me but for Yseult, he was to be her trial but I saw no harm in testing the water. Nobody saw me break the circle. I crept backwards until the shadows hid me and allowed our bodies to collide unobserved. He flinched and would have given out a cry had I not silenced him with my gloved fist. I rammed it hard into his mouth. I need not have used so much force but I wanted him to be sure that it was I who was in control and that he was at my mercy.

Night had not blunted the heat of day; darkness made it only more impenetrable. His sweat, sweet and sticky, glowed with an amber hue upon his creased forehead. He couldn't possibly comprehend and it was, I think, the apprehension that tormented him. He had been raised to accept the double standard: that all women were simultaneously virgins and whores; that they were to be both respected and abused; that they were, above all, subject to the whims and fancies of the omnipotent male.

I loosened my fist and let my fingertips fall down his cheeks, parted his lips and allowed my tongue to reach inside. One hand slipped underneath his waistband and ripped open his fly whilst the other unbuttoned his shirt. It was not subtle; there were no pretences to love or affection. His chest was a jungle of hair, thin and wiry, almost luminously white against the night sky. It seemed so surreal and immaculate that I was overcome with the urge to verify its quality so I dug my nails into his flesh. That's when the blood came, that's when he screamed and I felt the wrath of Lady P upon me.

'Well, well, well.' Her voice was soft but loaded with sarcasm. 'Who would have thought it? Miss Charlotte Crowsettle, so sweet and innocent – or at least that is what she would have us think but some of us know otherwise, do we not, Charlotte?'

I watched the arc of her arm as it scythed through

the air and I reeled back as her open palm caught my right cheek. I stood there mesmerised until she struck me again, with the back of her hand. I had not expected my transgression to be met with such unequivocal violence. I could not hate her for it; I loved and admired her all the more. I would have fallen at her feet had she not hauled me before the assembled throng.

'Remind me, Samantha, what are the seven deadly sins. I don't think Charlotte is acquainted with them.'

The poetess strode before me, taking pleasure in my disgrace. 'Pride, Envy, Anger, Sloth, Avarice, Gluttony and Lust,' she replied.

'Correct. And which sin, do you suggest, has she so brazenly committed?'

'Gluttony, Percy?'

'Quite right. Sometimes, my dear Charlotte, desire becomes misplaced, sometimes we are lost within the overpowering demands of our own lasciviousness. It is not our fault. Who are we to be blamed for our very human frailty?'

She was circling me like a hawk rounding in on her kill, the black hem of her skirts rustling into mine. They were all glaring at me with various degrees of disapproval. Samantha, her suspicions apparently confirmed, was gazing daggers. Liberty Belle, on the other hand, appeared mildly amused but would not, perhaps, have been so bold as to intervene despite Lady P's actions. This woman who had taken on slavetraders, bandits and brigands in the name of freedom would not so much as raise a finger to protect me from the unchecked wrath of nobility. But she was right, my punishment was merited, the chastisement was what I deserved. Who was I, a mere governess, to question the perpetual jurisdiction of the status quo ante?

'You must learn,' continued Lady P, 'to observe without feeling, to feast your eyes but curb your appetite. Your time will come, Charlotte, but not if you continue in this display of wretched petulance. I will not allow it, do you hear? Remember, you are still only a child and, as I consider myself *in loco parentis*, you will do as I say, abide by my every word. Is that understood?'

Her eyes were furnaces like the very fires of hell, stoked by an army of fallen angels whose ranks I would surely join once she had devoured me. I had come to despise authority, to rail against it and overthrow its primitive traditions. Now it was revealed in all its effervescent glory, blinding me with its unworldly beauty.

She raised her arm again as if to strike me but, forewarned and forearmed, I had already learnt my lesson. 'I said, is that understood?' she repeated.

I fell to my knees, took her hand with great reverence and placed my lips upon the elongated frame of her fingers. When she allowed me to kiss them a brief shiver of excitement ran up my spine then fizzled away in my mind like a roman candle. Lady P's stern façade slowly melted into an all-conquering smile; the stony heart of my ice queen thawed and embraced me in the ravishing light of forgiveness.

The battle was over and the war was won. To the victor the spoils, to the *conquistadora* every hidden treasure that lay within my unexplored domains, now conceded to her empire. Blessed are those who submit without question, for they shall inherit the earth and all her sublime and dew-drenched riches.

Glowing with triumph, Lady P returned to the fray. 'Now, to the mission that awaits us ... or rather, that awaits our neophyte. Yseult, please step forwards. Your trial must begin before the witching hour is upon us.

There are demons on the chase and spies in the woods. The former will seduce you and distract you from your cause; the latter will seize you and set you upon the path to self-righteousness. The Society of Sin acknowledges no friends or allies and swears a bloody vengeance on all who seek to break it.'

Yseult, the scourge of male academics across Europe and beyond, was trembling, her discomfort plain for all to see. I could not discern who was the more fearful, the Grail historian or the French sailor, neither of whom was now ignorant of their fate as Lady P handed her the lash.

It was woven, I learnt later, from the finest Argentine leather. Whatever the tool or the purpose, only the best would satisfy Lady P. Only she and Liberty Belle had ever wielded the whip before, for the remainder of us it was a barbarous novelty that filled our hearts with unease. I'm not sure we expected matters to spiral out of hand so suddenly. What had begun as a midnight picnic threatened to descend into bedlam, though it was, of course, a chaos cleverly manipulated by its authoress who directed the ensuing events with a choreographer's prophetic dexterity.

'I ... I ... cannot ... go through with this, Persephone. I cannot embrace cruelty for nothing more than its own sake.' Yseult's fractured pleas fell upon the silent ground like seeds on barren land. Lady P would not be denied. She had sunk every penny she possessed into this quest, she had invested in it all her heart, her mind and her soul. She would tear out the symbols of fertility and plunge them straight back, into the Earth's groin, if only she could achieve her ends.

'But we agreed, Miss Tredinnick. Have you and I spent many, many hours devising your examination only to be thwarted by a failing spirit? Think about it,

Yseult. You know full well the consequences should you fail. Your reputation will lie in tatters, you will be ostracised by all who have loved you, humoured by all who have feared you. I shall make it my business to make every hour of your life a waking misery. Do it! Do it now!'

And so she did, taking the three-tailed whip, feeling its cool cowhide in her hand, allowing it to feel comfortable in her grasp. Her Grail was in her reach, her quest was almost at an end. Like her hero, Perceval, she could hear the question reverberating through the wood: 'Whom does the Grail serve?' And, like Perceval, the answer suddenly revealed itself: 'It serves its seeker.'

Yseult began gingerly with light flicks of the lash until she had raised a series of raw weals on the Frenchman's naked torso. But she eschewed violence, preferring instead to inflict suffering with tender affection. In truth, the damage was barely skin deep. The scars would heal and the incredulous stranger, his senses numbed by opium, would awake only to memories of a lucid nightmare. His body gyrated to the rhythm of the whip, each stroke lovingly applied as she warmed to her task. She began to understand the allure and the attraction of pain; she began to envy him, she began to take exception to the spasms of agony that splintered his skin. She edged ever closer and the coarse leather strands found their way into ever more intimate locations until his moaning was barely audible.

And then tyranny got the better of her and she threw down the whip with such ferocity that I thought a madness had overcome her. Well, perhaps that was true, but more mania than lunacy. The previously serene and sedate Yseult was transformed into a woman possessed. She threw herself upon the sailor, unshackled the chains that bound him and dragged his convulsing body to the altar. Nobody moved to intervene, it was as if, by some magic of osmosis, we were sharing in her pleasure and, like her, would not be spurned.

They were both caked in dust and dried sweat. Freed from his torment, the sailor exploited his freedom and seemed set upon revenge, not understanding that a heady cocktail of alcohol and opium incites the imagination but induces a stealthy impotence. For all his desire he could not perform and in his frustration his clumsy lovemaking became ever more physical and impolite.

But Yseult cared not. She mustered all her schoolgirl French to spur him on. She belittled him, she questioned his manhood until his shame was so great I feared his anger might explode into savagery. She had divested herself of all she had been wearing and cast them into fire where their blackness dissolved into the white flames. From their obscurity emerged a tall and muscular figure, as pale as the angel of death, a shooting star that collided into his nakedness and sent plumes of pleasure singing into the sky. Liberty has claimed many victims, men and woman who sought it like they sought the Grail but were burnt by its blood. It is, after all, a poisoned chalice, but for some its venom is as sweet and thick as the finest wine. She imbibed and he, seeing how her body responded to its warm juices, imbibed too. He was determined to prove himself her equal but had not bargained for her perverted sense of chivalry. She was the knight, he was her squire. She sat astride him, shielding herself from his ineffectual blows. She rode him like a stallion, pummelled his thighs with her outstretched palms and rained kiss after bloody kiss upon his bruised and battered lips. I watched her sinews ripple with every wave of ecstasy that pulsed through her body. I watched as her breasts bloomed from small buds into a fruit that was ripe for the picking.

She worked tirelessly to evoke some response from his penis, which lay defiantly flaccid like a crushed obelisk in his groin. She spread her thighs wide open and his hands moved inside and waded through the sticky swamps that guarded the sacred space of her cavern. She gnawed on his ears, dug her teeth into his chest but still he remained defiantly unaroused.

It was only later, much much later, that I realised she had had no alternative. It was an act so grossly repulsive that I ought to have turned my eyes. The moment her tongue descended over his navel his protestations abated and he began to gurgle like an infant at his mother's nipple. She smiled at his response, watched with distorted fascination as she won an involuntary twitch from his member. It sprang into life as she took it in her fingers and squeezed hard. Only pain would suffice, only the grinding erosion of his will as she tugged hard upon his prick, which suddenly reared into life. She laughed with the wild eyes of a demented dryad, cupped her lips into the shape of an elongated 'O' and lowered them on to him.

I will never forget that scream, it will reverberate through the corridors of my mind when every other memory is forgotten. It pierced the heavens and shook the chapel's crumbling walls as if an earthquake had passed beneath us. Her head rose and a drop of scarlet blood dribbled down her chin; the vampire had her prey, had it stiff and prone before her. She took his wounded member and thrust it inside.

She barked at the moon, howled like a wolf on heat

until he thrust hard enough to bring her to a stinging orgasm. And then she collapsed, her body disappearing into a fog of billowing black smoke that Lady P, ever the sorceress, had procured from the flames.

I was still trying to catch my breath when the clouds parted and the celebration reached its climax. Yseult, now conscious, was cradled in Emma's arms as Lady P removed the brand from the fire. She flinched at the approach of its burning crown but Emma held her tight and the poor woman had exhausted herself. The iron made contact with flesh for no more than a second, the bitter smell of scorched flesh gave way to the sweet scent of burning applewood. Yseult's cry was only momentary and soon gave way to a long contented sigh. She lay back as Lady P laid a moist, soothing kiss on the wound. One could already see the outline beginning to form; it was larger and more elaborate than that which disfigured the arms of the existing three members of the Society. Some time later she proudly displayed her scar. Woven amongst the bold letters 'SoS' were the body of a snake and branches bearing forbidden fruit which a naked Eve reached out to taste. I wondered when – or if – my time would come. I was already moist with anticipation.

Chilcombe Bredy
17 June 1876

Dear Emma
You will, I suspect, be surprised to receive a letter from me. I am sure it's not the done thing but I need you, rather than Lady Persephone, to confirm the version of last night's events that has established itself within the otherwise vacant halls of my memory. My father has written to say he will be returning

home tomorrow, although for how long I know not. I do not want him asking questions I will struggle to answer and I do not want to tell him lies, neither of us has ever shirked from the truth. He is a tolerant man but he must be kept in blissful ignorance.

I beg you, do not show this letter to your mistress, do not even mention its existence. She has been so very good to me, so very gracious with her company that I feel disloyal in even putting pen to paper. I fear, even more, the wrath of her disapproval.

Please, you must write immediately and tell me what happened. I can remember walking down the hill with you at my side, we were looking up at the stars, telling ourselves we had never before seen the firmament in all its heavenly finery. I was rambling, I did not want to think about what I had witnessed; you, very kindly, humoured me.

I remember hearing the church clock strike three when we finally arrived back at Chilcombe Lacey. There was a thin band of golden blue light spanning the eastern horizon. I watched the sunrise with Liberty Belle at my side; we shared a bottle of wine and a cheroot – well, I know it was not a cheroot but she would not tell what we were smoking. When the first rays lay across the lawn we danced a waltz and a sea shanty and then, I think, I fell drowsy and she put me to bed.

And you brought me breakfast and coffee when I awoke; you dressed me and poured me a draught of foul-tasting medicine that brought energy and vigour back to my tired limbs. Lunch is no more than a blurred dream; you told me I matched everyone for intellectual debate but I am sure you were flattering me. I lacked nothing from your attention. I would have walked home, the exercise and clear air would have benefited me but you insisted on donning your *uniform and riding me home. How soundly I slept last night, with the taste of your sweat still on my brow.*

I do not deserve such selfless concern; your kindness serves only to heighten my anxiety. Tell me, sweetest, dearest Emma, that it was naught but a dream, that I am suffering from a fever that has corrupted my morals as much as my mind. If not I am lost in a nightmare of my own creation.

God help me
Charlotte

To say I feared the wrath of Lady P would be so very far from the truth but the truth was too complicated – and too disturbing – to own up to, even to Emma, even to myself. Besides which, however much I hoped my letter would be met by her eyes alone, I was taking a risk in assuming it would not be intercepted by her mistress. Perhaps, deep in the depths of my troubled psyche, I wanted her to seize it, to confiscate it and bury it amongst all her other intimate secrets. The truth is, I did not fear her wrath so much as adore it. She had struck me hard. It was neither an accident nor instinctive reaction but she knew how to inflict a blow without leaving any lasting mark. My cheeks stung for the following two days but the pain was warm and pleasant and stirred tectonic rumblings within my girded loins.

I was correct, the reply came promptly, within an hour.

Chilcombe Lacey
17 June 1876

My dearest Charlotte
It reads almost like a love letter. I do believe Emma is quite embarrassed. When I tried to tease her I

could see I had come across a soft spot. You have a way with words. Your wit and wisdom come as no surprise to me but the company were suitably impressed. Samantha, who had always harboured a certain suspicion, is completely won over and would like you to teach her Spanish.

You must not think ill of me for intercepting your letter; it is not that I approve of censorship, nor that I have no faith in my trusted servant. You must understand, Charlotte, that whatever my predilection for proscribed liberties, the likes of which polite society vehemently disapproves, I am, above all, the Lady of the Manor. As such I have a solemn duty to preserve, superficially at least, the ancien regime. It is a duty I undertake with great solemnity and pride, even if that means contradicting myself. It is, you must understand, a game; a game in which our allotted roles are inverted, subverted and the world is turned upside down. I cannot give Emma the free rein she deserves and, in her previous existence, enjoyed. I will not see her hurt. I am, for better or worse, her mistress; she is beholden to me and I, in turn, am beholden to her. We go the way of all flesh, Charlotte, the way of all flesh.

You will have seen, too, the means of control I am obliged to adopt to maintain my authority. I am sorry for striking you, it hurt me to hurt you but you must understand that I had no alternative. You transgressed, you disobeyed me, you flouted my instructions. However much it pains me, I cannot allow such behaviour to go unpunished. To you, a child of the enlightenment, it will undoubtedly seem cruel and unjust but, as far as Chilcombe Lacey is concerned, the concept of liberal democracy has never caught on, and is unlikely to do so in the foreseeable future. My people might detest me but *they trust and respect my superiority. They have grown to love the rigidity of order and duty and, as far as they are concerned, I am the earthly manifestation of that harmony. They like to know where they are in the overall scheme of things and in that overall scheme of things I am all things to all men and women – I am the law.*

But now to more earthly matters. I am called back to London on business that I can no longer trust to my lawyers. My good name and reputation have come into question and it is imperative I right the wrong immediately. I have plans for you, I am working on them even now, as I write. It is a scheme so grandiose and debauched that you will require an assistant, an accomplice, a partner in crime. In my absence I have entrusted this task to Emma. I know not what she has planned, only that she has stretched her imagination to the limits and, more importantly, decided to accompany you.

I wish you good luck and look forward to being the first to hear your tales of derring-do.

Your ever loving mistress

Slowly, Lady P's world began to slot neatly into place. The order and tradition she so carefully maintained allowed her to indulge in more unconventional passions. In doing so, however, she created the space she needed to undermine the very values that system espoused as being morally superior. She was, in effect, a rebel, in the most subtle and sensual manner I could imagine.

6

Dear Diary
I am so very, very exhausted. It is barely four o'clock
in the morning but I cannot sleep, nor can I bear to
spend another minute tossing and turning in my
bed, twisting in my sweat. Even in the heat of a
Spanish summer I was able to nod off at any hour of
the day, now, whenever I close my eyes, I am visited
by all manner of visions: some fey, some frivolous,
some of which I simply do not understand, some of
which I do not want to understand.

Is it fear or is it uncertainty? In truth I do not
know what I have let myself into, has what I wit-
nessed the previous night, on the chase, condemned
me already? Dear God, I have betrayed you.

Father is due to return this morning. I do not
think I can bear for him to set eyes upon my lifeless,
washed-out features. I do not think the truth will be
safe from his prying investigations. He will want to
know what I've been up to, how Lady P and myself
have been passing the hot sunny afternoons and
why I look like the very image of death itself warmed
up. He will want me to account for Mrs Bexington's
absence and I shall have to tell him a lie. He will
request my company but it is a request I am unable
to consent to; Emma has called me and I am com-
pelled to come.

Thank God I have managed to intercept the Reverend Lytton Cheney's reproving letter. What Father would have made of it I do not know but I dare not take the risk. That, on its own, would hardly suffice to persuade but were he to add it to all the other evidence his own eyes can see...

'Father! How wonderful to see you!' My delight was genuine and unbounded but my enthusiasm had waned. He was too wrapped up in his rocks to notice the lack of a spring in my step as I strode up the path to greet him.

'Charlie! How the devil are you? I am sorry to have been away for so long. I do hope you appreciate how busy I've been of late. You must blame Professor Walditch, he has been proofreading the book from sunrise to sunset – and then he insists on taking me to supper to discuss matters further. I have quite forgotten the days when I was my own master but such are the demands of an author.'

'Oh, Father, it's only a volume of local geology. You have hardly reached the ranks of Mr Hardy yet!' I could sense the regret in his voice so I teased him. He had recently made the acquaintance of Mr Thomas Hardy, a Dorchester architect whose novels were beginning to court controversy in the literary world. My father thoroughly approved of his latest work – deemed 'too racy' by at least one distinguished magazine – and had promised to invite him over for supper on his return.

My father had never been one for hiding his feelings, not even in the company of his peers and the moment I set foot before him he took me up in his arms and embraced me. He was a big man, as gentle as he was strong, and I would not have wished to have incurred his anger. When he put me down I noticed him looking me over, sensing that not all in the Bride Valley was as it should be. Concern spread through his face and he was just about to give voice to his unease when a second figure emerged from the carriage and I recognised at once the slim outline of Professor Samuel Walditch. My cursed luck was blessed. The distinguished academic would be my saviour, my father's attention would be directed solely at him.

It was midday. The sun was high over the oak trees, beating down upon me, pressing its heavy heat into every orifice. After a swift lunch my father and his companion had donned rucksack and boots and set off with their hammers in search of elusive strata. The reprieve, I knew, would be brief; I had only bought myself a short stay of execution with my ad hoc story explaining how Mrs Bexington had departed, perhaps indefinitely, to look after a long-lost sister whose exist-ence she had hitherto never mentioned. A more dutiful parent might have taken some time to question his errant daughter at greater length but not my father, too keen to indulge himself and his mentor. Much as I was relieved when they disappeared up Honeybun Lane, I resented the lack of due care and attention. It was tantamount to a licence to carry on in whatever manner I wished.

So be it. I had secreted the vicar's letter about my body with the vague intention of tearfully presenting it to my father and confessing to all in a desperate plea for forgiveness. I would, after all, be saving not only my own beleaguered soul but also those of my fellow disciples. From somewhere in my mind came the notion that if I flung myself at his feet and begged for his mercy he might finally come to his senses and take his errant daughter in hand. I was growing tired of my autonomy, tired of my own wilful disobedience. After all, what is the point of pushing against the boundaries of decency if there was nobody there to give a damn? Sulking like the petulant child I lay down against a tree and reminded myself of the vicar's recommendations that would now remain unheeded.

St Ethelburga's Rectory
15 June 1876

Sir
Please forgive my impertinence for contacting you on a matter so close to your heart as your dear daughter, Miss Charlotte Crowsettle. I write, albeit without her consent, only with her interests in mind.

Sir, I welcomed you to the village when you arrived here last summer. I paid you the customary visit and have, despite a certain provocation, always attempted to retain a Christian courtesy in our dealings. We have had our differences and disagreements, some more vociferous than others, but I have always maintained the greatest respect for your achievements and your contribution to the Empire. A man of your standing, Sir Napier, is a man of great value to our humble village. I would not want to see your dignity corrupted in your absence by a daughter who has, quite innocently, come under the influence of the strumpet who has taken residence in Chilcombe Lacey. You will, I am sure, have heard the local tittle-tattle regarding the criminal means by which she took possession of the estate; let me tell you that this is more than idle gossip. My own investigations are beginning to expose the truth and I intend to reveal all before the summer is out.

You will discover, on your return, that your housekeeper is no longer in residence. She has fled, Sir

Napier, fled! The poor woman sought refuge in my home until I found her a position in a respectable household in Dorchester. I cannot bear to go into the gory detail; it would pain you as much to read it as it would me to write it. Suffice to say that she came across your daughter in a state of undress in a comprising and very unladylike position. I hasten to add that she was alone but that does not exonerate her, indeed, in my opinion it implicates her all the more.

But, please, do not take Mrs Bexington's word alone for the truth. She is a trusted servant but a servant nonetheless and one who is prone to distortions of reality. I myself have seen Miss Crowsettle scurrying towards Chilcombe Lacey in the dead of night. I firmly hold to the principle 'innocent before proven guilty' but I am afraid the evidence against her is rather damning. Aware of the moral peril that now resides in Chilcombe Lacey, I and several other like-minded souls have taken to patrolling the lanes of Chilcombe Lacey, particularly those that border the estate. We have seen strange things: a procession of carriages racing through the darkness to deposit their contents at that unholy door, the comings and goings of strange-looking men and your daughter taking to the fields to avoid discovery.

Make of that what you will. I do not wish to gainsay you, nor be he who said 'I told you so', only to present you with the facts as I have seen and evaluated them. I repeat, your daughter is in such grave moral danger that I fear for the welfare of both her soul and, I am afraid to say, her body. This letter may, indeed, arrive too late, she may already be corrupted, perhaps in the most unthinkable and unnatural of manners. Be that as it may, I still have a duty to attend to her moral welfare; she is not yet beyond salvation. If she addresses her sin, confesses and begs at God's knee for forgiveness, if she promises to mend her evil ways and live the life of a righteous woman from hereinafter, redemption shall be hers.

Sir, I know nothing of your plans for the summer but, if you are to continue on your travels and your daughter is to remain without an escort, allow me at least to recommend a guardian to care for her. It is not appropriate for a girl of her age to be left alone; the devil does indeed make work for idle hands. My fiancée, Miss Grace Fitzpiers, is presently seeking a temporary position prior to our marriage this autumn. She is a wonderful lady, not much older than your daughter, sweet but strong with an incorruptible Christian disposition. I consider myself immensely privileged to be her future husband. She will ask for no financial remuneration, faith, alone will be her reward.

But we must also look to the future. I have stated quite unequivocally that, once wed, my wife will devote herself to domestic duties and Grace has agreed to obey my every command. I am afraid I cannot allow her to take charge of Charlotte but in any case, what the girl needs is a husband to take her in hand. My very good friend, Gideon Blackmore, is presently studying for the ministry and will be ordained later this summer. What say you, Sir Napier? A minister cannot hope to tend to the needs of his flock without a wife to minister to those of his own. He has been promised a parish in Weymouth and currenly resides nearby at Chilcombe Magna, so your daughter would not be so very far away. You would be able to observe her flower into a perfect specimen of Christian womanhood.

I would ask you, once again, to pay heed to what

*I have written. The circumstances are grave, Sir
Napier. Believe me, if you were in possession of the
full facts, as I now am, you would be doing your
daughter a profound disserve and neglecting your
duties as a father. I await your prompt reply.*

　I remain, sir, your obedient servant
　The Reverend Dr Lytton Cheney

It would be hard to imagine my father paying any
heed to a senior man of the cloth, let alone the wild
ravings of the local vicar. The two had locked horns on
more than one occasion and, during a public discussion
over the merits of Mr Charles Darwin and his *Origin of
the Species*, very nearly came to blows. Yet my father
was not, like myself, a vehement atheist, rather a mild-
mannered agnostic who enjoyed discussing matters
pertaining to theology. He disliked organised religion;
he disliked even more the Reverend Dr Lytton Cheney.

And so did I. With an even greater zeal now I knew
the extent of his deviousness and preposterous plans.
He had been thorough in his investigations; I had not
credited him with such resourcefulness. Much as I
craved my father's attention, much as I was prepared
to accept his paternal discipline, I would not be tamed.
As long as Chilcombe Lacey was standing, I would not
be locked in the parlour in the stifling company of
'modest' women. I would stride the Chase like a colossus, seeking out the soft and shady bowers where the
nymphs and the satyrs dwelt. I would hunt down
hedonism and imbibe myself upon it and no sanctimonious fool would stand in my way.

I tore up the letter and swore my revenge.

The vicar and his select coterie of vigilantes were not
the only inhabitants of Chilcombe Bredy exercised by

the presence of Lady Persephone at the house but, as most adhered to a philosophy of keeping their heads down and minding their own business, ignorance sustained bliss. On first taking occupancy of the estate every member of Chilcombe Lacey's domestic staff had lined up to welcome their new mistress; within an hour they had all been dismissed, albeit with substantial severance payments. It wasn't that Lady P was so radical in her outlook that she found the concept of servitude demeaning, nor that she was so self-contained that she needed no external help for she retained the services of most of her former employees on an ad-hoc basis until, one by one, they took umbrage and resigned. The truth was that in her pursuit of liberation she had learnt to trust none save those who shared her single-minded lust for desire.

Her ownership of Chilcombe Lacey broke a tradition of exclusively male tenure that stretched back over five hundred years and put the fear of God into the inhabitants of Ashley Chase. Her first visit was fleeting and before the day was out she disappeared back to London. But within those 24 hours she swept away the centuries of benign dictatorship that had characterised the de Mortehoes' jurisdiction over the chase for the family had looked after its vassals like a father and practised a feudalism that was conducive to all providing they knew and accepted their position in the hierarchy. They continued to defer to their superiors, they doffed their caps, curtseyed and bowed, but they were all gestures devoid of respect.

The discovery of a Frenchman, quite naked, in the woods hardly helped to improve relations between the matriarch and her vassals. They were not so simple that they were unable to put one and one together and come up with the obvious solution: Lady Persephone de Mortehoe. In her absence, Emma had no option but to turn to me.

'Charlotte! Charlotte! Please, come quick.'

She collapsed, breathless in front of me where I had slipped into an uneasy sleep under the shade of the rowan tree. I was irritated by both her audacity in not addressing me correctly and at being disturbed when I was in desperate need of rest but realised immediately that there were more pressing matters to attend to.

'What on earth is the matter?'

'It's the *matelot*, he escaped and they've apprehended him. You have to help me, Charlotte, the mistress will hang me for the ravens to pluck my eyes out!'

'Please, Emma, calm down. Tell me, who exactly has captured him?' I had met her pleas in a light-hearted tone until I heard her response.

'The vicar! Lytton Cheney and that vile and repulsive creature who has agreed to marry him. They have him secured in the church tower and intend to call the police.'

She was still gasping for air when I hauled her up from her haunches. For a second our eyes were level and our arms entwined. We were both consumed by a smouldering desire to learn more about each other, to explore how far we could stretch our limits before one or both of us broke. That was what intrigued me, that is what I longed to determine – just how far were we prepared to journey on the path to pleasure and pain.

But now was not the moment. The apprehension of the Frenchman threatened to destroy the Society of Sin before it had had the opportunity to proselytise and, more importantly, before I had had the chance to join its select few. The Reverend Lytton Cheney, of all people, would not be the man to bring us all down. I had already resolved that we would perish in burning glory, not fade into dust. Being fluent in French I, at least, had the advantage over Cheney's schoolboy Latin.

I took an immediate dislike to Miss Grace Fitzpiers and not only because she, as the future wife of a vicar, stood for all I despised. She was a cut-glass symbol of the piety I longed to overthrow; so plain in her mediocrity, so undistinguished and dull in her appearance that I might have felt pity had it not been for her self-righteous arrogance. And yet ... and yet ...

'And what are *you* doing here?' she barked like a vixen on heat when she found us striding through the cemetery. 'I would not have thought this a particularly appropriate location for the likes of you. Jezebels, slatterns and whores are not welcome here. Please, go, before I set the Reverend Cheney upon you.'

The faintly ludicrous, if not surreal prospect of being chased through the graveyard by a man so devoid of animation struck us both down with a fit of childish giggles, which did nothing to improve our standing in the upright opinion of Miss Fitzpiers. She approached us, glowering, consumed with angelic fury. The sunlight, directly behind her, sent shafts of heavenly fire sizzling down to Earth, chasing us like meteors thrown from on high. I have to confess that from that moment onwards Miss Grace Fitzpiers put the fear of God into me.

But not Emma. She was the consummate revolutionary whereas I was merely a rebel without a cause. She stood up to her foe, stepped forwards and, when Miss Fitzpiers refused to give way, crudely thrust her to one side. She fell into a rustling heap of creased black silk, most unladylike, her skirts riding over her knees as she struggled to retain her dignity. Emma marched past her, triumphant but I followed meekly, and only at my companion's insistence. I was reluctant to pass by, reluctant to exacerbate a hatred that I could feel already gathering within her soul.

'Come, Charlotte. Let us leave the immaculate virgin to stew in her own bitter juices. We have to free the *matelot* before Cheney realises who he's dealing with. He might be a prize fool but his darling fiancée is a more formidable prospect. She has a poisoned mind and heart so cold it would freeze the very gates of hell.' She feigned a booted kick in her direction and, thinking she might make contact, I flinched as her toe came within an inch of Miss Fitzpier's face. 'Don't worry,' she hissed, 'much as I'd like to I have no intention of causing her actual bodily harm. I would not sully my boots with her virtuous flesh; I would not give her the pleasure of pain.'

I could not move, I could not take my eyes from those of Miss Fitzpiers. The burning hatred within them consumed me, fascinated me, would not free me from its spell. And she knew, Miss Grace Fitzpiers, that she had secured over me a famous victory, the spoils of which she would reap at a later date, when circumstances were more inclined in her favour. And Emma knew, too. She took hold of my hand and tugged at it furiously and when I was at her side she grabbed my forearm so hard the bruises remained a week and a day. Her voice was low and threatening. 'I am watching you, Charlotte Crowsettle. I sense a turncoat in the ranks. I hope, for your own sake, it isn't you.'

It wasn't me; the traitor did not come from amongst us. She came, unlooked for, right from the heart of the enemy.

It had never occurred to me that Emma Chetnole and the vicar might have been previously acquainted, although both hailed from London I could not imagine them mixing in the same circles. But as soon as he swivelled around to greet us I could see his ashen face turn a whiter shade of pale.

'Good afternoon, Mr Cheney. I gather we have a visitor from foreign lands, a Frenchman, indeed. Perhaps Miss Crowsettle can assist you with your interrogations. She is fluent in several European languages. I am sure she will succeed where you appear to have thus far failed.'

The rector withdrew as if confronted by vampires baying for his blood; the Frenchman's eyes dilated with panic as the memories of the previous night's events, suppressed by drugs and alcohol, began to stir themselves.

'*Comment allez-vous? Je suis venu pour vous sauver, pour vous retourner en France.*'

I reached out my hand to take his. English has a harsh, unfriendly brogue; the softer tones of his native tongue appeared to soothe him and he shuffled away from the vicar's protection into the company of the women who had connived in his persecution. Even in the half-shadows of the vestry he looked a different man. He stood tall to greet me and allowed the coarse blanket in which he had wrapped himself to fall to the ground and reveal a towering figure of fibrous muscle, finely honed by a life of hoisting the mainsail. A profuse untended lawn of black hair descended from chest to navel, thickening into clumps of dark curls that guarded the gateway to his hidden topographies.

The Reverend Dr Lytton Cheney interrupted our shared reverie. 'I am about to send word to Inspector Lefebvre in Weymouth. This poor man's utterly confused, he has not the slightest clue where he is, where he's from or where he wants to go. And I cannot, for the life of me, account for his sudden appearance here in Chilcombe Bredy.'

'A miracle, Reverend Cheney? Or perhaps there is a simpler, but less palatable explanation. I salute the regard in which you hold your fellow men but even I understand that a sailor is a sailor is a sailor. The world over. They have needs; needs that remain frustratingly unsatisfied whilst out on the ocean wave. And wherever there is a need you will inevitably find a woman of dubious virtue to meet it. Am I making myself clear?'

'Miss Crowsettle, I'm sure I really don't know what you mean.'

Quite unexpectedly, Emma turned on him. I could see, confined within her fist, the unmistakeable silver flash of a blade she prodded into his vestments. Her voice was barely audible. 'Don't play the fool with me, Cheney. Don't pretend you haven't seen it all before. Let me offer you a word of advice – if you value your flimsy reputation you will hand over your detainee immediately and without further question.'

'But ... but ... I cannot possibly ... I have a moral duty.'

'To the devil with your moral duty.'

Emma's snarling mouth was right up against his, her voice so full of venom it blew wisps of his receding hair from his face. For one awful moment I thought she might actually strike him; she might well have done had not Miss Fitzpiers burst into the building. Emma pulled away with an all-knowing smile. 'I think you know what is best for you, for both you and Miss Fitzpiers.'

I cast an inquisitive glance at Emma but her returning scowl made it perfectly clear that I should keep my counsel. I knew not what influence she held over Reverend Cheney; whatever it was, it did not extend to his fiancée.

'Have you shown them, Lytton? Have they seen the marks on his back?'

Curse the woman and all her hellish offspring. But I wondered – for a woman so apparently prim and proper – had she really identified the nature of the sailor's wounds? They were now no more than a series of distended rosy stripes, less painful than the warm glowing remnants of Lady P's palm I could still feel on my cheeks. It was plain to all that he had been a victim of the whip but only the experienced eye would recognise that it had been wielded not by a sadistic midshipman but the dainty untrained hand of a woman.

'*Il y a un bateau partant pour Calais ce soir. Je vous ai fixé à bord un passage. Vite, nous devons partir maintenant*! Emma, fetch the carriage!' I had issued my orders with the authority of a demanding mistress and, much to my surprise, she jumped to attention. Bridport was a busy harbour – whether or not a ship was setting sail for France this evening hardly mattered. He could not be trusted in Weymouth, too many prying eyes, too many mercenary spies. I would ensure he had sufficient money to cover his lodgings and passage and, more importantly, to buy his silence.

Miss Fitzpiers remained reluctant to let the man go but her fiancé's altercation with Emma had transformed him into a temporary ally. Correspondingly, Miss Fitzpier's demeanour had undergone a symmetrical conversion from hard-faced harridan to a simpering, dutiful chattel. He despatched her to the rectory, almost as an afterthought, and she silently obeyed with a curtsey, head bowed, eyes fixed firmly to the floor. He followed soon after, unwilling – or unable – to engage in discourse, a sentiment I concurred with. It was only on departing that he finally summoned the courage to make reference to his letter, or at least to its intended recipient.

'Your father, is he well? I understand he has been in Exeter, is he returned yet?'

I saw no reason to lie, the entire village would already know, even if he did not. The letter was torn into a hundred tiny pieces; the Reverend Cheney was no immediate threat. 'He returned this morning, with Professor Walditch. I think they plan to spend several days wandering the countryside in search of their beloved geology. They're both very keen on Mr Darwin...'

I let the last sentence hang in the air, a less than subtle taunt he could usually not resist but he was learning the value of discretion at the expense of misguided valour.

'Will you kindly remind him that there are matters, urgent matters, I wish to discuss. Miss Fitzpiers and I would be delighted to have his company for supper. Perhaps when Professor Walditch has gone?'

God bless Professor Walditch, only he stood between liberty and oppression.

When Emma returned he was gone and the Frenchman mounted the carriage without fuss. I stole my skirts to jump in alongside him but my way was barred.

'You have had a trying time, Miss Charlotte. I have been warned that you have a tendency to overexert yourself. Might I be so bold as to recommend an afternoon's gentle repose in preparation for this evening? Oh! Did my mistress not inform you? I am instructed to accompany you to Weymouth where we are to search for a suitable accomplice.'

'Yes,' I replied, genuinely troubled by the announcement. 'Lady Persephone did write and tell me you had plans for me but I had hoped to dine with my father tonight.'

'Then I suggest you make alternative arrangements unless, of course, you intend to defy my mistress' express wishes.'

Defying Lady Persephone's express wishes was not an option I was prepared to contemplate, the consequences were, potentially, dire.

'Very well. At what time shall you call? Remember my father is home, you will have to be discreet.'

'Discreet!' she snorted. 'What on earth do you think I have in mind? You hold yourself in too high self esteem, Miss Crowsettle. Were I not charged with sole responsibility for your well-being I would be sorely tempted to teach you a lesson. Until sunset, then.'

7

Dear Diary
The heat shimmers on, a martyred saint, shimmers
up through the oolite and the clay; it breeds in the
bracken and bakes the dry earth. There is no respite,
everywhere I turn, it confronts me with its stale and
stifling breath. It is creeping up behind me, sur-
rounding me, reaching out with its fevered digits to
drag my body to its smouldering pyre. I can see it
lying there, prostrate, spent and devoid of sentient
feeling but I will have no grounds for appeal; there
are no mitigating circumstances.

No, it is nobody's fault but mine. I am perfectly
aware that I am freely and wilfully entering into a
pact to twist the laws of nature and defy all that is
considered decent and pure. Unlike, perhaps, Percy
and Emma, I am not an infinite force, there are
limits to my capacity to indulge but I am driven to
take pleasure and feel pain until each and every
sense is bloated and there is nothing new under the
sun.

My father returned as the church clock struck
seven, with Professor Walditch in tow. They ack-
nowledged my presence but paid little heed to my
fictitious account of Mrs Bexington's departure,
neither did they object to my intention to spend the
evening at Chilcombe Lacey on the flimsiest of

excuses. My father mumbled something about it being a shame but that as he and his companion had much to exercise their minds it was probably for the best. Besides, he was still insisting that my interests would be better suited in the company of Lady Persephone, not realising she was absent in London and it was a mere servant who would be entertaining me.

There. It is time to leave. I do not want her to come to the door. I do not want my father to set eyes on her. Why? I have to confess that I do not really know. She is part of a world without reason whose purpose is only to serve itself. I wonder what unseemly pleasures await me tonight?

'No! No, Emma. I object . . . I wholeheartedly refuse. It's a ridiculous proposal, quite preposterous. I will not go through with it, do you hear!'

She cackled like a witch and let the ends of her mouth drop into a gesture that was neither smile nor frown but glowed with menace.

'You have passed beyond that point where choice is an option,' she said sharply. 'Only one woman can free you from the covenant and that woman, although presently many many miles away, has deemed you worthy of her patronage. She took counsel from me dear Charlotte. Can you believe that? That one of so much wealth and privilege should seek the advice of a mere servant? Does it offend you greatly?'

'I am not in the least offended. It does not surprise me, nothing surprises me any more. I do not pretend to understand the nature of your relationship with Lady Persephone but I am beginning to learn that she is no more your mistress than you are her maid. Oh, I know that is what you would have them believe, the great and the good and the unwashed alike but it has become clear to me that for you it is nothing more than a game. Pray tell me, what recommendations did you make to your erstwhile employer? What was your evaluation of me in comparison to hers? Am I to be trusted? Am I considered loyal?' And then I added, almost under my breath, 'Jealousy is an unpleasant friend. I do hope I have not implanted the seeds of suspicion in your soul.'

'Ha! Jealousy?' she spat out in immediate response. 'You don't know the half of it, Miss Charlotte. Envy is spread by love and love alone. I cannot speak for my mistress but, as for myself, I no longer claim to have faith in such outmoded and impossible sentiments, they are naught but tools of tyranny. I am driven only by desire as, I believe, are you. Both Lady Persephone –' here she paused, looked up and added with great emphasis '– both Percy and I are agreed that you are in possession of all the qualities we admire: intelligence, acumen and, above all, autonomy. What we cannot be sure of is your constitution. Rest assured, you shall be subjected to the very same ordeals we have already endured and I am convinced you will pass with distinction. Your task has been selected and secreted in an envelope sealed with our own blood. I am not at liberty to reveal the nature of its contents but I can at least enlighten you as to the enormity of its undertaking. It will require an accomplice and sacrifice. That is the errand which awaits us tonight.'

'My, my, Charles. You do look quite the part. A toff and a Tory, I would wager, and a bit of a cad to boot.'

Emma – or should I say 'Gabriel' – inhaled upon her – I mean 'his' – cigar and watched with amusement as I choked upon mine. 'Charles Cromwell' was an obvious moniker but 'Gabriel Emerson' was a mystery Emma never satisfactorily explained. A former lover, perhaps? I think not. As far as I knew she was oblivious to the charms of men. She looked younger and quite vulnerable in male attire, a young man barely into his twenties. It was a curious and unsettling combination of masculine and feminine. I think 'Gabriel' was an attempt to maintain contact with the latter.

A gentleman driving his own carriage would have drawn unwanted attention whatever the true nature of his sex so we waited for the moonless night to descend upon us before we set out. A thick mist wafted in from the ocean; fortune was on our side, but then it always favours the brave, does it not? In the meantime we despatched a bottle of Lady P's finest port whilst Gabriel taught Charles the rudimentary habits of the upper-class male. It was a lesson I would have struggled to stomach had not Gabriel insisted on its veracity. The wine had risen straight to my head, aided and abetted by fatigue and an empty stomach; its influence soon extinguished my fears and curdled courage in my loins. What had, in the revealing light of day, drawn my most vociferous protestations was now nothing more than a splendid joke. Bravura was flowing through our veins, we were men in the making, drunk on liberty and licentiousness.

There will, I am sure, be those who use history to condemn the lot of women of my time and they will, for the most part, be correct in their assumptions. They will reprove us for our passivity, make light of our manners, ridicule our fashions and humour our reluctance to engage in sexual relations. But hindsight is an ambiguous tool and, truth be told, they will not know the half of it. Much as I struggled, perhaps vainly, to free myself from the shackles imposed upon my sex I was supremely grateful not to have been born 'Charles'. The crinoline was a cumbrance, so, too was the bustle. Every item of female clothing seemed designed to constrain. We were secured in a prison of our own creation and made our vulnerability the epitome of style. But never can there have been an item of clothing as tight and uncomfortable as the male trouser. Gabriel moved like a natural, but I could not come to terms with the lack of swirling skirts, the rustle of taffeta and the soft caress of silk against my skin – I felt naked and exposed. It was, as Emma later mentioned, a question of freedom – some are born to it, some are lost in its turbulence.

We took the coast road, shrouded in fog, and drove at great speed, clattering down Boot Hill towards the harbour. It was as if the very act of masquerade could change the nature of our chemistry and send waves of testosterone crashing through our veins. Gabriel jumped from the carriage and strode manfully along the Custom House Quay and into the King's Arms. By the time I had joined him, he already had a girl at his side. There was no questioning his good looks: a handsome, dapper dandy in his black velvet Albert, his silk waistcoat and newly fashionable bowler hat. He leant easily on his cane whilst supping at his wine and gazing into the eyes of his belle. All he lacked were side whiskers and a beard.

'My dear Charles, do hurry up or you will miss all the fun.' It was quite uncanny. To all intents and purposes Emma had disappeared but Gabriel had filled the very self-same shape. Even her voice boomed with male authority, rich and full with the languid rhythm of a poet. I joined him, but felt inadequate at his side. I found movement difficult in a stiffly starched cotton shirt with an impossibly high collar and whenever I turned my head I feared my top hat would topple from my crown. A cravat, that most ridiculous of all fashionable ostentations, chafed at my throat and I could feel an army of blisters raising itself within my buttoned brown leather boots. The binding around my breasts dug into my flesh and my nipples were sore and erect. Surely only a fool could fail to see through the disguise.

I lowered both my head and my voice in an attempt at authentic modulation. It seemed to do the trick. 'Forgive me, Gabriel. I thought it prudent to allow you first choice. I see you have wasted no time in making an excellent selection. Your name, my dear lady?'

She raised her hand. I took it and kissed her gloved fingers. She was an elegant creature but no more than a girl and when she opened her mouth the vision of beauty shattered in a thousand tiny fragments of coarse vulgarity.

'Chastity,' she answered in the thickest of Dorset brogues before breaking into a cacophony of hoots and guffaws. There is nothing on earth less attractive than a woman who laughs at her own pathetic jokes. Chastity was little more than a common trollop but that, I supposed, was the purpose of our exercise.

They say that necessity is the mother of invention and never was a truer word spoken. I pride myself on being a perceptive student of human nature with an eye for the finer detail and it was surely that skill that came to my aid for I know not from where else my mannerisms might have come. Each vowel, consonant and gesture perfectly mimicking that of the natural-born male. Gabriel and myself were soon surrounded by a gaggle of whores and strumpets: some quite repulsive, others of striking beauty but each set on divesting us of our conspicuous wealth. Who could blame them? Gabriel would have made a fine catch, a refreshing change from the constant procession of foul-mouthed, foul-smelling sailors who were their stock in trade.

I began to wonder just how far Emma was prepared to go and to what extent I was prepared to follow her. Gabriel seemed to be playing the girls at their own game. He knew how to charm and manipulate them, knew when to compliment and when to tease. I think they would have offered him their trade free of charge. And yet I could not prevent myself from speculating on a less palatable explanation for her sublime talents. Gabriel was just a little too clever, a little too knowledgeable. Where and how, I began to ask myself, had Emma acquired such experience.

They followed us en masse from inn to inn, the reputation of which became progressively less wholesome as we passed along the quay to where the larger foreign freighters were moored. I did not like the look in the sailors' eyes as we sauntered by – we had the prettiest girls in tow and we were wealthy enough to afford them all; they were left with the dregs and, in accordance with the law of supply and demand, vastly inflated prices. The mood was turning ugly as Emma was becoming reckless and daring. Even in a hostelry as seedy and squalid as the Dorchester Tavern, eyebrows were being raised as Gabriel's hands began to wander.

But I had my own problems to contend with, namely Stella Halstock who was not, she assured me, a lady of ill repute but the daughter of a wealthy farmer who, utterly against her will, had engaged her to a man she despised. She was, as they say, on the run. I must confess to believing her, to being taken in by her tragic circumstance, partly through intuitive female empathy but more because her darting, dancing eyes, as blue as the midsummer Mediterranean, mesmerised me and cast me into her spell. I quite forgot that under my manly camouflage stood a body that was unspeakably feminine and that my breasts were bursting from their bindings.

Yet these were not womanly emotions. They did not flow from the same source, did not stir my libido with the same sticky oceans. It was, instead, a love that sought to plunder, voracious in its desire. It wanted to seize her, to take her in its rough arms and bury itself in her skirts. It was grinding and bumping within me, a palpitating presence between my legs, reaching outside and swelling within my coarse, confining breeches. We, or rather she, had manoeuvred our inseparable shadows into a dark corner, away from the throng, out of the earshot of Gabriel's outlandish joshing. I began to apply a little pressure, gently at first, allowing my thighs to ride with hers, an exploring thrust here, an enquiring probe there, foraging through the petticoats of her dress until my knee was nestling firmly between her legs, pushing against her whilst my hands had reached down to her buttocks, concealed within a mass of silk but still peach firm and worthy of unimpeded exploration. She made no protestations, allowing my fingers to slide down her spine and rest upon the small of her back that arced like the crescent of the waning moon and was, in my eyes, equally virgin and pure. I took a firm grip on those two shivering orbs and thrust her pelvis against mine. Even through the layers of fabric that offered her delicate womanhood only nominal protection I could feel her body longing to succumb to my natural authority. Her agricultural thighs, stiff with muscle and flooded with the sticky resin of ecstasy, squeezed hard against mine until I yelped in discomfort and delight. She tossed back her head and a mass of thick brown hair tumbled over her shoulders.

'Oh my God!' she gasped, an almost silent cry that was soon drowned in my own long, mellifluous groan: 'Oh my dear, dear God!'

And from within me burst forth a torrent of hot liquid, an unstoppable stream in full spate that dowsed my nether regions and soaked through my underwear. She could feel it through her exposed pantyhose and then on the naked flesh above, wet and warm on the lips of her labia, flowing into the dribbles of her own pleasure that were now dripping from her swollen clitoris. In that instant of climax, driven by a physical chemistry that was not of my own sex, I drilled my empty groin deeper into her vulva. All the ranged armies of the Queen's empire could not have mollified me. The fragrant aroma of female sap rose up through the smoke and the din; it was mild and sweet-scented, not the bitter pungency of spent semen.

'Oh my God!' she cried once more, louder and with a hint of surprise. With an almighty effort she heaved me to one side. She held one hand before her, staring at the damp flesh, flexing her fingers in incredulity although she put them in her mouth and licked them all the same. She raised the other, clenched her fist and dealt me a well-aimed blow underneath my right eye. No more the clear-cut tones of a wealthy farmer's daughter, she was now revealed as the street-strumpet I should have seen her for.

'Who are you? What are you? You filthy little queer. I can smell a tom. I can smell the dirty, smelly seed of a tom on my own fucking hands.'

I was lying prone on the floor presenting her with the perfect target. She lifted her boot, her heavy boot of rough country leather, and propelled into that vacant area between my legs where she had, only moments ago, assumed my hardened manhood to be standing in expectation. It was a crude blow but delivered with sufficient force to send me sprawling into the corner.

Emma should have known better; she was not quite as clever as I had given her credit for. I had put my faith in her, trusted her implicitly but I had not accounted for her lack of foresight. If we had wanted to lavish money over women of dubious virtue we might have acted with a little more prudence. We might have chosen our venue a little more wisely. There were several inns on the more respectable Esplanade that, offered the 'gift' of a few shillings, would have turned a blind eye to our indiscretions. The Dorchester Tavern had a reputation as reproachable as the whores who frequented it and was raided by the police on an almost nightly basis. I could not imagine Emma being unaware of this unless, perhaps, she was possessed by an ulterior motive.

'I swear I'll swing for you,' cried Stella, her voice now loud with anger and fear. It echoed around the room but, unusually, no one came to fan the flames of the commotion she had created. They were scurrying for the exits, retreating into the shadows of the night whence they came. Just as she was about to strike me for a third time the shrill blast of a whistle brought her to her senses. Even I recognised the alarm and Stella would take it instinctively as a sign to join the exodus. She hurried to join the rest of the rapidly departing throng which clearly included my erstwhile companion. I lay alone in a pool of spilt wine and sweat until the police arrived.

* * *

God bless the Weymouth constabulary, as incompetent in dealing with their inmates as they were in investigating the deaths of the de Mortehoe family. I was not, it is true, a model of sobriety but I was able, once they had raised me, to stand on my own two feet. I shall never be sure quite why they took such an instant dislike to me, the more I protested my innocence as a victim of assault, the more they manhandled and insulted me.

'Well, well, well,' mused a rotund and bearded constable in predictable music-hall fashion. 'It's not often we get the chance to apprehend the likes of you in Weymouth town. It'll be a privilege to apprehend you ... sir!'

He slurred the 'sir'; it was an ironic and ambiguous form of address, loaded with menace. He knew, all right, and he made sure I knew that he knew. Resistance would be futile, would only aggravate my already calamitous situation. Every time I opened my mouth to speak, each clipped consonant and vowel articulated in my unmanly tones served only to increase his hatred. I represented all that the forces of law and order held in contempt. To them I was the devil incarnate, transcending the barriers of womanhood and encroaching on their own world. And I had come so very close, so close that I almost understood what it was to inhabit the raw angular confines of the male body and its equally unsophisticated mind. I had come so very close but I desired to go no further. I had had enough.

The Nothe Fort cells had not been designed for the likes of me. They had welcomed through their heavy padlocked doors a steady progression of murderers, larcenists, pickpockets, pirates and, for a while, prisoners of war. They had, I was sure, never accommodated a woman. They and all the other petty criminals who inhabited this underworld were usually deposited in the assizes and freed on payment of a token fine. The wretched flotsam and jetsam who frequented the nocturnal world of the quayside were a perennial affliction whose existence was tolerated because they, at least, provided a valuable service. Without the poor the rich could not enjoy their wealth; without the whores fornication would remain a part of that great unknown that was the sexuality of their frigid wives; and without the queens and the pederasts they could never hope to satisfy their most base desires.

But a tom? She was a dangerous libertine whose very existence threatened the foundations on which society was constructed, foundations that for centuries had remained fast and secure precisely because the likes of me had been proscribed, punished and cast into oblivion. I knew full well what fate awaited me, it was a universal panacea practised in the dungeons of Cartagena as much as the dark damp cells of Nothe Fort where morning never came.

Lying in a pool of cold liquid that was, in all probability, a pungent cocktail of urine and vomit I wished myself back to the wild wide spaces of Ashley Chase and the verdant pasture of the Bride Valley. I tried not to think of Lady P or Emma, the authors of my ruin. I thought of my father; when – perhaps if – I saw him again I would no longer be his pretty little daughter. I would have ceased to bear any vague resemblance to the free-spirited child he had raised, alone, in his own indomitable way, disregarding all those who offered him the advice 'spare the rod, spoil the child'. Mrs Bexington was amongst them, so, too, the vicar and, I suspected, his darling wife-to-be and it was she who, despite my reluctance, loomed large in my imagination. She floated in, dressed in white from head to toe, an apparition of impossible piety surrounded by a silver halo of blinding fury. Her face was stern and cruel, her eyes followed my gaze wherever I tried to look for solace like Our Lady of Perpetual Succour but she had come not to offer redemption but to gloat over my suffering and shame. I cowered in the corner and then the door opened.

I was expecting him. Well, not him but someone – anyone – and I was hoping he would arrive sooner rather than later. Grim anticipation is, after all, often more terrifying than the dull reality of pain.

I can still recall with startling clarity the only time I had ever been threatened with a whipping, not so long ago when I was, to all intents and purposes, a grown woman, although that did not necessarily qualify me as an adult. Not, at least, in the opinion of Mr Donald Fraser Urquhart, the self-proclaimed pastor of the Weymouth Congregationalist Church who had taken to making 'missionary' forays into the heathen lands of the Reverend Dr Lytton Cheney's high church parish. I forget precisely what sin I had committed. I think he had caught me in close conversation with Josh, the farmer's son, who had the eye for me. He was barely seventeen but I played him along, teased and sweet-talked him until he was convinced I was his own. When I made it clear that was never my intention he turned angry, struck out and called me a 'whore'. Like a knight in shining armour Mr Urquhart came striding across the fields but he had come not to rescue me but to save Josh from the clasps of a lascivious temptress. He was to blame but I was a woman. I was the guilty party and a whipping would teach me the error of my ways. He took me by the wrist and led me, kicking and screaming, to his erstwhile chapel, an outhouse belonging to one of his disciples. Its spartan décor, the grim images of a suffering Christ and biblical exhortations to comply without question left me in no doubt as to the sincerity of his intentions. I suspect he wandered the Dorset countryside in search of victims such as myself but on this occasion zeal got the better of him – we had arrived at the place of punishment without the means to carry out the act.

For a while he was utterly bemused. His simple doctrine that required strict adherence to the word had not prepared him for the extravagance of decision-making and now, it appeared, his instrument of torture had been mislaid or, even, perhaps, stolen. He turned on me again, his face black with rage. To misplace such a valuable implement would be tantamount to an admission of his own culpability and that would never do. If in doubt, blame the woman. There was no point in protesting my innocence, he was judge and jury and, more presciently, he had the superiority of strength on his side. And yet beneath that unyieldingly sanctimonious veneer he was no more than a mere male; as duplicitous as each and every member of his sex. He could fire off his virtuous inanities from dawn until dusk but they would not leave a mark on my corrupted heart. And when his powder keg was dry I would advance on him, a vision of comeliness wrapped up in the black velvet pelt of the devil in disguise. How could he possibly resist?

He was reaching out, he wanted to touch me, to run his fingers through the soft fabric of my gown but he was fighting with his angels for the welfare of his soul. I watched his ugly features twist and contort until virtue triumphed over vice and he turned hard on his heels, fled through the door and padlocked it behind him.

His wrath remained, it would not dissipate; it could not find an exit through the thick stone walls and neither could I. The windows were barred, the door secured on the outside with a heavy iron chain which rattled when I threw myself against the oak panels. I searched frantically for a means of escape but when it became apparent there was none I sat myself down and wept.

It was a statuary lesson – that the sweet fear of the unknown transcends the bitter tedium of reality. I allowed my imagination to assume control, gave it free rein to wander through the wide halls of wild reverie. Whatever fate conspired, I resolved to yield myself to it utterly, to the pain and the humiliation, to his clumsy hands, trembling with a shared anticipation, fumbling with my layers of frilled underskirts to expose my drawers, to the sting of the cane as it cut through the frilled lace and pummelled my quivering flesh. Being a member of that mollycoddled minority who had never been subjected to physical chastisement I could only imagine and squirm in my seat, waiting for his return. The longer I waited, the greater grew the thrill of anticipation until it became almost unbearable. When the door finally flew open I fell to my knees, pleading for a just and merciful chastisement. But it was not Mr Urquhart who stood before me, stern faced and cane in hand, only the slim figure of the farmer's son who, witnessing my almost hysterical confession, promptly fled from the scene leaving me prostrate on the floor.

I never learnt quite why I was reprieved, and I never set eyes upon Mr Urquhart again. To be perfectly honest I think fear got the better of him, I think his nerves twitched and bristled as much as mine as he marched across the fields considering the scene that awaited him. It was an alluring vision, my young lithe body draped over a pew, skirts raised, backside exposed whilst the rod was poised to strike. My relief was short-lived, metamorphosing into curious disappointment and anger. I regained my dignity and tried, as best I could, to stroll serenely out of captivity but deep down inside I was cursing the pusillanimous nature of men.

No such escape seemed possible now, the laughing demons were circling above, waiting to enjoy my long-foreseen and inevitable fall from grace. And angels singing, too; unsullied verses descending from on high, waiting to tell me 'we told you so'.

A sliver of dirty-yellow lamplight fell upon the floor and stretched its feeble finger towards me as the door creaked open. Curiosity got the better of fear. He was not what I had expected, he seemed to be a gentleman of quality and breeding but appearances, as they say, are frequently deceptive. I had expected a toothless flea-ridden vagabond, not the genteel apparition that stood proudly before me. What circumstances had conspired to deliver him here? I dared not ask, I was not quite as naive as I looked. Remember: all that glisters is not gold and not all those who wander are lost.

'Good evening, *sir*. I presume you are another innocent victim of the constabulary's fanaticism. Might I request the pleasure of your company?'

He did not wait for a response but bowed lightly and sat himself right at my side. His breath reeked of alcohol, tobacco and stale sweat, his fine and noble profile had been ravaged by years of loose living. It was immediately apparent that he was but a husk of his former self. Addiction had drained from him every modicum of decorum; had stolen the light from his bloodshot eyes; had turned this once affable squire into a shameless predator with a peculiar perversion that only the likes of I could satisfy. He had taken residence in the prison, emerging only between dusk and dawn. What little wealth he had not yet squandered he diverted to the pockets of my gaolers. They shared a symbiotic relationship: he the parasite feeding on those who society has already condemned, they the underfed, underpaid peddlers who provided him with his helpless prey. Nobody cared; why should they?

He was kneeling behind me now. I could feel his chill breath on the back of my neck and the rustle of his robes against mine.

'You dirty little whore! What is it with women like you, no respect and no shame? You never learn to obey, you have no idea what is good for you. They have sent me to teach you, to make you understand.'

He had one cold clammy hand clamped firmly over my mouth, the other was fastened tight around my throat until I began to choke. Then he pulled my head right back so that his filthy lips were at my ear. He had expected compliance but I was in no mood to concede.

'Get up!' he ordered, tugging at my breeches and pinning me hard against the stone wall.

He grabbed my belt and tore it in two, then ripped open my shirt and jacket until they slid off my shoulders and gathered in a crumpled pile round my feet. I watched with fascinated horror as his penis peered out, proud and erect, from his unbuttoned fly. There was nothing between him and my vulnerability. My breasts heaved in horror and I gasped breathlessly for air. His sinister smile that extended from jaw to jaw became etched like a carving in living rock. I would feel his hands as they groped and fingered their way through the crevices of my body, and then ... and then?

When I saw his manhood throb and quiver in nervous anticipation and felt his hands between my legs, the thin and fragile chord that had hitherto held my temperament intact finally snapped in a display of daring majestic rage.

In that split second of freedom I seized a burning candle and, before he had a chance to recoil, tipped its molten wax like a pellucid lava over the cherry-red helmet of his quivering penis. He screamed, quite naturally, but with a clamour that terrified me for I had no idea as to the sensitivity of that ironically tender and fragile organ. It reared up in agony, like a wounded beast, and I cackled with undisguised delight. He struck out and I managed to avoid his flailing arms but I had not counted on him being in possession of a knife. I was wild with panic but he was livid and more terrified than myself.

The silver blade flashed in the dark and caught my outstretched fingers but the searing pain never came; he caught me with the blunt edge and it merely stung. But I tripped on the heap of my discarded clothing and landed, prostrate and prone, flat on my back. I closed my eyes and waited for the end to come.

The iron grille rattled furiously, a clamour of angry voices echoed along the corridor. One, raised and indignant, was that of a woman – it was Emma's.

'I'm sorry, your ladyship, someone has made an awful mistake ... you can rest assured, I shall have his guts for garters ... I'll have him out on the streets with the rest of the garbage ... but you must understand, these masquerades you talk about, well, they're a London fashion, are they not? We don't have them in these parts, begging your pardon, but we don't go in for that sort of thing. Please, if you would wait here I shall release Lady Claridge forthwith.'

Emma's diction had a shrill, conceited clarity I had not previously heard. 'I am afraid I do not trust you at all, Mr Yeobright. I fear for the safety and good name of my dear friend. I shall not rest until I have set mine own eyes upon her.'

My assailant had sufficient warning to withdraw from his assault but I had only enough time to cover myself with a filthy blanket. The door was unlocked and eased ajar and in the space of less than a second her countenance passed from feigned concern to genuine undisguised shock. For that moment even she was lost for words.

'Lady Claridge! I cannot begin to apologise for the incompetence of the local constabulary. I shall make my vehement protestations to the relevant authorities first thing tomorrow morning. Mr Yeobright, who is this foul reprobate you have placed in the same cell as a woman of Lady Claridge's breeding? Begone! Let woe betide you if our paths ever cross again.'

My assailant needed no further encouragement and scurried away into obscurity. In my confused and distressed condition it took me a short while and a wink of Emma's eye to understand that I was 'Lady Claridge' but the gaoler was less easily persuaded.

'Forgive me, Lady de Mortehoe, but I'd not be doing my honest and solemn duty if I weren't to ask you for credentials. It's a sad reflection on the times in which we live but I've dealt with more than one fraud and impostor in the last seven days alone. Your ... friend has been accused of a very serious crime. I can't just let her go, you understand.'

Emma was magnificent, a perfect display of

controlled indignation and affected understanding. 'Certainly, Mr Yeobright. You are only doing your job and you are to be commended for it.' Realising I was no longer in imminent danger she warmed to her theme. 'Come, Stephanie, we can hardly blame the poor man for jumping to the wrong conclusion. You make a fine gentleman, make no mistake. Now, Mr Yeobright, I have here a letter addressed to myself from the Duke of Baltonsborough. I trust you will accept this document as proof of identity.'

She waved a sheet of handwritten paper in front of him, pointing to Lady P's signature. It was an excellent counterfeit, only a fine eye could have detected Emma's slightly stunted reproductions of Lady P's exquisitely formed characters. Mr Yeobright was still not convinced but I suspect Emma's sheer effrontery told him that discretion was the better part of valour, especially as she let fall a ten-shilling note from her valise and made no effort to retrieve it.

We journeyed home in an uncomfortable silence until safely beyond the boundaries – and the jurisdiction – of the borough of Weymouth. It was a fine night, the sea mist had been swept away on a warm breeze and a million stars gazed down from the glittering firmament. At the top of the Black Down, Emma shook the reins and brought the gig to a halt. She had divested herself of her male attire and had clearly raided her mistress's wardrobe to make good her deception but still insisted on lying back in her seat and lighting a cheroot. For several minutes I sat and watched her, barely attempting to conceal my fascination. She was perfectly aware she was being closely observed and, as was her wont, played to the crowd. Whatever role she played, she carried it off to perfection as if it were more than second nature, as if it were more than mere performance. She had been, to me at least, maid, driver, footman and elegant dandy but only now did I see her revealed in all her glory. She had selected for herself the reception dress Lady P had received from her costumier only three days previously and had planned to wear for the celebration that would mark her return. The black taffeta skirt was tiered and gathered in a delicate bustle; it accentuated her slim waist so much that I was forced to refrain from slipping my arm around it. Her ripe bosom was yearning to free itself from the heavily boned confines of her cream-striped and studded bodice, bursting at the seams so much I almost felt compelled to ... no, I cannot bring myself to say. That evening, under the stars, I could make out in every detail, every tempting nook and cranny.

She tossed the glowing remains of her cheroot into the undergrowth and, before picking up the reins again, turned to me. She giggled and I, who had for the past two hours been fighting back a surge of angry tears, instinctively joined in as her mirth was infectious. The gig rocked to our uncontrollable laughter all the way to Chilcombe Lacey. It was, after all, only a game, a game that tonight we had won by varying degrees of dishonesty, manipulation and clever skulduggery. That we had succeeded only by the skin of our teeth, that I had come within a whisper of succumbing to the unspeakable only served to inflame our enthusiasm. The greater the risk, the more magnificent our conquest over the forces of modesty and decorum we had sworn to wage war upon. We would, of course, take them on again and again but each and every time the stakes would be pushed a little higher.

I knew; Emma knew. Ultimately it would all end in tears.

8

The Royal Wessex Hotel
Winchester
18 June 1876

My dear Charlotte

I write in haste with important tidings and a warning you must heed without question. Forgive the lack of pleasantries, I do hope you are in good health and being well cared for, but urgency must take precedence over etiquette and in any case Emma is the most consummate of hostesses!

My journey to London has been delayed by events over which I have no immediate control but which disturb me greatly. I would return to Chilcombe Lacey without a moment's hesitation to rectify matters were not my business here far more pressing and, potentially, more devastating. Besides which, I have an appointment in town, with a lady who will interest you immensely but more of that anon.

You will be aware, I am sure, that I have reliable contacts strategically located in Weymouth, Dorchester and elsewhere who keep me informed of every coming and going that might be of interest. You might call them spies and consider me paranoid but I would counter with the need for vigilance. Forewarned is forearmed.

I have received word from a trusted acquaintance that a formidable foe is en route for Chilcombe Bredy, if, indeed, she has not already arrived for I fear that time, too, is conspiring against me. The woman concerned – she is no lady – goes by the name of Miss Grace Fitzpiers and has recently become engaged to the vicar of Chilcombe Bredy. Curse the wretched man. He is naught but a simple fool and what Miss Fitzpiers sees in him I simply do not know. She has surely an ulterior motive and it is that which concerns me all the more. I can think of only one rational explanation as to why she has chosen to take up residence in our neighbourhood.

In matters of beauty she is, in my humble opinion, quite wanting. In both appearance and style she is plain and undistinguished; she lacks the refinement and dignity that comes only with noble breeding. She is, in short, a charlatan and opportunist who has raised herself from her lowly origins by a combination of cunning and Machiavellian chicanery. If I have created in your mind the image of a most unpleasant woman you must take it as the gospel truth and not the ravings of a jealous woman. Me? Jealous? Of that self-righteous harridan!

My carriage calls, I leave for London without further delay. I have no time to explain in greater detail, perhaps that is just as well but I must warn you, once again. You must, at all costs, avoid contact with this woman. She will make herself known to you, I am certain of it. She will try to draw you into her well-baited trap. They say she has a charisma, a magnetic charm and, though I confess I have yet to witness it, I know of several who have been taken in. She has destroyed them, Charlotte, they are utterly ruined. I beg you, should you encounter Miss Fitzpiers turn immediately on your heel and, without saying a word, retreat to the sanctuary of Chilcombe Lacey. You know I do not generally approve of dis-courtesy but I give you my express permission to insult the dreadful woman as much as your fancy takes you.

Allow me to end on a brighter note. I hope to return this coming weekend with the above-mentioned exotic creature, quite the antidote to the likes of Grace Fitzpiers. I shall be convening the Society; she will be initiated forthwith but, do not fear, your time is almost come.

Until soon, my sweetness

P

The letter was addressed to me not at my father's cottage but care of Chilcombe Lacey and arrived on a breakfast tray prepared and delivered to my room by Emma. It was almost midday; when she opened the curtains the hot sun swamped the room, filling it with light so blinding I was forced to shade my eyes.

Emma fussed quietly as she carried out the perfunctory tasks a maid is obliged to attend to when her mistress is suffering from excess. There was clothing strewn across the floor and dishevelled sheets and blankets, which had been cast aside in search of cool air. She brought me water for a wash, a gown for the hot summer afternoon and a jug of hot frothing coffee to bring me to my senses. She was bright and friendly but said not a word about the previous night's events nor the letter from Lady P. Was she, I wondered, au fait with its contents? Had she, perhaps, intercepted it on my behalf? It was not until I finally descended the curving staircase that she requested my attention.

'Begging your pardon, ma'am, might I have a word?'

She had added a rural inflexion to her voice, as if to increase its authenticity. I was about to ask her to stop playing games with me, that I considered her a friend not a servant until her coquettish smile told me my protestation would be pointless and unwelcome. Nevertheless, the severe cut of her black and white uniform, frilled and overstarched, put between us a gulf that I struggled to overcome, that was not, perhaps, intended to be overcome. It was not unflattering but it did not appear comfortable. It was not an outfit I would have chosen to adopt had I the liberty to exploit my employer's absence.

I asked her to join me on the terrace and made sure that she sat in the full heat of the sun whilst I enjoyed the shade. I knew she would not have wanted it otherwise.

'About last night?' I asked, in an appropriately dismissive strain.

'Not so much last night, and if you are asking for an apology it will not be genuine. It is the nature of events that they sometimes become a law unto themselves, I cannot be held responsible, Miss Crowsettle.'

I held up my hand to indicate that no further explanation was required. Basking in the afterglow of my encounter with the voluptuous Stella Halstock I had quite forgotten that, had it not been for Emma, the evening would have ended in disaster. Had it not been for Emma? Had she not contributed to my predicament? But when it mattered she had been my saviour. I felt guilty for ever doubting her.

'I am afraid,' she continued, 'that I failed us in our mission. I am too easily distracted, too prone to give in to temptation. I cannot help myself.'

Her outburst surprised me. I had quite forgotten Lady P's instructions and it was true that, pleasure aside, we had returned from our errand empty-handed, without the required collaborator.

'You cannot accept all the blame. I am as culpable as you, dear Emma.'

'Don't be ridiculous. It was my duty to escort you and in that duty I quite clearly failed,' she snapped at me, perhaps angered by my intimacy. It was not, I realised, at all appropriate. 'My mistress will be furious, and so should you be, Miss Crowsettle.'

Although I did not feel in the least bit angry, it suddenly occurred to me that it was my obligation to do so. Furthermore, as Emma's superior it was my duty to express it in whatever means I felt appropriate. I would have happily spent the afternoon deep in sweet conversation, asked her to open a bottle of wine and share it with me but now was neither the time nor the place. And then, in a flash of inspiration I can only describe as divine, the obvious revealed itself to me.

'I am afraid *I* cannot abrogate my own responsibility and *you* have ideas above your station. Whilst I am sure she will deal with you leniently, I have no wish to incur Lady Persephone's wrath on your behalf. No, the solution is clear to me. You shall be my accomplice and sacrifice. I shall tell your mistress that in all the bordellos and backstreets of Weymouth I could not find a woman more worthy.'

I knew Emma would have protested had I not injected my lecture with power and presence. I sat up in my chair but lowered my voice to accentuate its authority. She had to understand that I was entirely in earnest and not taking pity because I loved her. I put my finger to my closed lips to indicate that the matter was closed.

'That will be all, Emma. I am sure you have work to do.'

It is all very well playing the landed gentry if one *is* the landed gentry and has some notion as to what the role requires. I could pull off the performance but it gave me no pleasure to sit alone in the garden, staring at the wilting flowers and the bleached-brown grass. Even at the height of summer, nature seemed to be withering and lying down to die. The incessant heat, weighing heavy on the Chase and the valley was draining my energy and dulling my senses, drip by drip, drop by drop. If Lady P did not act soon all my passion would be spent.

The afternoon dragged. I could feel Emma's presence in the house, hear her singing in the parlour and talking to herself in the scullery. The good Lord only knows how she managed such a large house almost single handed with only occasional help from the village. Tired of kicking my heels, I decided to make my way home, through the fields so as to avoid prying eyes and, more particularly, Miss Grace Fitzpiers. My father would be out in the field with Professor Walditch but as I was presently inclined to avoid his company that worried me not a jot.

I suppose that I am, by nature if not nurture, an inquisitive person. My father is fond of reminding me how I pestered and pestered him until he told me the story of my poor, unfortunate mother. He tried ignorance, euphemisms and deceit but I knew when he was lying and would accept nothing but the truth. Even as I child I was instinctively aware that I was different, that no matter how generous or caring my father was there was, within our family, an absence, a gaping wound. Ours was a lonely and nomadic existence. I did not adopt a sedentary lifestyle until arriving at Lady Elizabeth Varsfield's Academy for Young Ladies, an expensive but suitably liberal institution where I excelled despite an instinctive dislike of both my tutors and my fellow students. They were probably correct in attributing my rebellious nature to a motherless childhood but I took it as a slight on my father. The fact that he was several thousand miles away, lying wounded in a hospital in Calcutta, merely exacerbated my isolation.

For a curious young lady, well educated, brimming with confidence but with what many considered a louche disposition, my chance encounter with Lady P could only inflame my curiosity. During those long Spanish nights, confined to my room, I had mapped out my philosophy. 'Out of sight, out of mind,' as the duchess was fond of saying, not really understanding that my exclusion was breeding contempt. The mysterious, exotic Lady P fascinated me. In a world where women are deprived even of autonomy of their bodies, how, I constantly asked myself, had she assumed control of one of the county's largest estates? The news of the sudden death of her parents and two brothers in unusual circumstances had spread as far as Cartegana where it was the subject of idle discussion for a day or two. They took great pleasure in condemning her outright. I imagined her a heroine prepared, perhaps, to adopt extreme measures to claim what was rightfully hers.

I wanted to learn more about her. I would have passed the long afternoon exploring Chilcombe Lacey's every nook and cranny were it not for Emma who was, I supposed, fiercely protective of her mistress. But Emma was up in the east wing; I had gone there to bid her farewell. She was preparing the house for the weekend, engrossed in domestic duties and had barely acknowledged my presence. The great oak door that gave access to the servants' quarters stood invitingly ajar. Lady P's personal quarters would, I was sure, be securely locked. Perhaps the best way to her was through her trusted servant? As you will already know, I am not one to resist temptation.

The scullery was clean and well swept, only the most demanding of taskmasters would have found cause to complain. I noted nothing of immediate interest and dared not risk a more thorough investigation save a neatly folded leaf of vellum. Not, I considered, a material Emma would be accustomed to using for her orders and invoices and certainly not the stationery of choice for those who supplied her. It could only have been written by Lady P's hand. Even if it were no more than mundane instructions as to the running of the household it was still Lady P's elegant hand. I sat at the table and read.

The Royal Wessex Hotel
Winchester
18 June 1876

My dear Emma
Take heart, dear love. When I left, all too hastily, I was filled with foreboding and feared the worst. I am so sorry for unloading my worries on to you who have suffered so bravely and endured so much pain. I promised you a new life but I seem to have provided you with naught but distress. Rest assured, when this is over and done with I shall make it up to you.

I write, all too briefly, with news that will interest you. Our nemesis, Grace Fitzpiers is back! Yes, the cunning vixen has returned and is, I am certain, hot on my – on our – trail. I do not believe I will ever be rid of that cursed woman but if she hopes to get the better of me she will be sadly mistaken. I came to Winchester with a specific purpose: to engage the services of a private detective. He is a good friend of Inspector Lefebvre so I have high hopes! I would have liked to ask him to deal with Miss Fitzpiers but he has informed me that I am too late; she has already taken up with the vicar, of all people! But she can do no more damage to me or my reputation. She has done her damnedest to destroy everything I have fought for yet it has all been to no avail.

I know you are impervious to her charms but I am worried for Charlotte. Keep an eye on her, Emma. I fear Miss Fitzpiers might well hold a fatal attraction that Charlotte will be only too keen to fall for. Come between them, keep their prying eyes apart for they are cast from the same mould, extremes of the same emotion. You will recall that the Miss Fitzpiers of old was quite the reverse of what she now has become. Do you not concur that Charlotte could fall victim to the same process of conversion? I had hoped to allow her a little more time. I am inclined to share Samantha's suspicions and proceed, for once, with caution. Oh, I know you are Charlotte's greatest advocate and would soonest advise me to the contrary but you have grown immensely fond of her, have you not? Remember, dear love, she is mine to toy with as I wish.

But I am chiding you and I do not mean to condescend. Your well-being is of my utmost concern and even though matters of the heart are your own affair I would be obliged to interfere if I considered it to be for the greater good. That was, after all, the essence of our arrangement – that you and I should forego our individual desires if the needs of the society so required. I hope it will never come to that, that our individual desires are shared by one and all but woe betide she who comes between us. That much I must make clear.

To lighter matters! All being well I shall return in the early hours of Friday morning. I think it prudent to arrive in the hours of darkness so, pray, do not *wait up. All I ask for is a plate of cold meats and several bottles of the finest Chablis laid out for us. I will not be travelling alone. I have told you, more than once, of the Mexican lady, the Aztec goddess with whom I shared a berth on my return passage from Bordeaux? For reasons too complicated to discuss here we parted on indifferent terms but even then I felt sure our paths would cross again. Perhaps the residents of Chilcombe Bredy are correct, I have the premonition of a witch for I have received from her a long and elaborate letter and we are to meet at Holy Mass in the cathedral tomorrow. It is the feast day of Our Lady of the Orchards – quite appropriate, considering our imminent celebrations.*

I will say no more. I fear I have already disclosed rather too much information and thus guaranteed your undivided attention on our homecoming but I would rather you took your fill of sleep for a busy weekend beckons. There will be much work to do on both our parts but I ask you, please, do not request Charlotte's assistance. The events of the coming weekend must come as a complete surprise. By all means, stoke the fires of her imagination but reveal no more than you deem necessary. Keep her moist with anticipation, girl!

I leave you now, with all my deepest and dearest love.

Your servant and mistress
Percy

'Do you make a habit of reading private correspondence or am I uniquely privileged by your concern?' Emma's pitched tones were so laced with superiority that I spun around on my seat without thinking. She had stepped out of her servant dress into a robe and a role that commanded my immediate respect.

'I'm s-s-so s-sorry,' I stammered, feeling utterly inadequate before the magnificent, majestic image that towered over me. I do not believe I had previously seen a woman so sharply and severely dressed. Emma's finely tailored suit hinted at self-control, discipline and vigorous efficiency. It lacked the pompous passivity that had become popular in the provinces; it was a London fashion, not long off the dressmaker's dummy. It spoke of emancipation, of the dawning era of liberation that I never ceased to dream of and here was I, cowering before its black leg-of-mutton-sleeved arms.

Silence. What on earth could I have said? What excuses could I have made? She had caught me red-handed committing an offence that, between friends, was quite inexcusable. My guilt was unfathomable, justice was on her side. She said nothing but brought down her walking cane hard upon the table.

'I ought to beat the living daylights out of you,' she sneered, almost inaudibly. 'I ought to throw you out of this house and its grounds and never let you set foot in here again. Have you any idea what Lady Persephone would do to you should I have to reveal the circumstances pertaining to your expulsion? Let me tell you, it does not bear thinking about.'

Something in her intonation, the harsh tongue and the callous inflection caused me to sit up straight to attention, like a miscreant child accused by her governess of a heinous transgression. I did not, for a moment, imagine she might strike me but that was not what prompted me to beg for forgiveness. I had repeated the first woman's sin, destroyed her faith and trust. She had every reason to cast me from her Eden and leave me lost, wandering in a wilderness of my own creation. She was standing over me, so close that the rough silk of her jacket rustled against my bare fore-arms. I threw myself at her mercy.

'You have every right to deal with me as you wish, treat me as the scoundrel and villain I truly am. My behaviour is inexcusable, it warrants whatever punish-ment you consider appropriate. Please, please, forgive me!'

My pleas were insufficient, they fell on deaf ears. She stood aloof, stock-still and unmoved but I was infatuated by her cold austere beauty. I wanted her to bring the cane down on my back but it remained in her hand, resting on the table.

'Please! Tell me! Anything you request, anything you command, I will obey.'

I could stand her dispassion no longer. Her indiffer-ence tore at my heartstrings and played havoc with the emotions churning in the pit of my stomach. How could she be so cruel? I fell on all fours, sobbing and supplicant, at her feet.

'Get up, girl. I don't want my finery soiled with your weeping. Get up, I say!'

The second command was barked with volume and venom and I obeyed at once. When my face rose to meet hers I could see she was smiling, a thin self-congratulatory smile that spread wide across her taut jaw. I was still sobbing, my swollen, tear-stained cheeks were hidden behind a mass of dishevelled hair. Her fierce stare encountered my own reluctant gaze. Our eyes spoke volumes, mine lowered as an admis-sion of defeat, hers tearing into mine like daggers, glorious and triumphant. I would have followed her to the ends of the earth.

That was all she desired, tears and my abject contri-tion, an acknowledgement of her moral and spiritual supremacy. Furthermore, she had achieved her victory on her terms alone, without having to make concessions. She did not have to beat me. She could see that was what I expected and desired and she would not lower herself to oblige my baser instincts. It was enough to remind me that that was a universal panacea, the principal means through which insolence and importance would be controlled. It would have been so easy to resort to physical chastisement, it would have assuaged my guilt and given her pleasure but my guilt had to stew and her pleasure would have been short-lived, she would have wanted more.

'Enough,' she declared and her voice melted. 'I confess to being disappointed in you, Charlotte, but perhaps I have only myself to blame. I should have hidden the letter away. Don't worry. I shall keep your terrible indiscretion from Lady Persephone. It shall be our secret.' And then she added, with a mischievous glint in her eye, 'But I shall hold you to it when the need arises. You owe me, Charlotte, and I will not let you forget. Now, I have errands to attend to, errands that require me to spend the night in Weymouth. I would have asked you to accompany me but you have seen my mistress's letter, you have read her express instructions, I shall have to travel alone.'

She spun around and strode purposefully from the scullery. I followed close behind, at her heels, a slave in search of her master.

9

Chilcombe Bredy
19 June 1876

Dear Diary

The days drag, without the order of time or the discipline of chronometry. The sun rises, the sun sets, but the heat will not relent. It is like the plague, infesting everything with which it comes into contact.

I feel like a stranger within my own home. When I first arrived here I was convinced that the recent past was no more than a minor aberration. I was prepared to put it down to circumstances for I realise I am among those women who refuse to do as they are directed and only learn through bitter experience. I was quite prepared to take heed of my mistakes and find for myself gainful, respectable employment within less than a day's journey of my father. I missed him when he was in India and I in Spain. He was only an image and I a poor imitation of a dutiful daughter. I spent the lonely nights weeping for the mother I never knew and the father who had forsaken me. I dreamt of the day when we would be united forever and live out our lives, together, in the pastoral charm of Chilcombe Bredy. Yet now I welcome his absence. I would rather him exploring the fields with his partner in crime that tending to my crippled emotions.

The cottage is empty, a vacant husk with no

kernel, no heart and no soul. The cupboard is almost bare. I have been left to fend for myself, to make what I can from the meagre rations my father has purloined from friends and neighbours. What I wouldn't give for Mrs Bexington's return. I concede that I am quite incapable of looking after myself.

Dreams and reality, the two are surely moulded in one, what was fact and what is now fiction have become merged, blurry, indistinguishable. Last night I was visited by a vision, as fleeting as it was fateful. Emma stood at the gates of Chilcombe Lacey in mourning black, her slender cinch of a waist constrained and contoured by the miracles of corsetry. Behind her Lady Persephone, resplendent and regal, her arms raised towards the sun, as if in prayer. Is she not, after all, the high priestess of all that comes to grief?

And there was I, dirty and drenched in sweat. The heavens muttered thunder, and from the gathering clouds wept sad drops of cold rain as if mourning the completing of my mortal sin. I had been expelled from my own Eden and the archangels were guarding the gates to prevent my return. I could not look back, the image of what had been taken from me was etched into my soul but it would, from hereonafter, be as forbidden as the fruit on which I had gorged without dignity. Then I, in mutual accusation, spent the fruitless hours in a self-condemnation which would have no earthly end.

The written word should tell no lies – that is what I was taught, almost religiously, at college, by Lady Varsfield herself. The written word was sacrosanct, it could bear no untruths. Yet my diary is so full of falsehoods I can scarce believe a word of it myself.

Perhaps, as my story begins to move towards its sad conclusion, you might bear this in mind.

My father had cared enough to let me go, he had raised me to forge a life of my own, independent of others, to learn from my own mistakes, if needs be. And such is the nature of autonomy, help will not come of its own accord, it has to be summoned. My father could see that all was not as it should have been, but he trusted me to seek his advice as and when it was required. He was not normally a man to intervene but on that Thursday evening, whilst Professor Walditch was poring over a map in the dining room, he took me to one side to express his concern.

'I am so sorry, Charlie. Samuel – Professor Walditch – has been taking up far too much of my time but I think we are almost done. The finishing line is finally in sight. I promise you that once it is all over we shall spend a weekend in Bath and you shall have the choice of all the latest fashions.' His tone was apologetic. Those who did not know him might have deemed his generous offer blackmail, a pathetic attempt to win back the favour of his daughter. Those who did would have realised how much it had pained him to have been parted for so long.

'And I think a holiday together would do the both of us a world of good,' he continued, lowering his voice to keep out of his companion's earshot. 'In fact, I have been meaning to have a word with you for some time. I thought it might have been my imagination, indeed, I do not believe I have had the opportunity to take a good look at you since the day you returned. I thought then how you had grown, but that is what every father says, no matter how old his little girl and I am no different from any other doting parent. You know I prefer not to pry but I can't help observing how tired you look. No, not just tired, weary, exhausted, as if you had not slept for days. And now I come to think of it, you have not been sleeping well, have you? Is it the heat? I would have thought you would be used to it.'

I think I managed to conceal my surprise. How foolish of me to assume he would be so distracted as to not notice the pallor of his daughter's skin. He had trained as a doctor and doctors are trained to notice these things.

'Yes, Papa. I confess that I have not been feeling myself of late. The heat bothers me. It is not the same as it is in Spain: there it is heady and liberating, here it is muggy and claustrophobic. There are times when I feel I cannot breathe.'

I could see his eyebrows raised, my words had startled him. Or perhaps it was the heartfelt manner in which they were delivered. 'Well, be sure not to spend so many late nights at Chilcombe Lacey. I have no objection to your friendship with Lady Persephone, nor her maid, neither do I mind you staying over, that much makes sense when I am away such a great deal. But whatever your views on the aristocracy you should understand you are not one of them. They have a different way of going about things, it is the manner to which they have become accustomed, how they have been brought up to behave.'

His perception unnerved me. He knew far more than I had credited him with. How much more did he know that remained unsaid? He looked older and frailer, his forehead creased with concern. His salad days were fading away.

'Father, this has absolutely nothing to do with Percy ... with Lady Persephone. It is unfair of you to blame it on her.' My words were terse and my anger barely masked by an emaciated smile, a vain attempt at reassurance.

'Very well. I could not prevent you from going over there, even if I wanted to. I know, how about a picnic this Sunday afternoon? The weather looks set fair. We might ask Mr Drew to take us up on to the Chase and we can walk back together. I'm sure Professor Walditch can keep himself occupied for the afternoon.' I was ready to share in his enthusiasm, to use it as a means to excuse myself from Chilcombe Lacey but then his face dropped. 'Oh no, I am so sorry. I am afraid Samuel and I have been asked to lead a group of geologists from Southampton. I cannot possibly let them down. Perhaps the weekend after . . .'

He had tried so hard to win me back over. The troubled look on his world-weary face had said far, far more than his tactful advice but he had lost the moral high ground. He had, to all intents and purposes, relinquished responsibility for my welfare.

'I see your nerves are frayed, too. Please, Charlie, promise me one thing: if, come Monday, you are no better, allow me to call the doctor.'

I nodded in assent and we went our separate ways: he to the study, me to my room and the desk overlooking the chase. The sun seared the arc of its passage into the hazy evening sky; shadows crept across the parched lawn and fingered the flint walls of the cottage. Further up the valley, Chilcombe Lacey was stirring from its brief slumber.

She arrived in a chariot of fire, driven by Lady P and pulled by a quartet of silver mares whose hooves never once touched the ground. They rode through the village, kicking up a cloud of dust and dry flame, sending every other creature of darkness screeching into the cover of the night. Whatever was coming our way was as wicked as it was wonderful.

Lady P never drove through Chilcombe Bredy; both she and Emma avoided it as though all its inhabitants were infected with the plague. I never quite understood why. She preferred tongues to wag rather than remain silent and she courted the village's loathing with admirable gusto. In the absence of love, hatred would suffice.

Now she came crashing along Church Street in a cacophony of blinding light and ear-splitting sound, an army of dragons, driven by demons, in pursuit of their prey. I had slipped into a deep and dreamless sleep but the fingers of shimmering luminosity reached out and gently caressed my heavy eyelids. I was woken, drawn to the window only to watch the trail of blazing sparks pass up the valley, towards the chase.

But I saw her; she turned and lowered her hood, pointing in my direction. I watched as her profile rose up against the impenetrable obscurity which almost absorbed her translucent golden flesh. Even from my distant vantage point I could make out the noble silhouette of her forehead and the aquiline nose that curved elegantly like that of an eagle and rose like a crescent moon above the fecund earth. From the scarlet-edged fronds of her alabaster gown tumbled a torrent of onyx curls, each tress flickering like diamonds in an abyss. But it was the eyes that struck me, reflecting within them a supplicant girl bent at the feet of an Aztec queen, demanding to be her sacrifice. They held me in their thrall for what seemed like an eon and only let me free when I had pledged my allegiance to the dusky shadow of her soul.

The village returned to darkness, not a lamp was lit

nor a soul stirred. Either the world had turned its back on the mistress of Chilcombe Lacey and her latest apostle or I had been drawn into their dream. The valley was doused in an ethereal aurora; spectres or not, they were gone.

10

Chilcombe Lacey
20 June 1876

My dear Charlotte
*Come quickly! The world is moving fast and you and
I are both in danger of letting it pass us by; that
would never do. Did you watch us thunder through
the village this morning? They all hid behind their
curtains and their shutters, all except one.*

*I have mentioned already the existence of this
mysterious creature, perhaps you caught a glimpse
of her? Believe me, a mere glimpse is not enough,
does not do justice to her incomparable beauty. You
must meet her face to face as soon as possible. She
is, I am sure, an Aztec goddess, a direct descendant
of the earth mother Tonantzín. I spent much of the
journey telling her all about you, currying your
favour in her heart and she is so looking forward to
hearing your stories of Spain.*

*Come quick, dear heart. I cannot despatch Emma
to collect you; she has more pressing matters to attend
to as I am sure you will appreciate. Come quick, for
the wine is flowing and your advice is much desired.*

'Til soon, my sweet
P

In the broad daylight, under the spread of the horse
chestnut tree, the true beauty of María Inés de la Cruz
was revealed in all its exotic splendour. She lay like a

jaguar reclining in the jungle, her head resting on her elbow, her raven tresses trailing upon the picnic blanket she was sharing with Lady Persephone. They were deep in conversation but both rose to greet me when Emma announced my arrival.

'*Buenas tardes, señorita Crowsettle. ¿O puedo llamarte "Carlita"?*'

The informal nature of her greeting quite unsettled me. I threw her a fleeting, questioning glance that I hoped would go unnoticed but she missed not a single episode in the passage of time. Her omniscience flooded the valley with all-seeing, all-knowing essence, and left me no option but to let her illimitable gaze scrutinise every aspect of my dress and anatomy. A lesser woman would have withered before her but so desperate was I for her approval that I stood defiant in the eye of her hurricane.

'Good afternoon, Carlita. Much as I am impressed with Percy's Spanish, I think it more courteous to continue our conversation in your mother tongue. But you have taught her well. I hope you will find time to help me improve my limited English.'

Her English was near perfect and far more comprehensible than the grunting vernacular in which our neighbours, the peasants, muttered their banal greetings. Her light, lilting accent, free of the heavy Castilian lisp I had become accustomed to, ascended through the layers of thick heat to soar with the buzzard on the thermals that wafted up from the Chase.

'Good afternoon, madam.' I dipped a curtsey which amused her no end and made her hide her giggles behind the back of her cupped hand.

'Please, Carlita. I am only beginning to learn the customs of the English and I confess that as yet I do not really understand them. I suspect I never will.'

'What she means,' said Lady P, 'is that, like you and I, she has become an enemy of a system so archaic that it is rotten from the foundations upwards.'

'But you...' I intervened, hardly able to contain myself.

'Yes, Charlotte,' she replied. 'You are quite correct. I am part of that privileged hierarchy. Indeed, I am somewhere near its very peak which, in the opinions of some, condemns me as a hypocrite. But please, tell me, what on earth am I supposed to so? Abandon my position, give up my house and its grounds to the poor, the deserving and the dispossessed? I am sure my generous gesture would be welcomed with ungracious laughter and celebrations the length and breadth of Dorset. Not content with accusing me of murder, they have tried, and failed, to have me declared insane. Such an act would be all the evidence they needed to have me locked up in the asylum. What would happen to our select band then?'

'You are quite right, Percy,' said the Aztec. 'I know from my own bitter experience what happens when a woman tries to ... how do you English say? Upset the apple cart?'

Both Lady P and I smiled at her command of the idiom and shifted a little closer to her centre of gravity. I could feel her arm drape itself around my waist as she leant gently against me.

'I would very much like', continued Lady P, 'to be part of a revolution that overthrew the status quo ante and turned society upside down but if I put myself on the periphery I lose all my influence and authority. I become as helpless as those I seek to propel to power.' She spat out a mouthful of wine on to the bleached grass, her tone turning irascible and dismissive. 'Besides which, why in God's name should I raise a finger to come to the aid of the ignorant, narrow-minded masses? I hardly think they would carry me high on their shoulders and install me as empress of their republic. *Plus ça change, plus c'est la meme chose*, isn't that how the French would have it? Do you think they would tolerate a woman such as me, or Emma, or María or even yourself?'

She pointed her index finger at me and dug it with some force into my stomach. 'We have crossed our Rubicon, ladies, but we have also crossed theirs. They think us weak but we have our weapons and subtlety is our strength. We are more potent if we remain where we are, together and undivided. Change can only come from within. In any case,' she finished, looking only at me, 'there are those of us who enjoy the contradictory aspects of duty and desire, are there not ... Charlotte?'

It was half smile, half enquiring frown. Seeing Emma coming towards us across the lawn Lady P excused herself and left us to join her. Together they disappeared into the house.

'Lady Persephone has told me a great deal about you, Carlita. I am delighted to make your acquaintance and I am honoured to be invited to join such exalted company. *La Sociedad de Pecado*, as we would have said in the convent, though none of us would dare imagine what it might entail. Yet we are both to join its apostles in the coming days. I cannot wait.'

'A convent,' I replied, almost open mouthed.

Her long black lashes flicked over the dazzling embers of her pupils. I realised how naive and innocent I must have appeared but I knew she was teasing me and that if I lay back and let her tell her tale I would be seduced by this most beguiling of enchantresses. It was not that I was vulnerable, rather that I allowed myself to play the helpless, subservient little girl. It was only a game. She knew it, I knew it. She was the wolf with slavering wet tongue and sharp serrated teeth; I was her little Red Riding Hood, longing to be devoured.

María Inés de la Cruz licked her scarlet lips and ran her slender fingertips through the fronds of her hair. 'You would like to know, would you not, Carlita? I do not blame you. So many others have sat before me, demanding to hear my tale. I refused. They often became angry and cursed me to hell. But you are different and I shall tell *you* in intimate detail.'

20 June 1876
Chilcombe Bredy

Dear Diary
Do you remember when I passed through my religious phase? It was not so long ago, was it? Father mocks me now but at the time I think it disturbed him immensely. He feared having a puritan for a daughter. I wrote to tell him that I had, on several occasions, attended the chapel of the Strict and Particular Baptists less than half a mile from the college. I told him that the pastor was so impressed with my enthusiasm and demeanour that he had invited me to lunch the following Sunday. I suspect he replied immediately to the headmistress informing her of his disapproval which she would undoubtedly have shared as from thereon I was always given errands to run on a Sunday morning. I think I owe them both a good deal of thanks.

But If I had come across a creature as esoteric and urbane as María Inés de la Cruz I think my religious zeal might have taken off in an altogether different direction. If there existed nuns in England

I never set eyes on them. In Spain they were a more frequent sight, in the mornings and evenings dashing to prayer but they were aloof and covered from head to foot, even in the heat of midday, veiled and hidden from probing eyes. Their hidden forms, cloaked in black and white, rendered them infinitely appealing to my twisted curiosity. They might have walked stark naked through the streets of Cartagena but I would not have found them as alluring as the concealed unknown and unseen. The thrill of the forbidden aroused within my stirring libido a desire to explore and expose every secret that was denied me. There could surely be only one reason for declaring them taboo and that was sufficient reason for me to taste the sweet kernel of pleasure secreted within.

Temptation loomed large on every church and chapel step but only once, when I caught the eye of a novice not much older than myself, did I dare act on my whim. I asked her, in deliberately inept Spanish, how I might learn more of her vocation for I felt that I, too, had a calling.

Oh, I had a calling right enough, and it was as sacred and heaven sent as anything experienced by the martyrs and saints. And she was a divine revelation, despatched from on high to test my febrile flesh. Poor little Conchita, she was wavering when the abbess blundered in on our intimate discussions. I say intimate, it was, perhaps, a little more carnal than what she had intended. We knelt together, saying the rosary with our fingers on the wooden beads. 'Blessed art thou among women,' I mouthed, lowering my eyes and letting them rest upon hers. 'Pray for us sinners . . .' as our mouths edged closer to one another and I ran my tongue over my lips. I let my hand fall upon her tunic, so starched and stiff that I could barely manipulate the coarse fabric. I fought my way through the layers of harsh fibre that shielded her maidenhead from the vulgarity of the temporal world.

She flinched as I slid a forefinger inside her. She was slippery and wet, welcoming and warm. 'Dulce nombre de María,' she whispered, placing her willing hand upon mine and, like a pilot before the harbour, assisting with its entrance, for she was, by virtue of her purity, tight and intact but I was so gentle that her pain soon melted into pleasure. 'O clemens, o pia, o dulcis Virgo María,' she cried as a trickle of treacle-thick syrup dribbled out on to the flesh of her thighs, flesh that had never seen daylight let alone felt the warm and wandering flow of spilt love. 'Pray for us sinners...' Footsteps on the staircase outside, angry leather on hard stone. 'Now and at the hour of our death...' The door burst open, both heaven and hell were upon us.

Poor little Conchita. I never did find out what happened to her. I returned to the church a week later when I hoped any fuss might have died down but her iron-faced Mother Superior still stood guard in the porch, a switch clenched angrily in her left hand. She never saw me for I had adopted the same modest style of dress that her holy order prescribed. She was not as old as I had previously imagined, framed by her coif and bandeau one could see only the clarity of her skin, the proud nose and the eyes still delirious with rage. I stood at the foot of the steps, gazing up at her, entranced by the purity of her wrath. I dearly wanted to stride up to her, full of defiance, and confess to my heinous sin. But I was overwhelmed with the fear of the unknown so I turned and fled.

I wish, now, I had not.

'You have seen Spain but you have not yet seen Mexico. One day, when our work here is done, I promise to take you there. You shall return with me – we must both travel in disguise – and together we shall share the delights of Xochiquetzal, the Aztec goddess of love.'

María's eyes were wide open with exhilaration. How many times she had told her tale I do not know but I hung on her every word as if she had only just flushed them from creation.

'But Lady Persephone said . . .'

'That I was a nun? Yes, that much is quite true. I entered the convent of Las Carmelitas Descalzas – the barefoot Carmelites – on the day of my sixteenth birthday and I left exactly ten years later at the age of twenty-six. Can you imagine that, Carlita, ten years with only women for company?'

She paused and I dwelt on her last question. I could not quite decide whether it would be paradise or purgatory.

'No,' she continued with a wicked smile, 'that is not a question you are required to answer. I entered the convent not through any great love of God or the Virgin Mary but because it was the only safe haven I could find. My father had been trying to marry me off to a steady procession of fools and imbeciles but I turned down everyone. By the time I reached sixteen he had had enough; he chose a husband for me himself, without consulting me. As it happened, the man he selected was tall and handsome and from the richest family in Mexico City but that was not the point. I am, like you, a woman of principle. I will not be told what to do. On the eve of my birthday I packed a small case and with the help of my maid disappeared into the night. The nuns looked after me. The abbess was strict but she was kind and loving, too. It took my father four years to find me but by then it was too late. I was no longer his daughter. I had become Sor María Inés de la Cruz, a bride of Christ.

'Oh, you English Protestants! How I pity you. Your God does not smile and your Christ does not drink or dance. And you have banished Our Lady, the most beautiful woman the world has ever seen. So spartan, so sober, so unrelentingly dull. That it is not how to live, is it, Carlita?'

I nodded. I missed Spain. Were it not for the existence of Chilcombe Lacey I might well have returned. The sun was warm on my back; the somnambulant aroma of freshly mown hay drifted in on a gentle breeze and lulled me into the dangerous world of my dreams. María continued in her graceful Hispanic tones.

'You must not think me a hypocrite. I consider myself a good Catholic girl.' And then she added, quite thoughtfully, 'Within the limits of my conscience. Tell me, is it a sin to fall in love?'

I shook my head. 'I think not, but there are many who consider it a crime. We are in the minority, María. They hate us, they hate us every waking moment of their day and even their dreams are full of hate. Sometimes they think of nothing else but hating us and one day, perhaps one day very soon, they will come to crucify us, too.'

My voice was low and full of restrained passion. I felt María's fingers tighten around mine. She was seeing a different, quite unexpected manifestation of my character, one that surprised me as much as it did her. It was, I think, my Transfiguration, there in our very own Garden of Gethsemane, sweating under the shade of the valiant oak tree. It was at that moment I realised, I think we both realised, that I would be the martyr, that I would be she who suffered for her faith.

A martyr? Surely suffering was not supposed to be a pleasure? And yet pleasure in its extreme is a cross we all have to bear.

'He offered me protection,' she continued. 'He was the first man, the only man, I have ever encountered to treat me as an equal, to grant me the respect I yearned, the respect I consider my birthright even though I have been born a woman. He was also the Archbishop of Cuernavaca.'

María's voice was shaky, suddenly flowing over with bitterness. 'He betrayed me, Carlita. He betrayed me just when I had placed all my trust in him. I thought he was a saint. I would have been his disciple and followed him to the ends of the Earth but I soon learnt that he was no different from the rest of them. He abused me. I shall have my revenge and you shall be a part of it. If you so wish.'

'What happened?' I asked, unashamed of my naked curiosity. 'You do want to tell me, don't you?'

Her silence was her assent. After a moment, she went on but looking down now, not meeting my admiring gaze. 'He denied all knowledge of me, even though we were both caught, *in flagrante delicto*, on the little altar of Saint Catherine of Sienna, the patron saint of those who are faced with sexual temptation. It was the early hours of the morning, the very rich hours, which we had taken to sharing in the empty cathedral with a bottle or two of fine Rioja from the vineyards of Don Amancio Ugarte.

'He would call me his little angel then burst into laughter because I was a good deal taller than he. He called me his cherub and seraph, begged me to take him from alpha to omega as we lay under the image of Our Lady of Guadalupe. Her eyes were on me every minute of our assignation but she never once made plain her displeasure, only her concern for me, her inquisitive child. As I awaited my passage from Veracruz I learnt of his untimely demise, his heart pierced by a falling crucifix. And do you know? My prayers were answered. She struck him dead, Carlita.

'For a man of his years and learning, his body was surprisingly lithe and light, a temple to indulgence and illicit love. Yes, I did love him, I adored, worshipped him. I knelt before him, obeyed his every order because through his body I genuinely believed I might find salvation. I obliged his every need.

'It was, at times, a trial but whenever I moved to mouth an objection he held up his hand and blessed me: "Suffer the little children to come unto me, and forbid them not: for to such belongeth the kingdom of God." Then he invited – no, ordered – me to partake of his divine nature. It did not quite taste divine – warm and viscous but with a bitter aftertaste that stayed for days on end no matter how much I washed out my mouth with soap and water.

'He would tell me, the moment he began to remove his vestments, that it was all for my own good and it was true that the flashing of gold and silver, the scarlet cross of his chasuble raised me to the realms of spiritual ecstasy. He wrapped its fragrant silk around my naked breasts and gently drew me towards him. He was never violent, I should credit him with that, never crude, never without his dignity and I was never able to refuse, not even when I took his hot vibrating *bicho*. I took it in my hands, enveloped it with my lips and let my tongue lick the salty liquid from its tip.

'That was all. Not once did he enter me or allow his

hands to journey through my virgin territories. Not that I was wholly pristine, not having spent ten years in a nunnery. I begged him to, I prostrated myself at his feet like a Lenten supplicant. I would have been his disciple, his slave, had he only summoned the strength to share. He had already broken his vows; fornication could hardly have been more heinous than fellatio.

'Our liaisons continued, on and off, for the best part of two years. He promised to take me away with him, as his secretary and assistant, if only I would bide my time. But I grew impatient and greedy, so I suppose he had no alternative but to expose me as little more than a holy whore. Had matters progressed, he might have put his own position at risk. And shamed the Catholic Church. Kingdoms come and go, reputations rise and fall but the Church must be seen to be sacrosanct whatever sins it has committed.

'I was taken, shaking with terror, before an *auto de fé*. Knowing Spanish history you must realise what dread those words strike into heretics and believers alike and I feared for my life. They charged me with onanism, which is, as you may or may not know, a mortal sin that would scar me for life and condemn me to hell unless I was truly repentant. Do you not think that ironic that of all the nuns in the long history of convent I was the only woman to be accused of playing with myself?'

María allowed herself a wry smile which I returned. My emotions were torn between laughter and pity. I felt for her disgrace but I was desperate to hear the end of her story.

'Please, go on,' I urged softly.

'They were clever. Not only was the archbishop's name never mentioned but he was despatched to

Rome for an audience with the Holy Father. He was far from harm's way and any attempt to implicate him would only exacerbate my already precarious situation. In any case, as a publicly exposed sinner, I was quite clearly insane. They spared me the sentence of death; I was not even subjected to a whipping but was defrocked at dawn in the square of Santo Domingo in front of a thousand onlookers. They threw my habit into a pile and set it alight, covered me in a robe of horsehair and threw me into a carriage bound for Veracruz.

'Like Eve my sentence was exile – from my sisters, from my order, from the arms of my lover and from my homeland. At the time I was hysterical with grief, screamed out for forgiveness but it was the only gift they could not afford to offer me. If I remained in Mexico, if I remained on the American continent, I would have represented a constant danger, a bomb that might go off quite out of the blue and with disastrous results. In Europe I would be safe and, as handmaiden to the Comtesse de la Fayette, in the safe hands of France's most pious and respected Catholic family. But, I never reached her chateau. The moment I set eyes on Lady Persephone on the quayside at Bordeaux I understood my life had taken another turn, that fate was leading me and I should follow her.

'It was, I agree, rather presumptuous of me. With my last franc I persuaded the purser to billet me with Percy. She was not, at first, best pleased. They were spartan quarters for she was travelling incognito and doing her best to distract attention from herself. Matters deteriorated with alarming haste and we might have come to blows had not the captain himself intervened. I told him we could settle it ourselves, over a bottle of rum. She was not then quite the finished article, not the epitome of poise and self-assurance we see striding towards us now.

'I knew she had a secret, I could see the guilt curdling in her eyes. For all our foibles we Catholics have an uncanny ability to seek out guilt and latch on to it like a leech. It was clear to me that whatever transgression she had committed was on a far greater scale than mine. My sins, of lust and avarice, were merely cardinal but hers, I soon deduced, were mortal, without contrition she would be damned. We made a pact. I would tell her my story, she hers but both of us would swear to secrecy. We tossed a coin to determine who should start and I won. I spared her no detail. I was as explicit in my revelations as I have been with you and, like you, she was mesmerised, hung on my every word.

'And then she opened her heart, in floods of tears, poured out more than I might have deemed prudent but she had been holding back for far too long. Her narrative did not surprise me. I understood her motives although clearly I could not endorse them. But neither is it my place to condemn and as a Christian it is my duty to forgive. She asked me to hear her confession and I – yes I, the defrocked and disgraced María Inés de la Cruz – absolved her.

'We dissolved into a drunken heap and she told me of her vision, of her eclectic ensemble of friends and lovers. I did not, at first, approve and took umbrage. Oh yes, we have had our disagreements but good friends always do and she has been my salvation. London was not the city I had imagined, it took only a week of smog and destitute melancholy to bring me to my senses. She is a clever woman, she covers her tracks well but I was a determined and desperate waif; before long I had hunted her down.'

So came her tale to an end and the sun, having proceeded in its passage across the sky, opened her arms and showered kind and tender light upon us. I wanted to prise out from her at least the gist of Lady P's confession but I knew that, for all her faults, María Inés de la Cruz was as the personification of honour and discretion. She would say nothing.

And Lady P was fast approaching, with Emma at her side. She noticed that we had devoured the contents of several bottles of wine and shook her head in mock reproach.

'When the cats are away.' She laughed, tossing back her head. 'Emma and I have been hard at it, on your behalf, I should add, and what thanks do we receive? An empty bottle and a couple of half-cut hosts. Come along: María, to bed, Charlotte, to home. On foot, I think: the walk will sober you up. Sleep now, for tonight we feast.'

20 June 1876
Chilcombe Bredy

Dear Diary
They are closing in on me – the forces of good and the forces of evil. Oh! But I wish it were that simple. What is right and what is wrong is all blurred and I can no longer see clearly. Yet my fate is out of my hands, I have relinquished all responsibility and I shall let Lady Persephone take control. She – they – have plans for me, for myself and María Inés de la Cruz and I have waded in too far deep to withdraw.

The ante has been upped, the stakes raised. I returned, woozily, through the parched meadows over which wafted wisps of smoke from a bonfire Emma had lit in the stableyard. Burning, burning, burning. The stench was stifling and acrid.

Why is he at home? And where is Professor Wal-
ditch? I had to sneak in the back door, like a servant,
creep up the stairs to the safety of my room. I had
planned to lock myself in there and, if unable to
sleep, feign it. But there was another voice, agitated,
drifting in through the opened windows and seeking
me out. It was not my father's, it was not his friend's;
though it was firm and strong it was not that of a
man. I recognised its autocratic intonation – it was
the eternally upstanding Miss Grace Fitzpiers.

And my father was listening, murmuring his
assent. How could he bear her presence on his prop-
erty? How could he stomach her nonsense and lies?
Does he not realise she is a sad cantankerous
woman, full of bitter untruths?

Or is she? I can no longer distinguish between
truth and mendacity. She is more subtle than the
serpent; she has my father in her grip.

I will not believe a word of her gibberish: that
Emma – or rather, Lady Melcombe – is the disgraced
daughter of the Duke of Sherborne who refused the
hand of the Queen's cousin, fled and turned to har-
lotry. That her mistress is under investigation from
Scotland Yard on suspicion of murder and that
Inspector Lefebvre is hot on her trail. I can hear the
strain of concern in his reply. He is telling her I have
not been myself of late, that I have looked weary
and withdrawn. And yes, I have been spending much
of my time at Chilcombe Lacey, perhaps too much. It
could be that the two are related.

He should not be sharing such intimacies with
her, he should not be telling her that Professor Wal-
ditch has returned to Exeter and that he would
presently be leaving to join him for a few days when
he has not yet informed me of his plans. He says he
is worried that his daughter has fallen into bad

company, that he had trusted Lady Persephone, as a member of the landed gentry, implicitly and that he had dismissed the village gossip as idle rumour. She is reminding him that there is no smoke without fire. He is concurring, 'I am not the world's most dutiful father, Miss Fitzpiers, and this would not be the first time I have neglected my daughter's interests.'

She has him now, putty in her hand. She has been thorough in her research, she knew he would be going away and leaving me alone. She delivers her tour de force.

'My fiancé busies himself in his parish whilst I am left to twiddle my thumbs. I confess I am at a loose end and, as a newcomer, I have few friends here in Chilcombe Bredy. I am told Charlotte is a charming young lady, intelligent and witty. I believe I would very much like to know her. But I realise it would be audacious of me to assume her friendship and I am, after all, several years her senior. In the absence of yourself and her dear departed mother, might I volunteer my services as her chaperone, perhaps? If you are satisfied with my performance I am prepared to offer my services on a professional basis, until my marriage, at least.'

He intends to give her proposal his full consideration. She is to return this evening to learn of his decision. I fear it will go against me. Her final words, stern and serene, send a shiver down my spine.

'Rest assured, Sir Napier. I would take care of her. I would watch her like a hawk.'

11

I watched them all arrive, the same faces, each one animated and radiating anticipation. They filed past me, offering admiring glances, for Emma had spent the best part of the afternoon scrubbing and preening and arranging my new frock until I looked more duchess than doctor's daughter. She had chosen it herself, had passed several long hours in Madame Sosostris's Emporium in Crewkerne in pursuit of a gown that would best suit my awkward frame. I had, on first sight, shied away from its iridescent beauty, its red silken flames that would surely burn anyone who approached me with amorous intent. The plunging neckline, edged with black Venice lace and sequinned beading, thrust heavenwards even my petite breasts and created between them a deep riven valley. 'Don't be silly,' Emma had mocked me. 'You mark my words, once you've tried it on you'll never want to take it off again. Besides, *I* want you to wear it. I want you to outshine them all.' She had been sweetness and light all day and I was, once again, quite smitten.

Lady P had taken me to one side and sat me down so close that I could feel the blood pumping through her veins. Her face exuded concerned appreciation. She had turned me around and around, silently examining me, scrutinising my attire and comportment in great detail. I felt like a helpless mannequin, a plaything in her hands as she ran her fingers over the thin fabric. I wondered what would happen should I fail to meet her approval.

'That servant of mine will put us all in the work-house,' she said with a laugh. 'Madame Sosostris's gowns do not come cheap and that, I should imagine, is one of her more expensive designs. Never mind, we do not want to associate ourselves with the nouveau riche, do we? Those who know the price of everything and the value of nothing.' She leant over and kissed me gently full on the lips. 'And you are my protégé, I begrudge you not a penny.'

I blushed and even under the light dusting of rouge I could feel my pale skin turn scarlet. 'I promise I will not let you down, Percy,' I murmured into my fan.

'It never occurred to me that you might,' she replied, a little tersely. 'That is exactly why you were chosen. I hope you do not feel jealous or usurped. Tonight was to be yours and yours alone but that was before María Inés de la Cruz walked into our lives. I should have realised that the equation was not quite complete, that there was something missing. She is here now, the one who will go before you. I am the prophet, she is the evangelist, but you are the anointed one, my messiah.'

She was talking in riddles but, however implausible she sounded, I was finally beginning to comprehend. The realms of Lady P's amoral empire were closing in on me, its borders were being pushed to their limits, something would have to give.

'Will I have to wait long? I almost feel time is against me, against us.' My voice was hollow and wavering, it drew concern from her ladyship.

'What do you mean?' she asked, halfway between a hiss and a whisper. Her mouth was half-hidden by the back of her hand but Emma was close at hand and made no attempt to remove herself from earshot. And why should she? She was as deeply inveigled as Lady P and myself. 'No, please do not tell me Grace Fitzpiers is still in pursuit.'

I nodded. 'She came to see my father this afternoon, with a proposal I do not think he will refuse. He is leaving for Exeter tomorrow and in his absence Miss Fitzpiers has offered to act as my chaperone.'

Lady P looked alarmed. Unnoticed, Emma came to join us on the sofa. 'Your father? But he has always been a bastion of compassion in a valley where primitive justice still reigns. I would have sworn by his liberal intransigence. What on earth has she told him to turn him against you?' Lady P asked.

'Not against me, Persephone; he has taken against you!'

'The cantankerous little cur! But how short-sighted of me. I had not looked for this, in our own backyard when I had assumed trouble to be outwith the borders of our fiefdom. This is important, Charlotte. What did she say?'

'He had already noticed that I have looked tired, pale and wan. He asked whether I was wise to spend so much of my time in your company and made me promise to see a physician if, by Monday, I felt no better. But it was she who fuelled his doubts. She said . . .' I faltered, I had half a mind to believe all that Miss Fitzpiers had said to my father. Lady P was no innocent, that was her attraction and I was, by now, perfectly aware that Emma's present, perennially ambiguous status belied her noble lineage. But a murderess and a whore?

Lady P had taken hold of my wrist and was squeezing it hard. She sounded agitated, consumed by concern.

Her voice was metered with unease. 'You must tell me, exactly – word for word if you are able – what Miss Fitzpiers told your father.'

'I cannot!'

'You stupid little tom. Do you not understand? Even you must realise that catastrophe is staring us directly in the face.' She shook my body so violently I feared she might well throttle me. 'Tell me!'

The tears that had been massing in the corners of my eyes welled up and trickled down my cheeks. 'She said ... she said ... that you are under investigation from Scotland Yard on suspicion of murder and that ... that Emma, my beloved Emma, is the disgraced daughter of nobility turned to prostitution.' Then I broke down in a sobbing fit.

Lady P let go of my arms and rose abruptly to her feet. She addressed her remarks to Emma, as if I were an irrelevance.

'I think it is time for a council of war. I have had enough of Miss Fitzpiers and her temerity. I have given her too much slack and in doing so I suspect I may have underrated her. She must be dealt with severely *tout de suite*, before she sabotages our plans.'

And then her wide smile returned, consumed every inch of the angst and anxiety that had crossed her face. 'It can wait until tomorrow. This evening we are safe and anyone foolish enough to intrude into the grounds of Chilcombe Lacey will suffer the consequences. Ah! Here comes our monarch of the high seas, Miss Liberty Belle. Madam, I fear Miss Crowsettle has been a little unnerved by recent events. I wonder, perhaps one of your tales might calm her down. I must attend to my guests and Emma has a sacrifice to prepare.'

She was right, my nerves were fraught, and talk of sacrifice hardly soothed them but Liberty Belle was carrying a large flagon of rum, a drink of which I had become over-fond the previous time we met. The pirate queen had made a rare concession to femininity and she swept to my side in a swirl of swishing scarlet silk. Her bodice was cut so low I could almost make out the pink whirl of her left nipple which rose above her ebony skin. There was, above it and to the right, the most delicate of tattoos – not, as you might imagine, a skull and crossbones nor a silver cutlass dripping with blood but a hummingbird sucking nectar from a flower. She caught my gaze and tugged her neckline a little lower. 'Pretty, isn't it?' she asked. 'Shall I tell you the story behind it? Of the battle with my sworn enemy, Dr Merengue, who I pursued through the islands of the Caribbean?'

I nodded and allowed her to pour me a large glass. From the corner of my eye I watched Emma and Lady P leave together, deep in conversation, and I knew that a conspiracy was already afoot. But the alcohol soon went to my head. I leant back and let Liberty Belle's heroic images envelope me.

We were joined, over time, by Samantha Poorton and Hildegard von Bingen who sat at her feet, hypnotised, like small children, as Liberty Belle brought her history – our history – to life in visions before our star-filled eyes. She drifted in and out of reality, as if she had existed since the very beginning of time.

Liberty Belle had come to the end of her tale and a sedative silence had fallen over the company.

'Come, ladies. The hour is almost upon us, the hour when we are called to celebrate, to celebrate and make our offering.' She was shrouded in the gathering gloom, we could see only her face, which shone under the torch she held high above her head. Lady P's invitation, baited with temptation and delivered with an irresistible come-hither look, lured us all towards the great hall. In single file we followed whilst Emma took up the rear to ensure no one fell behind.

Or, perhaps, to deny any means of escape.

I cannot say, for certain, that what I went through that night was dream or lived experience but I can, without doubt, confirm that it revealed Lady Persephone de Mortehoe in all her unheavenly grandeur, that she possessed qualities beyond the comprehension of a mere mortal such as myself.

Neither could I say, for certain, whether she is magician, illusionist or bona fide sorceress. Had they been able to get their hands upon her, they would surely have burnt her as a witch. All the untoward events that would blight the valley later that summer, all the unforeseen and unfortunate circumstances that set neighbour against neighbour and tore the village in two were blamed upon her sinister practices. I can well imagine that they were indeed the work of Lady P, exacting her revenge.

The great dining room burst into light as we passed through its doors, accompanied by a cacophony of sound. Roman candles, firecrackers, flares, every conceivable form of pyrotechnic filled the chamber with a riot of exploding colour. And there sat Lady P on her throne, tall, proud and stunning, before the roaring fire and behind a cascade of crimson crystals pouring from the ceiling and landing in dancing sparks on the floor. She was 'Flower Feather', Xochiquetzal, the Aztec patroness of erotic love returned from her underworld, surrounded by a retinue of butterflies, glowing with searing heat.

Xochiquetzal sat lifeless, silent, majestic. From the drawing room emanated a turquoise mist, along the beech floorboards, rising into curled columns of clouded jewels before dissipating above our heads.

The doors opened and the entire company, awe-struck, retreated as one as María Inés de la Cruz entered the room.

But she was no longer María Inés de la Cruz: she was Coatlicue, the goddess of earth and fire, accompanied by a phalanx of white-clad virgins. Her terrifying beauty filled the hall with its exquisite brooding anger. Some averted their gaze from this grotesque deity; others, myself included, could not take their eyes off her.

Her skirt, so short that it exposed the very top of her firm thighs, was a writhing mass of serpents, her tunic a mosaic of claws and snake heads. Her breasts were covered with feathers of every colour and hue and round her neck hung a necklace of human hands and hearts.

Coatlicue marched to the fire and if any of us had dared to stand in her way she would surely have burnt us to a cinder. She carried in her clasped hands an obsidian dagger that flickered in flames whenever and wherever she wielded its blade and carved her name in the smoky, suffocating air. Coatlicue the insatiable: the source of all life who takes the dead back to her body.

There was one more to come, one who would bring with her the sacrifice, gagged and bound. Xipe Totec, Our Lady the Flayed Servant, burst into the throng with lightning flashing about her. Somewhere, beneath the silver and the gold, was the pale figure of Emma although, to all intents and purposes, she no longer existed, she had been usurped by her alter ego.

Save for a flimsy loincloth wrapped loosely around

his waist, Father Oliver Powys was naked. He had been stripped of every other garment but his crucifix which he clutched in his right hand. Even he, the most corrupt and shameless of all prelates, felt intimidated by the atmosphere and the crowd of unholy women who gathered around him. Lady P considered herself fortunate in having as her local priest a man from whom money could purchase almost anything, although, had he been made vaguely aware of the nature of the ceremony in which he was to participate, he might well have had second thoughts.

If Father Oliver did not share the Vatican's uncompromising attitude to women, he hardly considered them his equals. As a minister he took great pleasure in hearing their confessions which, depending on what was owned up to, he would probe for the most intimate details. He always kept a pencil and paper at his side and would jot down the more salacious stories to feed his one-handed fantasies late at night. His definition of celibacy rested on the assumption that he had not engaged any woman in holy wedlock even though he had a string of mistresses across his parish. How he longed for Lady P to join his harem; despite his constant flirting she had consistently refused. Perhaps he thought this his moment for the sum he accepted from her would have bought him a passage to the New World. Perhaps that was her intention. Father Oliver would soon learn that it was hardly commensurate with the task in hand.

Absurdly handsome, square-jawed, his face dappled with a mat of coarse stubble, Father Oliver Powys barely resembled the archetypal Roman Catholic priest, not least because at the age of 32 he was England's youngest minister by several years. That he rarely went about his business in cassock and dog collar served to exacerbate the ambiguity as to his role. When it was convenient, he donned his holy garb; when his faith might have told against him he played the gentleman and scholar. His manly, muscular figure and his easy manner won him the hearts of many ladies in his own diocese and beyond so that, despite a constant barrage of rumours, his bishop chose to turn a blind eye to his extra-curricular activities. Not for nothing did the diocese of Sherborne boast the highest numbers of converts in the Holy See. Nevertheless, it was symptomatic of Lady P's influence and power that, through a combination of subtle persuasion and blatant blackmail, she had secured his services. He might well have been a gigolo but it came at a cost.

And yet, for all his earthly prowess he could never hope to match the celestial temptations of María Inés de la Cruz. Lady P had deliberately underplayed the nature of the gathering she wished him to attend and the suave Lothario had simply assumed that each and every member of the weaker sex would have fallen at his feet. He could never have imagined his nemesis' insatiable desire for retribution; a retribution directed not only against the Church, which had humiliated her, but at a faith that had sought to deny and suppress every free thought she had ever dreamt up. They had planned it meticulously: she, Lady P and Emma. Her revenge was to be the revenge of all women, in a ritual so ancient it is almost forgotten they would go the way of all flesh, he the sacrificial victim, she the omnipotent, all-devouring goddess.

Emma – or should I say Xipe Totec – secured the young priest's wrists and ankles to a pillar before the blazing fire. Soon he was soaked in sweat and his calm self-assurance had metamorphosed into a fear so tangible it transmitted itself to all the women surrounding him. We closed in on him but Lady P warned us off, making way for María Inés de la Cruz.

She approached her victim, eyes set firmly on the prize, the dagger so close to her lips that with one slip she might have punctured them and left a trickle of blood behind her. She would not have cared, the unholy scream that came forth would still have echoed around the room and pierced the hearts and the souls of all who stood within its range. It would still have shattered the glass and crashed through the windows to waft on the wind down to Chilcombe Bredy where each and every man and woman still awake at that unearthly hour listened fearfully and crossed themselves.

It was a cry from a language unknown to all save María herself but its meaning imprinted itself unforgettably in our minds. *'Tlecuauhtlacupeuh'* in the tongue of her ancestors and then, in her native Spanish, *'La que viene volando de la luz como el águila de fuego'*: 'She who comes flying from the light like the eagle of fire'. She raised the knife before him and plunged it deep into the heart of Father Oliver.

Father Oliver put his hand to his chest and felt on his fingers a warm and viscous liquid. He fainted, María fainted. She swooned into the arms of Lady P who held her tight. The onlookers, to a woman, stood watching with mouths gaping, not wanting to believe what their eyes had just witnessed. The wild and the willing were called to prove their worth; only Samantha Poorton stepped forwards.

She was almost as skilled in the fine art of pleasure as Lady P herself and, with hands as delicate and as determined as a surgeon, she coaxed life back into Coatlicue's limp body. She twitched as Samantha prised her thighs apart, quivered as her healing hands lay like limpets upon her golden flesh, then shuddered as she felt her lips upon her labia. What had been arid was now dripping with the luscious dew of a Mexican dawn. Samantha withdrew without tasting for it was Father Oliver's sole prerogative to make amends for the sins of his Church.

Did he know whether he was alive or dead? He had recovered from unconsciousness and was gazing in wonderment at his 'blood'. 'A miracle? he asked himself. 'A miracle!' he declared at the top of his voice, barely able to contain his relief at still being alive. A curious declaration from a man who seemed to fear heaven as much as hell; a man whose eternal destination was far from a foregone conclusion. But Coatlicue was in no mood to allow him more than a moment's self-congratulation; what Samantha had begun Father Oliver was required to complete. And, unlike his God, she was an impatient deity with a thirst for sacrifice, those who denied her were inevitably destroyed.

How sweet to watch the roles reverse themselves, the conquered become *conquistadora*, exploiting the rich treasures now returned to their rightful heiress. The priest had relinquished his power, handed it over to the woman who now had him in her charm. He might not last a minute unless he obeyed her every instruction.

He knew what he had been called upon to do but moved with too much sloth for her liking. She unhooked a snake from her belt and waved its fanged jaws before him.

'No! No!' he yelled and Lady P smiled contentedly, congratulating herself on correctly guessing his phobia.

Coatlicue cocked her head approvingly; she was enjoying his debasement. 'What do you fear more,

Father? The venom of the serpent or the venom of a woman wronged and scorned? Come to me,' she whispered. 'Is it not better to give than to receive?'

She took his head in her hands, firmly but with no great force for she required him intact. 'Do you sense it?' she asked, as she drew it towards her vagina. 'Its aroma is all around the room. It is driving me mad with desire, Father. How about you? The scent of my fresh papaya. Can you feel it, yet? Has it settled upon your taste buds? Has it pervaded your empty soul? No? But then you must sup and sup deep before the well runs dry.'

His tongue leapt into her deepest crevices. Not the all-conquering army of the aggressor but a single secret agent who knew exactly what to look for, where to find it and, most importantly, how to tease and torture it from its secret hideaway. She was offering up to him the ultimate pleasure but just when he thought it his for the taking she would snatch it from his grasp.

'Lick, you bastard! *Hijo de puta*. I do not think you are man enough for me. Have you never had the privilege of a woman like me? I am not like your floozies and harlots, am I? Those cheap little tarts whose loose and saggy quims you fuck day in day out. They are but dried prunes compared to my juicy papaya. My lover, Xochiquetzal, has told me all and I am inclined to feel sorry for you. I will empty your libido, drain it dry for my revenge and you shall take not an ounce of love in return.'

She pushed hard. Her nostrils flared and her eyelids slammed shut. The madness was close at hand. It was beginning to take hold of her body and she tore at her necklace and flimsy bodice, scattering jade pearls across the room. She could barely stand on her own two feet. I reached out not, perhaps, to offer support but to plug into whatever juices were flowing through her veins. I cared not that there was blood on my hands, it was only blood; it was not the precious, hot and sticky liquid of life.

'*Santa María, Madre de Dios, ruega por nosotras.*' She had entered her trance and was no longer of this world. 'Holy Mary, Mother of God, pray for us,' she repeated, her eyes closed, raised towards heaven. And then in a voice, a shriek, that was not her own: '*Ay! Nuestra Señora de los Dolores; perdóneme! Perdóneme!*'

She doubled up violently, as if racked with pain, and pushed Father Oliver from her with such force that he was sent sprawling across the room. He crashed hard into the table but no one looked out for him; his job was done, he was superfluous to requirements.

'Hold her tight!' barked Lady Persephone, her gloved hand poised on the branding iron. 'Hold her tight!' she cried again.

I gripped hard on to her arms, while Emma held her legs. Coatlicue was bound to us both; all three watched in horror and fascination as the white-hot metal rod was lowered and pressed into her bare bronzed skin.

I shall never forget the stench of burning human flesh nor the cry that shook Chilcombe Lacey to its very foundations. It was too much for me. Overwhelmed by events, I fell into a deep faint.

'Wake up, sleepy head!' Emma's voice was clear and fresh and washed like a pure spring tide through the stagnant waters of my mind. I coughed, spluttered and turned over in my sweaty sheets. The midday sun boomed into the room, the air was already stale and still.

'Come along,' she enthused. 'Your presence has been requested and I am about to serve breakfast.' She paused, smiled and checked herself. 'Or should that be lunch?'

'Please, Emma. What on earth happened last night? My sleep was plagued with nightmares, that is, if I have slept at all.' I opened my eyes and saw blood-stains on my hands. 'So,' I said with a sigh, 'it was true. What have I become involved in? Am I lost forever?'

She sat on my bed, took my hand and dabbed my moist brow. It was not enough, I needed physical contact. I wrapped my arms around her and held her so tight that she struggled to breathe. The door clicked open; so tight were we entwined that we scarce had time to tear ourselves apart before Lady P entered. Emma leapt to attention.

'Are we not forgetting ourselves, Emma? Miss Crow-settle is a guest and should be treated as such, not as one of your ne'er-do-wells from the city. I shall have words with you later.' She spoke with a smile but it was cruel and condescending. I ought to have owned up there and then but I could not rid my mind of the image of the mistress chastising her servant. I was quite sure that Lady P would never raise a finger to harm her but the scene was sweet all the same. Emma looked daggers at me but I remained tight lipped.

'Now, I should imagine you have more pressing matters to attend to. I am sure Miss Crowsettle can dress herself.'

I offered a dumb, tight-lipped nod in agreement, feeling both Emma's humiliation and my own, the shame of a small and insignificant child reprimanded by her superior. My face reddened into a rosy blush and a warm disgrace fermented deliciously in my lush forbidden territories. Lady P had a wonderful talent for letting her subordinates know their place. I knew I would never, could never become her equal. I had no desire to do so.

'Come along, then!' she snapped and I wallowed in her disdain. She would not take her gaze from me, followed me around the room until I had no option but to remove my nightclothes right under her nose. Just as I was about to select a light and loose summer frock from the wardrobe she intervened. I was not, so it seemed, considered sufficiently adult to decide on my own clothing. Lady P rummaged through the racks of assorted garments but could find nothing that matched her purpose. 'Tsh, none of these will do. Wait there, Miss Charlotte, I have something more appropriate in mind.'

She disappeared into the corridor and left me alone, naked. I dared not deviate from my location, stranded in the middle of the room with the sun drenching my uncovered form in hallowed light. I was neither voluptuous nor curvaceous, I lacked the full silhouette that was currently in vogue. In the eyes of the law I was a grown woman, responsible for my own welfare and I had years of experience to draw upon should I be required to prove my maturity. Yet I knew I remained, deep down, little more than a child. No matter how my nipples bulbed like buds on a bay tree the unforgiving stare of the sun cruelly emphasised their lack of prominence. I was no longer the slender figure who strode confidently down Weymouth quay less than two months ago; I had become a scrawny shadow of my former self, an emaciated ghost who, in another, less privileged life would have been dismissed as a waif and a stray.

She was gone a long time, and when she returned I realised why.

'You wish me to wear ... that? It is a child's dress.'

'I do not wish you to wear it, Miss Crowsettle, I am telling you to do so. And if it is a child's dress, how might it possibly fit you? You might, at least, try it on.'

She handed me the dress but I let it slip through my fingers. Her withering stare rooted me to the spot. She would not let me alone until I had obeyed her instruction but I was stuck fast between subservience and rebellion. It was I, of course, who was first to yield.

'I will not be treated like this,' I said with a sob, stamping my feet. 'I am a grown woman, not a little girl.'

'But you are beginning to resemble one,' said Lady P, satisfied. 'And I do believe you are behaving like one.' She looked so stern and severe, like the governess I had promised myself I would never, ever become. And then suddenly her dark-clouded façade broke into a beaming smile.

'Oh, my dear Charlotte, I am such a cruel taskmistress to tease you so. Listen, child. There is always method in my madness. Emma and I have been deep in conversation –'

'You have been discussing Miss Fitzpiers?'

Lady P frowned; even in good humour it was not done to interrupt her. 'Amongst other matters,' she answered. 'But, yes. Miss Grace Fitzpiers was very much at the top of our agenda and, clever girl that she is, Emma came up with the obvious solution. And that is why you are taking to disguise, dear niece.'

'Niece?' I repeated incredulously. '*Your* niece?'

'That is quite correct,' she replied, frowning. 'Most would consider it a great honour to be made a member of the proud de Mortehoe family.'

'I am indeed honoured,' I responded quickly, mustering as much conviction as was possible in my utterly confused state. 'But please, I do not understand. Miss Fitzpiers and I have already met and, although we did not exchange words, she knows full well who I am. She seems an intelligent woman. I do not see how you can fool her.'

'Both you and Miss Fitzpiers underestimate me at your peril. She might well know more than you but Emma and I have managed to stay one step ahead. Your cousin is well acquainted with Miss Fitzpiers. In fact, I would not be lying if I let slip that they both have an intimate knowledge of one another.'

'My cousin? Emma?' I wanted to add, 'Have you taken leave of your senses?' but I thought it prudent to keep my mouth shut.

'Your cousin, Emma,' she confirmed, flourishing two sheets of parchment emblazoned with fine legal manuscript and the family seal. 'Your cousin, twice removed!'

And so she was, at least in the eyes of the law. I scrutinised both documents certifying that we were, indeed, bona fide members of the family. To the educated if untrained eye they appeared genuine. They were near-perfect forgeries. I didn't need to ask who had engineered them.

'These are all very well,' I protested, 'but they are hardly likely to stay the legal profession if Miss Fitzpiers calls upon it for assistance. Concealing Emma's identity is one thing, pretending I am not my father's daughter is quite another matter altogether.'

Lady Persephone put her fingers to my lips, pushed them together and sealed them tight. 'You forget that Emma and I are both mistresses of the masquerade. Why, did she not even make a passable man of you? No matter how much I admire a woman who can put two and two together and make five, no matter how perceptive she might be, there are times when ignorance is the best policy. I can reveal no more, suffice to say that we have only to stall Miss Fitzpiers for a further forty-eight hours. When we are done with you, Emma and I will have the delightful prospect of dealing with her at our leisure. And rest assured, she will suffer.'

'But ... but ... my father will always vouch ...'

'Hush, child,' she whispered, running her hand over my puffed cheeks, delicately brushing locks of hair from my eyes. She was the eye of the hurricane, a haven of calm and serenity immune from the battering gales that had brought confusion and uncertainty into my life. Her every consonant sounded safe and secure; her graceful vowels oozed assurance. 'Your father leaves early this afternoon, he will be gone for a short time but long enough to confound Miss Fitzpiers and her mealy-mouthed fiancé.'

Were it humanly possible to remove the bile and venom from Lady P's anger, it would surely have been sufficient to poison the entire village. I let her hands slip to the nape of my neck and loosen my hair. She began to brush it with long firm strokes.

'All I ask is that you confine yourself to Chilcombe Lacey. Stay close to the house, do not stray too far into the grounds. Emma will keep an eye on you but she will be busy entertaining our guests. I would ask you to assist her but no niece of mine will be seen in the scullery. Besides which, you would spoil your pretty white dress.'

'But if she is my cousin, surely we are equals?'

'Indeed, but some cousins are more equal than others. Emma had grown tired of domestic bliss, she had become a petticoated prisoner. She is a woman before her time and the world is not yet ready for the likes of her. She might play the servant but at heart she is a wild beast and with me she is free.'

Lady P held out a chemise, drawers and frilled underskirts. They had been precisely ironed and starched stiff and I stepped into them with difficulty. The dress, too, felt harsh and unyielding. It was a simple but dainty garment: the white taffeta clung to me, the high frilled collar reached right up to my chin, the neckline was a ruffle of flounced lace, the waist gathered tight, digging into my waist and the layered flared skirts fell scarcely to my knees.

She was pleased with herself, stepped back and took great delight in her recreation of girlhood innocence. I felt as compliant and vulnerable as she had intended; I was a manifestation of her power and my lack of it. When I sat down beside her on the sofa swathes of lace and taffeta rose up and enveloped me. I had to fight my way through the fabric to make myself seen.

'Your time is almost come, my sweetness. Tomorrow will be yours and yours alone. I am looking forward to being seduced. No man or woman has yet succeeded but I have every faith in you.' Lady P unpinned from her breast a tiny heart-shaped brooch and fixed it to my bodice. Her voice dropped an octave, its tone was low and ominous. 'But you should understand that, if you are unable to satisfy me, not only will you be barred from Chilcombe Lacey and the Society of Sin for ever more, you will be required to submit yourself to the unpredictable urges of its members and, under such circumstances, I am afraid I cannot be held responsible for your well-being. Do you understand?'

I nodded. The events of the previous evening were emerging from a smoky fug, the blood and the dagger and the screaming priest. I desperately needed to know what happened but felt unable to open my mouth in her presence. Lady P smiled victoriously. I was behaving just as she wished and, when my voice finally came, it had lost its adult confidence and conviction.

'Well, what is it, girl?' she snapped.

'I ... last night ... was it a dream ... or a nightmare ...? The priest, is he dead?'

'Certainly not. Father Oliver Powys is very much alive and well, although still a little shaken.'

She took my hand and led me to the window. A carriage was waiting at the door, Father Oliver, deep in conversation with Emma, was about to climb aboard. Above the midday silence we could just make out their words.

'My mistress asked me to pass this on to you,' said the servant. 'She trusts it will be sufficient recompense for your services ... and any discomfort you might have experienced.'

She handed him an envelope, bursting at the seams. A note slipped out and glided on to the gravel. Within seconds he had grabbed it and stuffed it in his wallet.

'Well,' he said uneasily, 'it was not quite what I had anticipated but never mind ... eh?'

He made his farewells and tried to embrace Emma but he was clumsy and she would have none of it. He was obliged to retreat with his tail between his legs.

As his carriage rumbled up the drive, Lady P turned from the window and sighed. 'Alas, Father Oliver does not come cheap, but he was worth it, was he not? I think that for a moment he was really convinced his time had come. I am a woman of many talents, Miss Charlotte, magic and illusion included. But you have not yet seen the half of it; I am saving the best until last.'

'And María? How is she this morning?'

'Happy, satisfied and revenged. She has gone for a

stroll with Liberty Belle. They have, it appears, much in common. I think she would have liked you to accompany them but I told them you were suffering from lack of sleep. Oh yes, I remember – María asked me to give you this.' She placed in my hand a small phial of silver shimmering liquid. 'This will encourage your dreams, but use it sparingly, it is extremely potent.'

'Should I enquire as to its contents?'

'Best not. But now I must go. Do not ignore my instructions and remember who you are, Lady Charlotte de Mortehoe. Remember who you are and behave with the appropriate decorum.'

12

Chilcombe Bredy
21 June 1876

My dear Charlotte
It is with great regret and not a little distress that I take my leave of Chilcombe Bredy without the opportunity to say farewell. Professor Walditch has called upon me once more; for the last time, I hope, and by the time you read this I will be en route to Exeter. I anticipate being away for no longer than a week, perhaps much less. Samuel's instructions are vague, as always!

I have seen so little of you since your return from Spain that I barely know where to begin. You have changed, Charlie. Perhaps that is inevitable and if your dear mother were here she would surely put my mind at ease but in her absence I have had to act with your best interests at heart. Forgive me if I have done wrong, I am so worried about you.

I was visited last night by a young lady by the name of Miss Grace Fitzpiers. I understand she is betrothed to the vicar of Chilcombe Bredy, the dreadful Lytton Cheney, but she did well not to disclose that fact until the end of our conversation. She is bright, well educated, I would imagine. I confess I took to her straight away. God knows what she sees in that simple fool but each to his or her own, as they say.

To cut to the quick, Miss Fitzpiers made me an

offer I felt unable to refuse – to act as your custodian – in loco parentis – until my return.

I can already feel your indignation! You have always been a self-contained and independent daughter and I have never done anything to curtail your freedom. I beg you to bear this in mind as I attempt to explain myself.

Two matters concern me. The first: that your friendship with Lady Persephone de Mortehoe is perhaps not as healthy as I first assumed. She is several years your senior, from a background you and I can only dream of. It is not that I am against aristocracy per se, it is just that I do not think their influence wholesome. They may be well bred but they breed rudeness and discourtesy in those they befriend. Yes, I know you consider yourself an adult but you are as impressionable and naive as a young girl.

The second: both you and I have dismissed the rumours concerning Lady Persephone and her 'servant' Emma Chetnole as mere gossip and tittle-tattle but now, it seems, there is more than an ounce of truth in them. I was inclined to believe Miss Fitzpiers but not to trust her with my daughter's well-being until I had made further enquiries. I telegraphed Inspector Lefebvre in Weymouth and he sent, by return, confirmation of Miss Fitzpier's good character and recent investigations he has been making into allegations against Chilcombe Lacey. It seems new information has been uncovered, courtesy of our friend Miss Fitzpiers. In the light of recent events he strongly recommended I engage her services whilst I was away. I can hardly ignore the advice of the law, can I?

The inspector will be visiting Chilcombe Bredy to conduct interviews with some of its residents. He has promised to call in and make certain that all is well *as I still have a nagging doubt that my judgement is poor. I am sure he will be proved right and me wrong, and that you and Miss Fitzpiers will get along famously.*

Your ever loving father

I sat on my empty bed and read the letter several times over before bursting into tears. Even if, by the mores of polite society, I had fallen into a company of nymphs, dryads and devils, in the eyes of my father I was still an angel. I had reluctantly disobeyed Lady P's strict instructions to remain at Chilcombe Lacey. I sat upon the bed trying to square my devotion to Lady P and my love for my father.

'Surely,' I had told myself, 'it would not matter if I slipped away for half an hour to bid him farewell?'

Chilcombe Lacey lay empty and quiet, its inhabitants and guests had taken refuge in its gardens. I entered myself into a pact, between my heart and my head, between duty and decadence, and wandered slowly towards the front door in the hope of meeting my vigilante.

But Emma was nowhere to be seen and no matter how tortuous and winding I made my way to the exit, no matter how long I dawdled before the portraits of Lady P's ancestors, no matter how heavy my step on the groaning floorboards, her divine form failed to materialise. I had promised myself that when she eventually apprehended me – as her mistress had promised me she surely would – I would come along quietly and make no mention of my intended mission. In Emma's presence any anxiety I felt for my father would surely vanish into the ether that surrounded her.

There were tears in my eyes as I passed through the

gates, unobserved and, as far as I was concerned, unloved. I picked up the pace and strode along the lanes with grim determination, caring not a jot who might have seen me and what they would have made of a grown woman dressed as a young girl. Blinded by sweat I ran up the garden path in a vain attempt to catch my father before his departure. But he had long since gone and the cottage smelt unoccupied and musty. It had not been cleaned or swept since Mrs Bexington's departure.

I do not believe in hindsight, I refuse to trade with regret but I think I can say, in all honesty, that never before have I made such a grave error and I hope to God that I never repeat my mistake. You might call me a fickle creature; I would not hesitate to plead guilty, guilty but insane. I had become addicted and I needed a desperate fix to satiate the passion pulsing through my veins. In hindsight it is clear that my desire drove me to distraction, drove me from the arms of those who loved into the arms of she whom I despised. My poor little soul, starved of the affection it yearned for, simply turned from one extreme to another.

The cursed creak of my father's ancient front door signified her entrance. Her footsteps were deliberately loud within the hall and upon the stairs. She knew I was there, upstairs, and that I was trapped with no means of escape. She knew that alone, without Emma or Lady P, I was utterly impotent. She knew she had fomented within me the seeds of discord by exploiting my fascination with all that was contrary to my liberal convictions. I was an easy target; the soft white underbelly through which she could damage – or even destroy – the Society of Sin. Miss Grace Fitzpiers had come to claim what she considered rightfully hers.

Her supercilious tones rang out triumphantly

through the house, echoing in every nook and cranny. I hated her still, but I hated her with a vehemence that might, at any given moment, metamorphose into infatuation.

'Good afternoon, Miss Crowsettle. I know you are there, why not save us both the time and trouble by at least having the courtesy to greet me. I cannot imagine your father approving of such insolence.'

There was no lock on my bedroom door, until recently there had been no need to shut myself away. Now I had to jam a flimsy chair under the handle to keep the tyrant out. I knew that any attempt at resistance would be futile; she would camp out on the landing for weeks if it served her purpose.

'Get out, you dirty little whore. You have no right to be here. Wait until my father returns, he'll give you what for.'

'Sticks and stones, Miss Crowsettle, sticks and stones. Your father has given his express permission for me to be here and I have it in black and white, signed and dated. It is all quite legal and above board. For the time being I am your guardian and my word is law. Is that clear?'

She tugged so hard on the handle that the chair collapsed into a pile of worm-infested wood. My defences were crumbling equally rapidly. I eased the door open, just a crack, a couple of inches wide, no more. I simply had to catch a glimpse of her, to see her face again, to remind myself of its handsome cruelty. What do they say, 'Give them an inch and they will take a mile'? The breach was wide enough for her to thrust her boot into. I tried to slam the door back on her but she was too strong for me and forced herself into the room.

She was too strong for me. Is that really the truth?

Who am I trying to fool? I am a member of the weaker sex but I had never considered myself a particularly delicate creature. From Cartagena to Chilcombe Bredy I have always been able to take care of myself. Even if she was indeed divinely inspired and received her strength from on high, if it had come to fisticuffs between us I am sure I would have bested her. Had I not run the cavalcade of strumpets who lined the Via Dolorosa, taken a few well-aimed blows but given out as good as I got? Why, I had even locked horns with the Guardia Civil and lived to tell the tale, so the prospect of sparring with the considerably less burly Grace Fitzpiers should have held no fears.

Unless I allowed it to.

The following few hours I can still recall with great clarity. I shall be able to recall them for the remainder of my life purely because I have no desire to forget them. She moved with grace and determination, spoke with the eloquent severity of a martinet. Her face was veiled, her hair gathered severely above the nape of her neck. There was not a square inch of her frock, tight fitting and narrow skirted, that was not of the darkest mourning black. For whom, I asked myself, was she grieving? She had the upper hand – surely it should have been a celebration?

'Is it any wonder that Lady Persephone has taken to dressing you as a little girl? I think that for once I am in agreement with her, your outfit suits you perfectly. I do not take kindly to insubordination, Miss Crowsettle, and petulance I consider to be an infantile vice that should have been dealt with many many years ago. That sort of behaviour I had anticipated, I had even devised a means of correcting it that corresponded with the liberal views of your father, however much I might disagree with them. But I am sure that even he would be shocked by your use of such foul and abusive language, that even he might have been provoked to adopt more drastic measures. If I were able to consult him I would, but as he has invested in me total responsibility I shall have to act of my own accord.'

Without a word she grabbed my left ear and dragged me downstairs to the kitchen and there she washed my mouth out with carbolic soap and water.

You are wondering, why did I not protest at such humiliating and cruel punishment? Why did I not struggle? It would not have taken a superhuman effort to break free from her grip and make a dash for Chilcombe Lacey and freedom.

The truth is that I knew full well there was worse to come and much as I knew I would come to a sore and sorry end, I could not beat down a fatal curiosity.

Her power and control were absolute. With one hand she seized my hair and pulled it tight until I was stood upright, with the other she took an old wooden brush that Mrs Bexington had used to clean her pots and pans, doused it in soap and forced it into my mouth. I felt no pain, merely discomfort as she scrubbed and scoured until suds began to dribble down my chin. She carefully replaced her utensil in the kitchen sink and pushed my face up before a dirty rusting mirror.

'There, let that be a reminder of what happens to those naughty little children who utter wicked profanities.'

She let go of me and I felt a shiver of disappointment along my spine. Was all her passion spent? Had I overestimated her? Not a jot. She seized my ear once more, this time with such force that I yelped loudly and brought to her face a vindictive, self-satisfied smile.

'I would hate you to think me a tyrant, Miss Crowsettle,' said Miss Fitzpiers with more than a hint of irony. 'A disciplinarian, yes, but a bully I am not. I ask for ... no, I *demand* respect and obedience without question. Providing you submit to my authority you will find me a fair and, I think, charming chaperone.'

She had placed me in the centre of the lounge in a beam of bright sunlight. When I held my hands together before me, she took umbrage and slapped my face hard with her open palm.

'Hands by your side!' she snapped. 'And stand up straight! Woe betide you if you move a single muscle without my express permission. Do you understand?'

I said nothing. She struck me once again.

'I asked, "Do you understand?"'

'Yes,' I replied, almost inaudibly. I saw that her hand was raised, poised.

'Yes, what?'

'Yes ... ma'am.'

She lowered her arm. 'Excellent. At last we are making progress. Now I have some questions for you. I would like you to answer them in as much detail as you possibly can. It is imperative that I – we – put a stop to Lady de Mortehoe's vile activities before it is too late. I am afraid that both she and her accomplice are beyond salvation but it is not yet too late to save you. We have not a moment to lose. Provided you tell me the truth, I promise you shall come to no harm but remember: I know more about your so-called friends than you imagine. I shall know instinctively if you are lying.'

She sat down on the sofa and paused for a while to admire her handiwork. I wondered if I hadn't conceded too quickly. I would hate her to be disappointed in me.

'Tell me, Miss Crowsettle. What happened last night

at Chilcombe Lacey? Was a Roman Catholic priest involved?'

I said nothing, kept my head straight and still. It was a tactic guaranteed to provoke her but I could not – I would not – betray my friends.

'Very well. Let us try something a little less complicated. You were there, that much I know for certain. The others – a dozen or so strumpets and charlatans, the supposed intellectual elite of our nation's womanhood – must be tracked down and apprehended. Their names, Miss Crowsettle. Their *real* names, please, no aliases or fancy pseudonyms.'

Not a word. I held my head high, my stare fixed into the distance as if utterly ignorant of my persecutor. I had to know just how far I could push her before she snapped. The room was taut with tension, fraught with nerves so shredded that the merest wrong move on my part would unleash the full might of her wrath.

Miss Fitzpiers shifted uneasily in her skirts; she was teetering on the edge. Despite my dedication to decadence, she had not accounted for my inner resilience. Deep within me lay the soul of a martyr and the heart of a stoic. I steadfastly refused to confess.

'You are doing yourself no favours,' she told me, her lips pursed and thin. She was struggling to contain herself. It would be only a matter of minutes before she erupted like a dormant volcano and I would witness the magnificent splendour of her rage unleashed. 'I shall give you one last chance. I do not think I need explain the consequences should you continue to defy me.'

Ah! The sweet taste of defiance. Miss Fitzpiers's master plan had proceeded like clockwork. Until now. It suddenly occurred to me that her weakness lay in her strength, and vice versa. Her carefully woven tapestry was beginning to fray at the edges, the threads were loose, the weft was coming undone.

It would have been easy to take the whole thing apart and consign it to the dustbin. Too easy. It would have broken the spell and released us both from its bondage. Neither of us wished for that to happen.

No, what was required called for subtlety and discretion. The work was restored but its pattern was slyly changed. You would not have known it but her power was slowly ebbing, transferring itself to me.

'Tell me, Miss Crowsettle. Have you ever embraced another woman with improper, dishonest or immoral intentions?'

I maintained my dignified stance but the smile said it all. 'I really don't know what you mean, ma'am,' I said.

She was shaking. Her body convulsed with paroxysms of controlled rage. Then the dam burst and Miss Fitzpiers suddenly leapt to her feet.

'You evil witch! You know full well what I mean. I should have known all along you were too stubborn to listen to reason. I suppose you think you are clever? I should never have listened to your father's petitioning. I have been too lenient, allowed you to push me too far. I will not be toyed with a minute longer. Where does your father keep his cane?'

I was certain it would come. From the moment we first set eyes on each other this moment had been inevitable. Still, when the word finally slipped from her lips it sent my pulse racing with fear; mine would be a Pyrrhic victory. Her pupils flared with excitement and I saw within them that my own dark reflection was exactly the same.

'He has no cane, nor any other implement of chastisement. He has never needed one, has never lifted so much as a finger to harm me. With the greatest respect, ma'am, the year is eighteen seventy-six, we no longer resort to brutality to control. Your methods are part of the past, quite Neanderthal.' I was warming to my theme, goading her, not caring for the consequences should I overstep the mark. 'In any case, I am no longer my father's daughter and you have no authority over me. He abrogated all his paternal rights when he appointed you as my guardian. I have been adopted by Lady Persephone de Mortehoe. I have become her niece, it is all legal and above board.'

'Ha!' she crowed, her face beaming with incredulity. 'You fool, you sweet, stupid, ignorant little fool. You do me great disservice, Miss Crowsettle. I had hoped you might find in me an ally but I see you are as two-faced as I feared. Being engaged to a simple country vicar does not make me a simpleton. You do not know the half of it, young lady. I am as educated and emancipated as your so-called friends and I am quite the equal of Lady Persephone de Mortehoe, though she would fain admit it. This is not the first time she has tried to play this trick on me. You might well admire her; I consider her beneath my contempt.

'Now, what does it say in the Good Book? Spare the rod, spoil the child. If only your father had listened to his betters instead of believing a lot of modern stuff and nonsense. No society can exist without rules, Miss Crowsettle, not even your perverted Society of Sin. And every society must exert its authority in whatever way it sees fit. There will always be those who refuse to conform, who persist in their insubordination. For those we reserve the ultimate sanction. You might call it cruelty, we consider it a kindness.

'I should have known,' she remonstrated with herself. 'I should have known that kind words and gentle persuasion would cut no ice with the likes of you. I shall have to return to the vicarage and fetch the vicar's cane. If a job is worth doing it is worth doing well. I will not lower myself to administer a servant's beating. For all your faults, Miss Crowsettle, you are a young lady of quality and I intend to teach you the error of your ways. It would be remiss of us both to start off on the wrong footing. You shall wait here and consider your fate.'

She let that final sentence slip out slowly and hang in the hot sultry air. I think she was testing me, wondering whether I might, after all, be a worthy opponent. I had no intention of escaping, she knew I had no intention of escaping, yet neither of us was prepared to acknowledge it. She marched me to the scullery; I entered without a prompt and listened as the door was locked behind me. A moment later the front door slammed shut. For the time being, at least, she was gone but unlike Mr Donald Fraser Urquhart she would not shirk from the task in hand. I was certain she would return.

21 June 1876
Chilcombe Bredy

Dear Diary
She has thirty-six hours to save my soul. The others are beyond redemption but I am still a child – just look at me – and she has a duty to save me.

Will they come looking for me? Do they care? I think not for I have let them down and put myself beyond redemption. I do not deserve their forgiveness. I do hope that in time they might come to realise that I cannot possibly match their mettle. I do hope that in time Lady P will come to understand the contradictory motives that drove me into Miss

Fitzpiers's bower in pursuit of pure untempered desire. She was an abyss, dark and deliciously dangerous, and she knew perfectly well that once I stood on the precipice I would be unable to resist the temptation to fling myself in.

They will be preparing the sabbat; the night when the ghosts of all those who have fallen into disgrace will return to walk the Earth. I watched them this morning, laughing, and as if already possessed by demons. I could see it in their eyes, they could hardly wait.

Will they come looking for me? Perhaps: but to punish, not to liberate. Does it not say in the Good Book, thou shalt not suffer a witch to live'? If they assume I have passed over to the enemy they will surely not stand for betrayal. If what my father says is true – and still I refuse to believe it – then I am a liability; a liability that must be silenced or removed. They need a sacrifice, perhaps it shall be me.

Listen! I hear the front door scrape open. Something wicked this way comes.

She was not alone. To my intense horror she had brought with her the vicar. I recognised his limp tones as they passed along the hall. His presence would put an entirely different spin on proceedings, change the rules of the game. I was prepared to submit to Miss Fitzpiers, her elegant, irrefutable superiority had pervaded every inch of my psyche and, I should add, the less well-travelled expanses beyond. I was ready for her, but not for him. I panicked and tried to hide the fragment of card upon which I had poured out emotions somewhere about my person. It was quite impossible. Whoever had designed my dress had done so with a specific purpose in mind: to keep my sacred feminine hinterlands safe from prying hands – including my own.

'And here's the wayward child,' announced Miss Fitzpiers, opening the scullery door but with her attention turned to her fiancé. Once she caught sight of my frantic and futile attempts at concealment she let loose a laugh that filled the whole house. It put the fear of God into the Reverend Lytton Cheney. I could see it, she could see it and I could see, too, that she found his unmanliness quite distasteful. She threw him a sharp and disapproving glance. I knew she would take out her displeasure on me.

She dismissed him with a wave of her hand and snatched the parchment from my grasp. 'Interesting. Very interesting,' she murmured as her grin grew wider and turned magnificently malevolent. It was only then that I saw the cane – a long, thin, whippy wand she bent before me. Without a word I followed her to the place of correction.

The vicar was sitting uncomfortably in the corner. He rose to greet me until Miss Fitzpiers hissed angrily at him that a woman of my ill repute did not warrant his respect. I was overcome with the desire to spit in his pale and insipid face. I think I might have even done so had not my nominal chaperone reminded me of my already precarious position.

'I shall offer you one final chance to confess. If you tell me everything, here and now, I am sure the Reverend Cheney will be moved to clemency. Well, Miss Crowsettle? What have you to say for yourself? Has the cat got your tongue?'

She brought the rod down hard upon a cushion as if to signal her intent. The mesmerising whistle of rattan and the harsh thump it made on contact rendered me dumbstruck. I was trying to imagine what pain such an instrument might inflict upon my poor untutored body but I was overcome by the desire to taste it. We all have our pride and a point beyond which we are not prepared to bend it. I would not accept the vicar's compassion, even were she to whip me within an inch of my life.

Which is more or less what she did.

'This,' I told myself, 'will be my sacrifice. I shall suffer so the Society of Sin can survive.'

Her hands were hard on my hips. For the briefest of moments her breasts came into intimate contact with my own and, because I so much wanted to be there, I backed instinctively into the beckoning curves of her bosom. She cast me a frown so severe and full of contempt it would have frozen the heart of the bravest white knight dashing on his steed to rescue me. I passed beyond salvation, yielded to her powerful, irresistible grip as she manoeuvred me over the arm of the chaise longue. Her face flashed momentarily before me, her previously undistinguished countenance, now flushed with flame, transposed into the ethereal visage of heaven's most terrible avenging angel.

The Reverend Lytton Cheney had sat himself down in a most advantageous position allowing him uninterrupted views of my rear. His fear had been subsumed by a most depraved curiosity. He did not comprehend the situation, did not appreciate the ritual, its significance was utterly lost on him. Yet between Miss Fitzpiers and myself there was a tacit, perhaps implicit understanding. I resented his presence as much as I desired Miss Fitzpiers's. I promised myself a revenge as sweet as that of María Inés de la Cruz.

It was not enough for Miss Fitzpiers to have me draped over the chaise longue with my posterior raised high in the air, a sublime target for chastisement. It was not enough to debase me so thoroughly before the man I hated more than any other. Oh no. There was no limit to her ingenuity, the lengths to which she would go to truly humiliate me. Her fingers rustled through the stiff lace of my petticoats and lifted them up and over me so that the frilled hems fell over my face in a cascade of white taffeta and lace. She took a pin from her hair and secured them.

It was not enough for Miss Fitzpiers. I knew better than to protest when she reached for the waistband of my drawers and eased them down. I tried hard not to move a single muscle or sinew but I knew that the instant she laid a finger on me I would not be responsible for my bodily reactions. Sure enough, her touch, although brusque and uncaring, raised a frisson of desire within my shivering flesh. With her hand poised delicately underneath my vagina, fiddling – a little unsteadily, I thought – to undo the buttons, I instinctively snapped my thighs tight shut, trapping her within such close proximity to my swollen moist labia. And I would not, for the life of me, let go until I provoked the intended reaction. With her open palm she dealt me a hard slap on the top of the leg, so sudden it went unseen by our onlooker. The pain was sharp but soon dissolved into a warm glow, which spread along the length of my outstretched limb and lulled me into a false sense of security. I felt it a secret between us. The scarlet handprint remained for hours, a trophy I wished would never fade away.

The first cut is the deepest, unexpected, arriving as if from nowhere. The first cut is also in many ways the worst, as, whatever it might think, the body is never quite ready for the shock that follows. I could hear the cane carving through the air, gaining velocity on its rapid downwards trajectory. One would imagine that in that split second there would be insufficient time to contemplate one's fate but to me the entire passage of history seemed to be encapsulated in that minuscule infinity. I tensed my buttocks and steadied myself.

And that was wholly insufficient. Nothing could ever have prepared me for the devastation the first stroke wreaked as it exploded upon my skin and sent ripples of trembling flesh across the exposed orbs of my buttocks. I reared like a horse in a stable and reached instinctively for my injured regions but Miss Fitzpiers would have none of it and rapped me hard on the knuckles with the cane.

'Any more of that and I shall double the discipline,' she snarled and pushed me firmly into the coarse fabric of the cushions. The second stroke followed swiftly. Based on the evidence of the previous, my body had rapidly come to the conclusion that there existed on Earth no pain greater than that she had initially inflicted on me. How wrong. Every raw sensitive nerve felt under attack, and once more I rose in an involuntary spasm.

'Please, Miss Fitzpiers, no more ... no more ... I promise...'

'What do you promise, Miss Crowsettle? How am I to believe you?'

The rod came down once more with a stomach-churning thud. The pain sliced through me once more; I recoiled violently and let out a curse I had picked up in Spain. '*Hija de puta!*'

Even whilst writhing in divine agony I had the presence of mind to wonder when and where Miss Fitzpiers had come across an insult so offensive that the only time I had ever uttered it before, completely by mistake, it earned me a swipe across the face from the Duchess of Crewkerne's riding crop. The manner in which Miss Fitzpiers proceeded to lay into me left me in no doubt that she not only understood the profanity but had once been the recipient of its disgrace. Or else, heaven forbid, she had had cause to utter it herself. She rained down blows upon my poor defenceless backside until I was unable to choke back the tears and began to blub helplessly. Still the whip came down but by now the pain was such that it had begun to act as an anaesthetic. Every time the rod struck my buttocks I hoped it might be the last but she refused to relent until, sensing victory, she began to lecture me, interspersing her sermon with judiciously timed blows.

'Let me tell, you, Miss Crowsettle ...' down came the cane, I gasped in distress '... that if I ever catch you within a mile of Chilcombe Lacey I shall be obliged to discipline you in a similar fashion and I will not cease from disciplining you until you have learnt your lesson ...' the cane cut into the top of my thighs, a sharper and almost intolerable pain '... as long as you wish to remain in this village, you will have to abide by my rules and respect my authority. I will not tolerate insubordination. It has to be nipped in the bud, straight away.' One last stroke, convulsing my limp torso. She took a step back and handed the cane to its rightful owner, the vicar, who had been observing the incident with barely disguised delight. Whatever modicum of dignity he had was lost as his forced frown faded and he licked his lips with anticipation.

It was a perfect punishment, applied with a dexterity that could only have been acquired through years of practice. There was no point in pretending otherwise, order had triumphed and she had indeed beaten out of me any notion of resistance and rebellion. I had no desire other than to submit myself to her creed and, even though I did not like its rules, or the way in which they were enforced, I understood that they had to be obeyed, and that one must accept the consequences if one transgressed. Never before had a chastisement administered by Miss Fitzpiers failed to achieve its objective and, as I lay prostrate and supine across the chaise longue, gently weeping, I was as convinced as her that I would succumb to the inevitable.

'Get up, child,' she rasped.

However, much as I wanted to comply with her instruction immediately, my crumpled figure, racked with agony, failed to respond.

'I said, get up. Do I have to repeat the process all over again to make you understand?'

That much I did understand. I promised myself that I would be so good, so righteous and obedient that Miss Fitzpiers would never find reason to beat me again. With great difficulty I slowly unfolded myself.

'What do you say?' she asked, her voice still vibrating with authority.

'Thank you,' I replied, without thinking or hesitating.

She smiled, victory had always been assured but the speed with which the discipline had taken effect took her by surprise. 'Now,' she continued, slipping into a more soothing tone, 'are you ready to confess?'

I would have done so there and then had I been physically able to do so. But I was clutching my stinging buttocks, wondering when the pain would subside. I tried to speak but could only suck in great gulps of air. Seeing that my distress had rendered me temporarily mute, Miss Fitzpiers was moved to relent.

'Well, well, well,' she ruminated. 'It seems your remorse might well be genuine; Let us both hope so – for the sake of your soul ... and your skin! I shall give you an hour to recover and make yourself decent. I shall hear your contrition on my return and woe betide you should you fail to convince me.'

And then, so unexpectedly that I recoiled from her touch, she leant over and ran her fingers through my tousled hair. More than that, her fingers brushed over my face and rubbed out my tears.

'I am sorry, Charlotte. Believe me, I am sorry. I take no pleasure in playing the despot and I try, whenever possible, to avoid brutality. You must appreciate that sometimes it is unavoidable, that to be kind one must give the impression of being cruel. I am not cruel,' she insisted, her moist breath condensing on my cheek. 'I am only trying to save you.'

And with that Miss Fitzpiers departed, securing the door behind her. Her fiancé followed like a lapdog at her heels.

Far from being beaten into submission, by surrendering to Miss Fitzpiers's chastisement I had, on the contrary, liberated myself from the tyranny of fear and apprehension. Nobody, nothing could harm me now. The transformation begun by Lady P was almost complete and, much as I loved and admired her, Lady P could not have offered me such bittersweet torment. Only the enemy could have chastised me so, taken me from pain to pleasure without pretence. And now, having surrendered myself to Miss Fitzpiers's authority, I was ready to subvert it. Lady P would have been proud of me.

The sun burst through the cottage windows, illuminating the reflection of my posterior in the mirror. It was blushed scarlet with a dozen and more raised angry weals, each perfectly placed and evenly distributed. I gazed lovingly at my blotched cheeks, my puffy eyes, my dishevelled mass of long black curls and was overcome with the desire to capitulate to curiosity. The thought that Miss Fitzpiers might return at any minute merely egged me on. I draped myself back over the chaise longue, exploring what were previously forbidden territories, igniting within me a million tiny fires until, without warning, my body arched as it erupted like a long dormant volcano.

I was asleep when she returned, without, I was relieved to note, the vicar. Once more, I caught my image in the mirror, simmering and self-satisfied, all it lacked was a pair of pointed horns. It was clear to me that Miss Fitzpiers was still troubled but her rage was all spent and she approached me with a distinct wariness, almost on tiptoe. I resolved to do all I could to placate her, to have her remain within my presence. I pitied the Reverend Lytton Cheney; he would be seeing precious little of his beloved wife-to-be over the next day and a half. If the plot I was hatching in the unvisited depths of my mind ever came to fruition, he would be seeing precious little of her until Judgement Day.

'My dear Miss Fitzpiers, I cannot thank you enough for making me see the error of my ways. I had sinned and you punished me. I hope you will find it in your heart to forgive me and accept my penance in good faith.'

She remained suspicious, looked me up and down, aware that all was not quite what it should be but unable to ascertain exactly what it was that was awry. But I had always fancied myself an actress. I upped my performance accordingly and fell to my knees before her. How could I have possibly dismissed her as dull and unattractive? She was Ceres, she was Prosperine, she was Ariadne: she was the majestic manifestation of all three and I worshipped the very earth upon which she walked.

I put my hands on my heart and fed deep, deep upon my mistress's peerless eyes.

'I swear to you, madam, I swear on the very heart of the blessed Virgin Mary. I renounce all the depravity of Chilcombe Lacey and I will tell you all you need to know about the abominable activities that take place there. I wish – I desire – to become a model of feminine Christian virtue. I beg you to be my mentor and guide and chastise me in any way you see fit.'

She was drunk on the heady scent of victory; she would not have noticed the dissident spark in my eyes.

13

22 June 1876
Chilcombe Bredy

Dear Diary
What has she done to me? Or rather, what have I permitted her to do to me? All that I stood for, all that I have learnt through experience, bitter and sweet, overthrown in the events of one afternoon. I cannot understand it, but only because I do not want to understand it. I have only to accept my lot and do as I am bidden by Miss Fitzpiers.

I am waiting for her, sitting in the warm sun that floods the lounge, illuminating the flecks of dust that eluded my Herculean tasks. I could not sleep so I set about cleaning the house from top to bottom. She suggested it, did not order it, but I must please her in every possible way.

I want her to be proud of me. I will stop at nothing to win her favour. I have no suitable attire, only the uniform presented to me by the Lady Borthwick on my first assignment as a governess. It was demeaning, it usurped my individuality, reminded me I belonged to her and nobody else. I was up all night washing it. Just before it was dry I starched and ironed it, then starched and ironed it again. It is stiff, tight and uncomfortable but cleanliness is next to godliness, is it not?

She is come; I must stop. There is much in here she would find interesting, much that would offend

*her, much that would earn me another beating. I
could save myself the shame, burn the book and let
its profanities rise to heaven and beg forgiveness on
my behalf from the Father Almighty.*

*But I am not yet ready for that; somehow it does
not seem quite right.*

But it was not Miss Fitzpiers at the door. Nor Emma
nor anyone acting on Lady P's behalf, only an envelope
that lay invitingly on the now polished floor. A twinge
of longing twitched within me, somebody, somewhere
was stepping over my empty grave, the self-same
person who had written the letter. If Miss Fitzpiers
herself had been striding purposely along the garden
path I would not have cared. I tore it open.

*Chilcombe Lacey
22 June 1876*

*My dearest Charlotte
Do not fret. I know where you are. I have no need to
despatch Emma on an errand to locate you, nor do I
need to send out a search party to discover your
whereabouts. I am sure Miss Fitzpiers is taking inor-
dinate care of you. It is curious, is it not, how one
woman's sworn enemy can be another's chaperone.
Or is she more than that, Charlotte? Yours is a
perverted passion, but one that I can readily
understand.*

*Much as you might desire it, I am neither angry
nor disappointed in you. You have forsaken us. You
have chosen to follow what you consider to be the
way of righteousness but, rest assured, our paths will
cross again.*

*Until then, my sweetest heart
P*

I am quite sure that Emma's arrival at the cottage was preordained, or rather that fate, in the guise of Lady Persephone de Mortehoe, had begun to insert her spanner into the works. There were three probable explanations but, as always, it was impossible to second guess Lady P's mind or anticipate her next move. Indeed, to do so incorrectly might place the willing victim in even greater peril. Perhaps Emma had been sent by her mistress to remind me that, no matter my location or chaperone, I was still very much hers and I was not, for one moment, to forget it. Or maybe she had come looking for me of her own accord, not realising her every move was being monitored. It would be easy to portray Lady P as the ultimate puppeteer, exerting total control over her obliging marionettes or moving her acolytes like pawns on a chessboard. Only for Emma could the third option be considered feasible for only she knew Lady P well enough to be able to elude her for any substantial period of time.

In truth she was not unlooked for. I had half expected, half feared her visit and had spent much of my waking hours devising an elaborate trap with which to greet her, setting myself as the irresistible bait. Dressed in a lurid fiery scarlet, her appearance was as provocative as her timing was immaculate. Miss Fitzpiers would return within minutes and I would ensure that Emma was caught in the very act my temporary guardian considered the most heinous of all.

If Miss Fitzpiers had endeavoured to keep an eye on my every move she had fallen uncannily short of the high standards she usually adhered to. Despite my apparent conversion, it was plain to see that she could not rid herself of the nagging suspicion that I might yet be feigning my born-again righteousness as part of some grander, malignant design. Even now, as her svelte figure approached the gate and looked on as Emma took me in her arms, she would be congratulating herself on her perspicacity. But I was acutely aware of her vigilance and beckoned Emma to embrace me knowing that the moment our bodies made contact she would be upon us.

'As I suspected, Miss Crowsettle. Back to your despicable habits the moment I turn my back. How could you be such a fool? I had thought better of you. It seems my judgement was badly misplaced.'

She was about to pass sentence once more, a punishment that would undoubtedly be more severe and applied with greater vigour than the first. I had hardly recovered from that. It still pained me to rest my sore buttocks on anything other than plumped-up cushions. For a fleeting moment all my carefully laid plans flew out of the window and I withered before her seething beauty, ready to accept my fate.

It was Emma who brought me to my senses, her wet lips on mine like the rush of springtime streams in full spate, as refreshing as snowmelt on the summer's hottest morning. When I pushed her away from me, violently, the incredulous look that crossed her face nearly broke my heart in two but then she heard Miss Fitzpiers's abrasive tones and allowed a smirk to sneak out. 'I know what you are doing,' it said. 'Perhaps you are not as stupid as you look, after all.'

She was quite right. I was not as stupid as I looked. Indeed, I was an awful lot smarter than she had given me credit for. Lust and hate, extremes of the same emotion, pulsed through my veins as I looked from one woman to the other. I could not decide which I desired the more, nor upon which I wished to inflict my long-fermenting frustration. Until I remembered how Emma had humiliated me in the scullery, exposed my pathetic love and brought me to tears. Revenge upon Miss Fitzpiers could wait. Right now I desired nothing more than to take retribution on the self-styled servant girl. Perhaps, in the process, I might finally unearth to the truth.

'Unhand me, you filthy queer,' I cried, with as much conviction as I could muster. Then I turned to Miss Fitzpiers, wiping my hands on my frock in a forced gesture of rejection for in all honesty I wished to have my wicked way with her right there and then. 'I beg you, ma'am, she came uninvited and when I rebuffed her she launched herself upon me. I am too ladylike to fight her off.'

I denied all responsibility, placed all the blame upon my friend. I begged, I implored, as Emma lay straddled on the ground in silence. Just one word from her and my elaborate scheme would have collapsed as quickly as the Caribbean sun sinking beneath the horizon, leaving me stuck fast between duty and desire. Miss Fitzpiers took her time surveying the situation, in issuing her judgement and in appropriating innocence and guilt. And yet her hands were tied, to condemn me before Emma would have been tantamount to washing her hands of my soul and casting me back into the hands of the devil herself.

'There is only one way for you to prove your fidelity to me and to God,' she finally announced. Her verdict, perfect and sublimely appropriate, shocked us both. 'Emma is to be whipped.' That much I had expected and wanted. 'And you, Miss Crowsettle, shall administer the chastisement.'

We gawped like simpletons until the awful reality became clear. Emma instinctively attempted to flee but

I was too quick and too strong. Small wonder: Miss Fitzpiers's pronouncement had opened up vistas of unforeseen gratification, which I was determined to exploit to their full. Such was Emma's loathing of my chaperone that it took every ounce of strength I could summon to bring her to submission. But subdue her I did, much to the delight of Miss Fitzpiers who stood by smiling intensely as her arch-enemy was overpowered by her nemesis. She might still have escaped my clutches had I not been visited by divine revelation.

'If I were you,' I whispered, 'I would not dig myself into a hole any larger than the one you are currently staring into. I have told Miss Fitzpiers all I know about you and Lady Persephone – and a great deal more besides. After all, why let the truth get in the way of a good story?'

'You liar,' she hissed. 'You don't know what you are talking about.'

'That's not the point, is it, my love? Fact or fiction, I have said enough to bring about the downfall of Chilcombe Lacey, let alone the end of the Society of Sin. Can you not see? Your fate rests in my hands. Do you see how much Miss Fitzpiers hates you? She will stop at nothing to have you brought to justice as a fraud.'

'Pah,' she spat, but with sufficient restraint so as not to draw attention to herself. 'Do you think I can be moved by such threats? You do not understand, Charlotte. I am of Quality and Quality never, ever rejects its own, whatever crimes they might have committed.'

'Even murder?' I retorted. 'You might well be able to bribe yourself back into favour. I doubt whether polite society will take such a lenient view of Lady Persephone's transgressions.'

'You would never be so stupid . . .'

'Really?'

I felt her muscles relax and her body acquiesce. Victory was mine.

Miss Fitzpiers, the while, was considering the logistics. She had come ill prepared for this eventuality. Her cane still hung on the lounge door, to retrieve it placed her in a conundrum. To fetch it herself required her to put all her trust in me and she was not yet ready for that. Instructing me to collect it would leave her alone with Emma and she feared her more than she suspected me, much, much more. I sensed her hesitancy.

'I have an idea, ma'am. Miss Chetnole shall make a rod for her own back.'

I marched Emma to the row of silver birches that divided the garden from the orchard beyond. Despite it being Midsummer's Eve, following a wet and late spring the newer branches were still slender and supple, perfect for the task in hand. When I snapped the twigs in two a trickle of sap rose to the surface.

'Your choice, Miss Chetnole, a dozen will do,' prompted Miss Fitzpiers. 'I am sure you would rather not require my assistance.'

Emma cursed under her breath, thus guaranteeing herself a more thorough beating but she had no alternative other than to comply.

One must give credit where it is due. Emma did not baulk from her objective and went about her business with the appropriate solemnity and ritual. The most experienced martinet could not have selected twelve finer wands; nor could the most penitent of victims have handed them to her tormentor with greater shame. Having accepted her role, she was determined to carry it out with modesty and decorum. She handed me the birch, her eyes staring demurely downwards. I unloosed the black silk ribbon that held up my hair, wrapped it around the birch and secured it in a bow.

Buoyed by approving nods on the part of Miss Fitzpiers, I began to warm to my theme. The prospect of Emma as my willing victim sent waves of elation rippling through my heart and my soul. I had to fight hard to restrain myself, to convince her that what was a sober duty had not become a frivolous pleasure. She must not catch sight of my salivating fangs or my wild roaming eyes; a wicked wolf with her very own Red Riding Hood to devour.

As it says in the Good Book, it is more blessed to give than receive. How true, how so very, very sweet, so very blessed. Emma's arse, tight within seething mounds of cotton and silk, was manna from Heaven.

'Miss Chetnole,' I snapped, attempting a passable impersonation of Miss Fitzpiers, 'please oblige me by removing your skirts and your undergarments.'

'What?'

'You heard. Do I have to repeat myself?'

I was surprised how naturally authority came to me and how effortlessly I assumed its mantle. The instructions tripped from my tongue and reverberated about the ancient orchard creating a symphony of passion unspent, of timeless, eternal desire.

She dared not disobey. Like a sorceress I had her trapped within my hex. Emma acquiesced, twisting and turning in her tight corset until her clothing fell to the parched earth in a dazzling scarlet heap.

Miss Fitzpiers, now very much my partner in crime, tossed me a length of coarse agricultural rope, the likes of which restrain livestock in the stockyard.

'You had better secure her tightly, Miss Crowsettle. This little whore has a reputation for sweet-talking herself out of impossible situations. You would have us believe you are indestructible, Lady Melcombe Regis. Is that not true?'

'Lady Melcombe Regis? Tell me, Emma. Tell me, *Miss Chetnole*. I think Miss Fitzpiers speaks the truth. You have deceived me, Lady Persephone has deceived me. She is no more your mistress than I am your lover.'

She nodded but smiled defiantly. 'You can protest until your heart is content, Charlotte. You might pull the wool over Miss Fitzpiers's blinkered eyes but you should remember this: she would not recognise the scent of semen even if her insipid lover shot his load down her throat. But both of *us* are parties to the pure and unblemished truth. You wanted to play the game but once you found the rules not to your liking you jumped ship, from a den of iniquity to a haven of insufferable virtue but it would not surprise me if you were unable – or should I say unwilling – to tell the difference. I recognise a fellow traveller. I am a fraud, you are a fraud and poor little Grace will have her heart broken in more ways than one. It's just a game, Charlotte, just a game.'

'Enough!' I shrieked but it sounded hoarse. She had dampened my fire and it was all I could do to muster a callous edge to my instructions. 'Enough! Do you hear!' But she had turned her face towards the oak tree I had led her to and offered no resistance when I fixed one end of the rope around her left wrist, looped it around the bough and tied the other around her right. Her uncovered flesh flinched as my hunting hands probed and explored without hindrance, clearing the ruffled hem of her chemise to allow a clear view of my goal.

She eased her thighs apart, tempting me, taunting me, knowing full well that Miss Fitzpiers's stare was fixed firmly upon me and any rash move on my part would reverse our roles. Even in the unbearable heat of noontide a swarm of goosepimples rose up from her unblemished skin.

'Come along, my dear love. Touch me, touch me where I will feel it the most, touch me until I am sore with longing and my succulent secretions begin to overflow. Touch me and taste with your lips.' Her voice was low, almost inaudible, but carried sufficient volume to reach Miss Fitzpiers's ever-alert senses. I had no option but to shut her up. I brought the birch down hard on Emma's taut buttocks.

She laughed. A shrill and harsh cackle that was infinitely more cruel than any verbal rebuke and far more cutting than the stroke I had just administered. I tried again, summoned up all the strength I thought I possessed but the blow left little more than a rosy tinge as evidence. 'Is that the best you can do?' she snarled through clenched teeth, as if I had let her down.

'Is that the best you can do, Miss Crowsettle?' asked Miss Fitzpiers, 'I am beginning to think you have been misleading me, that you have no intention of disciplining Lady Melcombe Regis in the manner she so clearly deserves. I wonder why. Is it, perhaps, that you are too fond of her? Perhaps a little over-fond? Perhaps unnaturally, unhealthily fond of her?'

She had turned menacing, prowling around the tree, poised to snatch the birch from me. 'Would you to like me to show you how it is done? I would have thought that yesterday's episode might have offered a perfect demonstration, even if you were on the receiving end. If you cannot bring yourself to punish her I will do the job myself. But you mark my words, young lady: if your reluctance compels me to do so you can rest assured you will be next, whatever the delicate state of your rump.'

It was not pretty, not compared to Miss Fitzpiers's elegant chastisement; if she was a pure thoroughbred I was a feral stray. It was as clumsy as it was brutal; a flurry of wild and poorly applied blows that I rained down upon her with barely a pause in between. I know not what motivated me to use such force, whether it was Emma's mockery or Miss Fitzpiers's continued misgivings but when the latter reached out to take charge I turned on her instinctively, waving the instrument of torture before her, threatening, a woman possessed. Terrified, she took two steps back and looked on with numbed gratification as I set about my business.

Within less than a minute Emma was screaming for mercy, her body bent into trying desperately – pathetically – to free herself from the ties that bound her. I might have taken leave of my senses but I was not so insanely distracted that I was unable to observe, thrilled and fascinated, the vicious reaction of her angry swollen flesh as the birch twigs cut into it with merciless intensity. The more she twisted in unbearable agony, the more she thrust her backside this way and that in order to avoid each excruciating cut, the harder I, intoxicated by my own cruelty, wielded the whip. I would thrash her to within an inch of her life, I told myself, as the willowy branches lashed the backs of her thighs and dug into her most intimate crevices. Her tortured behind had passed through several shades of pink and red to reach a dark distended hue. I widened the welts into weals and set about bruising every square inch of her behind.

I could see, from the corner of my eye, Miss Fitzpiers

creeping closer and closer but I merely assumed she was admiring my handiwork. But I was wrong, there was not at hint of praise in her voice as she suddenly threw herself between myself and my victim. 'Stop it! Stop it!' she cried but when I raised the birch to apply another stroke she retreated. The tempest immediately abated, I let my arm fall to my side and Emma's blood-curdling cries subsided into simpering sniffles. It was utterly unheard of for Miss Grace Fitzpiers, patron saint of cruel righteousness and scourge of unrepentant sinners, to grant mercy or spare suffering but there was method in her madness.

'Give me the birch,' she demanded, without explanation. 'And be quick about it! Tell her to put her skirts on.'

The balance of power between us was beginning to change: her undisputed authority was beginning to wane while my star was on the rise. Much as I wanted to obey her I had not quite completed my mission; the rite was not over and to break off now would be tantamount to heresy.

Freed from her bondage, Emma collapsed into an untidy heap at the foot of the great oak. Her eyes were wide open and brimming with pity. Much to Miss Fitzpiers's undisguised consternation, I would have none of it. Indeed, I took great pleasure in watching Emma squirm before me. I could have stood there all day relishing her indignity and shame.

'Kneel before me,' I commanded, taking the birch in both hands and running my fingers over its frayed bark. I wondered which had suffered more – the implement of torture or its victim.

She did as directed. The worst was over but she, of all people, realised that the spell was still in place.

There was only one way to break it. Keeping her head lowered and her eyes firmly on the ground she kissed the birch.

'Thank you, Miss Crowsettle. My gratitude knows no bounds. I shall be forever in your debt.'

She spoke with great sincerity; only a true kindred spirit would have understood the subtext and read between her lines. And I was beginning to understand – Lady P's ambiguous epistles, her elusive manner of speaking, Emma's own ever-changing personalities were all part of an elaborate performance in which what remained unsaid had a greater potency than anything mere words could express. Its beauty, grace and sophistication lay in subtlety and subterfuge. Its appeal lay in grand understatement and diffident gesture.

Emma's vote of thanks was genuine but her body language spoke to me with a greater volume. The moment I first encountered Lady Persephone I was awarded right of entry to a world in which give and take were dished out in equal measure. It was a world in which pain and pleasure, suffering and satisfaction were all part of the same complex equation, an equation only an elite and exclusive chosen few could resolve. It was an honour bestowed with an unspoken agreement that at some point I would be called upon to make payment in kind. Both Emma and I knew full well that that moment was nigh and that, notwithstanding my newfound addiction to Miss Grace Fitzpiers, my debt would be recalled imminently. For every action there must be an equal opposite reaction and, as sure as the sun would rise tomorrow, Emma would have her revenge.

Miss Fitzpiers could wait no longer. She grabbed the birch and, without removing my ribbon, threw it unceremoniously into the undergrowth whilst endeavouring to push Emma and myself out of sight – and perhaps out of mind – behind the hedge.

She was too late. The lean figure of Detective Inspector Lefebvre had already emerged from the shadows and was striding towards us, into the unforgiving light of midday.

I am quite convinced she did it deliberately. It was a challenge she could not resist and, like me, Emma was fast running out of invention. At some point in the near future we – me, Emma, Lady Persephone, each and every member of the Society of Sin – would exhaust experience and be forced to seek out pleasure in some other, as yet undiscovered, realm.

If that time had not yet come, Emma was becoming increasingly desperate. Exposing herself to the inspector was hardly worthy of a woman of her breeding, it was crude and unbecoming but from the look on Miss Fitzpiers's face it was clearly quite worth it.

She left nothing to the imagination, sitting against the tree, legs wide open revealing her chestnut-coloured forest of frizzled fur. Furthermore, with the inspector's arrival I had collapsed beside her in a vague attempt to protect her dignity. I failed miserably. She had deftly manoeuvred herself so that when I tried to break my fall I tumbled right into her lap, my mouth brushing against the swollen pinkness of her moistened labia. She thrust her pelvis towards me with such sudden force that the sugary sap dribbling from her deepest recesses oozed on to my lips. I could not resist one swift surreptitious taste and let my tongue explore the dew-doused cavity she opened up to me.

I know not what Inspector Lefebvre made of our unfortunate contretemps. It lasted no more than a minute, for Miss Fitzpiers struck out with her palm and caught Emma full in the face. She leapt to her feet, gathered her skirts and fled into the woods making no attempt to conceal her crimson rear. The policeman reached into his jacket and took out a notebook into which he scribbled a short observation. And then, tipping his hat, he was gone.

14

My dearest Charlotte
Do you know what they used to tell me when I was a little girl? Day in, day out, every time I expressed a desire or ambition?

'Good things come to those who wait.'

What utter tosh and balderdash. And then they told me that patience is a virtue to be respected and upheld but when I replied that I preferred vice to virtue my father beat me and my mother locked me in my room for a week. Let me warn you, my dear Charlotte; that was a lesson well learnt. Those who procrastinate, postpone or generally drag their feet are not welcome in my company and as for those who keep me waiting – woe betide them.

Today is the day, the longest day. I hope you are fully prepared, I hope you will not keep me waiting. Another word of warning, I do not expect to have to come looking for you. I have hired hands covering every road into and out of Chilcombe Bredy and a price on your chaperone's head. It would give me great pleasure to pay out.

Well, well, well. What a mess you have made of my servant's behind; you have certainly given her what for. I have half a mind to reconsider her conditions of employment and insist upon corporal punishment but Emma already enjoys enough pleasure at my expense! She is a glutton for punishment. I wonder, come midnight, whether we shall be able to say the same of Miss Charlotte Crowsettle?

She is not, of course, my servant but I am surprised it took Miss Grace Fitzpiers to expose Lady Melcombe Regis as a charlatan and fraud. No doubt she has done her best to blacken my character as well. I care not a jot whether you heed her advice, I expect Inspector Lefebvre to exonerate me. You might want to ask her: Who are her witnesses? Where is the evidence? Perhaps she is not yet aware that I have had them silenced or destroyed.

As I said, I cannot afford to wait.

Until tomorrow, my sweet

P

I had expected a rapid and irretrievable fall from disgrace; I had expected to feel once more the full force of her rage or, worse still, to be excluded from her immediate coterie but when Miss Fitzpiers finally returned, still flustered, late in the afternoon, she said nothing about the farcical events that had taken place earlier. In fact, she said next to nothing all evening and set me to reading the Bible at the back of the sitting room, as far from the window as possible. She sat herself at my father's desk, forehead furrowed, writing furiously, only occasionally looking up to ensure my concentration was fixed on the task in hand. The sun had not yet set when she despatched me to bed, a pointless exercise as curiosity had got the better of me and I felt so very far from sleep.

Miss Fitzpiers remained awake all evening, still scribbling away, past midnight and into the small hours of the morning. With each chime of the church clock I crept along the landing, down the stairs and peeped through the gap of the half-open door. She was too engrossed in her writing to notice me and, eventually, I became sufficiently reckless to remain there for more than half an hour; watching her, plotting, immersing myself in anticipation. Lady P was quite right; patience is for the foolish and the faint of heart.

I had worried that my Sunday best might not have met with Miss Fitzpiers's approval. I need not have for when I finally fell into sleep Miss Fitzpiers looked in on me and hung from the door a quite stunning visiting dress, bedecked with ribbons and bows and the most elegant of bustles that would not have looked out of place in Lady Persephone's wardrobe. The black silk shimmered in the early-morning shafts of sun that burst through the windows and layered the wooden floor with a thick veneer of blinding light. The cut was perfect, taking my gaunt and undernourished frame and, with the aid of a stiff and heavy-boned corset, squeezed a little here, pinched a little there, producing a shape most women would have sold their soul for.

Miss Fitzpiers disturbed my reverie before the mirror and, disapproving of my vanity, took my arm and frogmarched me down the stairs. But her power had dissipated. She had marched into the Bride Valley with the intention of usurping Lady Persephone from her throne but her reign had proved to be ephemeral. I was her only triumph, a short-lived prize about to betray the very sovereign who won her. She no longer held me in a thrall of fear.

It was but a short stroll to the Church of St Ethelburga but one which Miss Fitzpiers extended to take in almost every street in the village. She had intended, I think, to parade me before the populace like a trophy, a tamed warrior turned into her slave and, although they came out of their shacks and hovels to gawp and gaze, it was not with the admiration and respect she so fervently desired. News of the Reverend Dr Lytton Cheney's latest misdemeanour had spread rapidly and when we finally reached the porch we were greeted not by Miss Fitzpiers's quick-tempered fiancé but the considerably more mild-mannered Canon Barrington Merryfield. As my chaperone paused to exchange pleasantries with the locum I allowed my thoughts and my eyes to drift towards the chase and Chilcombe Lacey. From my vantage point I could just make out the balustrade, the thick, squat, ornate columns that lined its rooftop. From that direction, all seemed silent; a languid, indolent stillness as Lady Persephone and her guests recovered from the excesses of the night before and prepared for those of the evening to come.

But Emma, still smarting from the previous day's discipline, was not content. On the contrary, scuttling around, cleaning, scrubbing and removing the detritus of hedonism, she was deeply upset at her lot, angered by her mistress's treatment of her and confused by my eagerness to thrash her. She considered herself a Cinderella and resolved to exact her revenge. After serving breakfast she had made her excuses and taken off in the direction of my father's cottage, waiting until she was out of sight before diverting to the vicarage.

Though doing my best to appear alert and attentive, I sat through the service unmoved, the vicar's drone at times almost lulling me to sleep. I was tired, weary to the point of exhaustion and the incessant heat sapped every last ounce of my energy but the end was now in sight, it was just a matter of time. Miss Fitzpiers kept her ears on the sermon but her eyes on me. I would, from time to time and quite deliberately, shuffle on the unforgiving pew so that the crisp rustle of satin and taffeta on rough wood drew from her a withering, censorious stare. Her patience finally snapped when, driven to distraction by my restless fidgeting, she took my hand, slipped off the glove and, to my immense surprise, struck my outstretched palm several times in quick succession with a small leather tawse she had secreted in her handbag.

So, she had not lost all her magic; not for nothing had she acquired a reputation as an imaginative but effective disciplinarian. The sharp pain soon receded but the shame would stay for many hours yet. We were sitting towards the rear of the chapel and every face had turned when they heard the crack of leather on uncovered flesh. While parents looked on approvingly, pleased that my comeuppance had been delivered in public the faces of their children expressed the very same sense of dreadful trepidation that permeated through my veins when I was in the presence of Miss Grace Fitzpiers. They had my pity. Though each lived under a similar reign of terror as that recently imposed on myself, none would have experienced that delectable frisson of apprehension that manifested itself whenever she was near.

Had the Reverend Dr Lytton Cheney not been regrettably detained in Dorchester gaol, had he been able to assume his rightful place before his adoring congregation, I think Miss Fitzpiers would not have lacked the temerity to march me to the altar and demanded the good pastor himself administer a very public chastising. I had no doubt that, should my audacious plan fail to materialise, I would be subjected to another thrashing before the day was done.

How did I fail to notice Emma dashing across the vicarage lawn? Was I too wrapped up in my reverie?

As we left the church the vicar uttered a swift

farewell as his housekeeper passed him a written note. He apologised for having to leave us at such short notice, but he had an urgent visitor to attend to.

Morning passed into afternoon and the sun beat down without mercy, her heat unbearably stifling and sultry. Miss Fitzpiers and I took drinks on the lawn and, whilst I was restricted to a small bottle of ginger ale, she permitted herself a sherry. She was instructing me as to the correct behaviour a young lady should display. I was listening intently, there was still something vaguely appealing in her philosophy, something about a creed that demanded total obedience I found fatally attractive; *la belle dame sans merci*.

But the heat and the sherry went straight to her head, not least because every time I refilled her glass – as instructed – I laced it with a drop or two of the tasteless but treacherously potent concoction María Inés de la Cruz had bequeathed me. I did not have to wait long for the medicine to take effect; Miss Fitzpiers's stern lecturing soon became a rambling, intrusive examination of my morals which, with each fresh glass of sherry, became increasingly voyeuristic. She had begun to lose control. When she rose to attend to her ablutions she let slip from her jacket pocket a letter from my father, clearly addressed to me. The moment her back was turned I tore the envelope open.

The Royal Clarence Hotel
Exeter
22 June 1876

My dear Charlie
  What have I done? What terrible mistake have I made? To have left you in the care of a harridan, a virago whose only pleasure in life comes from inflicting pain. Will you ever be able to bring yourself to

forgive me? I would not blame you for never speaking to me again. I am about to take my leave of Professor Walditch and return home immediately. We are only halfway through our revisions but I have been such a fool to put pleasure before duty and Samuel will have to do without me. I am sure he will understand.

I have little time to go into detail; my coach is about to leave and I have not yet put away my rocks and stones. Suffice to say that since I took leave of Chilcombe Bredy without even saying farewell to my one and only daughter my heart has been troubled, though I could not, for the life of me, fathom why. My mood was hardly lightened by a casual glance at the Western Gazette which mentioned that our good friend Dr Lytton Cheney, the vicar of Chilcombe Bredy, had been apprehended by the Weymouth Constabulary for assaulting a young woman and accusing her of harlotry. It is not, I gather, the first time his puritanical streak has landed him in trouble.

I have just received an urgent telegram from my good friend Detective Inspector Lefebvre; you may remember that it was on his recommendation that I employed the services of Miss Grace Fitzpiers as your chaperone. It is a rather scrambled message, composed in a hurry and I confess that I cannot quite make head or tail of it. It seems that Miss Fitzpiers, far from being a paragon of Christian virtue, has been expelled from the Tabernacle Ministry in Dorchester for excessive cruelty. This, I should add, from a church which firmly believes that sparing the rod spoils the child. Furthermore, I understand that the inspector, acting on recent information, has himself witnessed such acts, although he does not elaborate sufficiently for me to make any more of his account.

It disturbs me all the more, not knowing the exact nature of events.

The long and short of it, dear Charlie, is that he has asked me to meet him tomorrow evening at seven o'clock in the church porch. That is all he said; the plot ever thickens.

I trust this letter will arrive before I do. I hope it is not intercepted by Miss Fitzpiers for it is now perfectly clear that the woman is not to be trusted. Please, take care; do not, at all costs, do anything that might provoke her.

I must go. Until tomorrow

Your ever loving father

It was as if nothing mattered any more, as if every law that governed polite society had been twisted and distorted until bent out of shape. Even that which we hold most sacred and divine: natural law itself. Miss Fitzpiers was close beside me, mouthing the silent words, unable to comprehend the import of my father's concern. However much she recognised her own cruelty, she did not, could not, perceive it as wicked. She did not consider herself a martinet and she could not understand those who criticised her ways. She was, in short, a despot, but a despot overwhelmed with the desire to love and be loved.

Sainthood, I would surmise, had never been her forte, however hard she aspired to piety. It was not that heaven had forsaken her, rather that she, or rather María Inés de la Cruz's most efficacious medication, had split wide open the narrow horizons of her universe and found her world irretrievably wanting.

The church clock chimed four. I suggested to the now almost incoherent Miss Fitzpiers that we take a walk in the meadows that bordered the translucent chalk waters of the River Bride. She nodded her agreement, her eyelids were heavy with the illicit, undreamt dreams of her formative years, and we set off in the direction of Chilcombe Lacey.

Though the village was deserted, the scent of freshly mown grass still lingered in the air. My father's apple trees, each surrounded by a lovingly tended flower bed were still in full blossom. A thick impenetrable haze shimmered and flickered with such intensity that it drained the parched grass to a bleached insipid yellow. The whole valley seemed to lie under a self-imposed siege of silence. The sun was consuming everything, each and every one of us, the fragments and fractions of our erring souls.

The alluring meadows of the young River Bride, even in this driest of summers, were still lush and luxuriantly verdant, replete with relentless growth, still heady with fecundity and desire. We wandered together through the waist-high grasses and flowers, omniscient nature, blood red and predatory, hungry in tooth and in claw.

By their soft gliding waters she lay down and wept. I laid down my arms. My resistance was breached; lulled into a deep and delicious sleep, I dreamt of nectar, of wandering into dark impenetrable forests and drinking from their fragrant and fast-flowing streams.

Or was it a nightmare?

I woke, hot and dishevelled, clothes twisted around my sweat-soaked body, Miss Fitzpiers's face hovering directly above me. I made to scream but no sound came. She pressed her wet palm hard against my mouth, stifling my cry. Although still under the influence of the potion, her lethargy had evaporated into the soft and sultry ether and she was overcome, now, by an insatiable yearning. Thus far, my machinations had proceeded according to plan but this woman, who introduced me to the pleasure of pain, having awakened a previously unknown lust, was about to cast her spanner into the works.

The years of subjugation and self-denial her faith had instilled in her at once unloosed and liberated, like a torrent of molten lava that burns all in its wake.

'And you are the cause,' she hissed, racked by emotions she could not comprehend. 'You, of all people, bear sole responsibility for my freedom. On you I shall wreak my revenge.'

Like a satyr she came on to me, a poor little wood nymph trapped in her shady bower. Fed by the fear in my eyes she poured herself into and over me; her rich anger, her fragile ice-cold indifference, her savage beauty had passed into madness.

But it was too late. Like a *conquistadora* in search of gold, like an Eve in search of forbidden fruit, she wreaked havoc on every inch of my body which, despite my protestations, promptly surrendered before her advance. Not even the fiercest Romany curse or the most obscene blasphemy would discourage her. I tried to fight back but she caught the wrists of my flailing arms and, with one hand, pinned them behind me.

Her lips locked into mine, our tongues tied themselves into knots that might never unloose themselves. I swear she would have suffocated me had she not finally stumbled upon those previously unknown provinces where, doused and drenched in her very own sticky sap, she let out a cry so loud and shrill that it must surely have pierced the heavens. So implacable was her determination to satiate herself, so exhilarating was my fear of that self-same infernal desire that neither of us noticed Emma passing by on her way back to Chilcombe Lacey, nor her loitering behind the wall when she came across this most unlikely and unexpected discovery. Oh, to have seen the smile that passed over her face.

We lay together in silence – she drained and exhausted, myself in a state of shock – until the sun began to sink behind the hills, oblivious to events unravelling in the valley around us. Determined to avenge herself on the two women who had slighted her, Emma had returned to Chilcombe Lacey to inform her mistress not only of my whereabouts but also, in all its explicit vulgarity, of what gross activities Miss Grace Fitzpiers and I had been indulging ourselves in.

For all her broad-mindedness, Lady P was, still is, a proud and haughty woman; when crossed she becomes a formidable foe, a woman for whom disloyalty is strictly taboo. Who on earth can blame her if she did not, at first, believe Emma's news? She slapped her hard across the face, sent her reeling across the floor and accused her of spreading impossible and treacherous rumours. But it did not take long for the maid to convince her otherwise, another unconventional display of her devotion, on her knees before her mistress's taut upright frame. The minute she was done Lady P became consumed by a jealous and violent rage. I had been reserved for her pleasure and her pleasure alone, that I should choose to fritter away the ripened fruit of my lusts on a mere governess infuriated her all the more. It was an unwritten rule as sacrosanct as the Ten Commandments: nobody, but nobody, snubbed Lady P and remained unscathed.

At the very moment I stirred and emerged from my fragrant trance, Lady P was resolving to deal with me.

She called to her side her closest allies – Emma, Samantha Poorton and María Inés de la Cruz. The Society of Sin would indeed convene to celebrate its first anniversary, but the nature of the festivities would be radically changed.

Hand in hand we ambled, disjointed and dreamlike, towards Chilcombe Lacey. In the crepuscular light and half-shadows, my countenance took on a fearful hue. Far from being repulsed by Miss Fitzpiers's abrupt turn of character, her demented debauchery spurred me to a greater greed and the desire to sate it upon Lady P and Lady P alone.

As to what happened next I am not proud, but Miss Fitzpiers had become surplus to my requirements and had to be dealt with as effectively. Given these circumstances, what would Lady P's reaction be? I had asked myself the question over and over whilst waiting for my victim to become intoxicated. I had come prepared. Mrs Bexington's breadknife was lying on the kitchen table and I seized it by impulse, not thinking for a moment that I might be foolish enough to use it. I feigned to embrace her but as soon as she responded, closed her eyes and parted her lips to receive me, I dug the blade into her ribs. Having duped and then drugged Miss Fitzpiers, I had intended to incarcerate her in Chilcombe Lacey's walled garden before making a stunning entrance to the sabbat.

They say that, given time, victims turn into their captors, that constant exposure to deprivation and violence eventually drains them of all the pity they ever possessed. So it was with me – I was becoming a watered-down reproduction of Lady Persephone, devoid of love and humanity. Miss Fitzpiers's bewildered confusion would have moved a woman of greater empathy.

'W – What are you doing? Are you going to kill me? Why do you hate me so much?' Her voice was quivering with fear, her eyes blinded by confusion.

'And why would I want to squander any more of my precious energy on a wastrel like you, Grace Fitzpiers? Let us be honest with one another, you are nothing more than a jumped-up little whore. I have had my fill, you are quite disposable. I have a goddess to serve.'

'But, Charlotte, you do not understand. I have seen the light, you have converted me. I am your Saul on my road to Damascus. You don't understand. I love you, Charlotte, I love . . .'

Enough! Too much! I could not bear to hear another word of her pathetic pleading. If I had listened a moment longer even my stone-cold heart might have melted into clemency. Love? I would not allow myself to be held hostage to such puerile emotions.

I bound and gagged her. I left her helpless in the greenhouse.

15

Night was closing in on the Bride Valley with the silent sophistication of a hawk in pursuit of her prey. The cerise skies leeward of the Chase were still clear but from the sea crept a thick fret, languid and malevolent. From the far distance I could make out the comforting sounds of the countryside as it moved effortlessly from day into evening. The sharp thud of an axe on wood, the thin croak of the roding woodcock and the bawl of a child reluctantly called to bed. But then the mist enveloped all and muffled every movement.

The Society of Sin had, I supposed, already convened so, consigning the memory of Miss Grace Fitzpiers to history and experience, I made my way through the thickening fog towards the house, navigating by instinct rather than design. I knew the grounds well; I knew where they would congregate to glut themselves on wine and opium before setting out on their task. At least, that is what I had assumed but arrogance had got the better of me, I had become complacent.

I meandered aimlessly and erratically, expecting, at every turn of step, to come face to face with my mentor. They would greet me with open arms, the prodigal daughter returned from exile and though I would feign contrition I would not be required to atone for my misdemeanours. Had I not, I would tell them, conquered our nemesis? Had I not sacrificed myself at her hands, suffered her punishment in the cause of all that was wicked?

At last! It was all becoming clear, a prophecy come true. I was a martyr, the chosen one. I was their messiah, they were my disciples with whom I would do as I pleased.

That, at least, was the theory. In practice I was a rebellious child in league with the enemy, a mutineer. They came in search of me and I only felt their presence when they were near, the eerie glow of their lighted torches, a silent angry mob in pursuit of their prey. I was no fugitive; I marched proudly into their arms. Then, and only then, could I make out the hatred in their eyes. Fuelled by alcohol and Lady P's rousing rhetoric, they immediately closed ranks and surrounded me. When would I ever learn? I had walked, without thinking, right into her trap. One swift glance at her ladyship told me I had made an awful mistake having committed, in her eyes, the most heinous and unpardonable crime.

For the first time that summer I was overwhelmed by a genuine sense of terror, a sense that my very own life might be in danger. Lady P, with Emma at her side, was dressed from head to toe in black but her silver, gold and diamonds flashed ominously in the firelight. Her comrades closed in, menacing, but they need not have bothered. I still had my pride. I neither backed away nor pleaded for mercy. I knelt at the feet of my patroness.

'At least you had the courage to return. I never doubted your integrity but there are those here that did. You have at least proved them wrong but that is the least of your concerns.' As smooth as velvet, silver tongued, her voice was soft and persuasive. It would have taken a woman of extraordinary fortitude to resist her. I was not such a woman.

'I am sorry, your ladyship. Whatever I have done to offend you, I humbly beseech your pardon.'

'You are sorry, child! Sorry! Is that the best you can do?' She rocked with contemptuous laughter, a cackle so harsh it surprised even her closest friends. It seemed to echo around the hills and return to the valley with added malevolence.

'Words alone cannot save you now. Confess. Tell us everything. Supplicate yourself, beg for a just chastisement. If we are sufficiently entertained I might find it in my heart to be less severe in my treatment of you.'

'I do not ask for leniency, only justice.'

'Leniency? Justice? They are not words in my vocabulary, dear Charlotte. I am judge, jury and executioner and I shall do as I wish. Your personal welfare is no longer my concern.'

It was evident that Lady P was in no mood for games and that she had no intention of sparing me. Pleasure had been removed from the equation, at least on the part of her victim. I was perfectly aware that I would not be the first to pay the ultimate sacrifice; a skilled and efficient practitioner with friends in high places, she had already taken care of her family and survived the ensuing investigation.

So I told them my tale, from beginning to end, from the moment I left Chilcombe Lacey against Lady P's express wishes to the moment I laced Miss Fitzpiers's sherry with María Inés de la Cruz's Aztec sedative. They sat and listened, diligently at first but then with rising disbelief. Warming to my theme I spared them no explicit detail and embellished some of the less lurid incidents. As my story reached its end, I had them all enthralled, their mouths watered, they licked their lips and their eyes rolled wildly. I think I might have won them over, even Emma and Lady P, had I not omitted two crucial events. The first, Miss Fitzpiers's vicious act of seduction in the meadow, which unbeknownst to me Emma had witnessed. The second, the details of her present whereabouts. I was quite prepared to accept whatever chastisement Lady P sought fit to administer for I would suffer to point of death at her hands. They were like a pack of wolves baying for blood; God only knows what they would do with Miss Fitzpiers were they to set their lecherous hands on her.

'Oh Charlotte! If only you knew how much you are tearing my heart in two.' Lady P brushed her hair from her face with the back of her hand, her voice so laden with pathos I thought she might fall into a swoon. Maria Inés de la Cruz was at her side, regarding me intensely. She was intrigued, fascinated, in all her travels she had not yet encountered the likes of myself and Miss Grace Fitzpiers. Her arm tightened around Lady P's waist, her nails dug into her flesh.

'Is your memory playing tricks with you, Charlotte? You seem to have forgotten a vitally important episode. Allow me to remind you. How much did you enjoy dallying in the meadows with your erstwhile lover or, should I say, Miss Fitzpiers?'

The gathered mob paused in anticipation. Addressing her audience like a judge before a condemned convict, Lady P continued, 'Emma stood watching you both for a full ten minutes. She might well have come to your aid had you not so callously betrayed her at the instruction of your chaperone. She is no more than a vulgar little charlatan, common as muck; you, however, are an altogether different proposition, not least because ... because...' She paused. A murmur of surprise passed through the throng. No one recalled Lady P hesitating before. 'Because I do, indeed, love you. I love you very much indeed.'

There was a collective gasp of horror. Tears welled in the corner of my eye and despondency was writ large on her face.

'But love is a listless child, languid, impotent and programmed to decay slowly without adding to the ever-dwindling list of hidden pleasures. I cannot afford to let romance defeat retribution and revenge. I cannot even allow you the satisfaction of meeting your end at my hands; that is to be Emma's privilege. We have planned an elaborate and appropriate demise for you but first we must locate your accomplice.'

I refused to tell them, not only because I was reluctant to reveal her whereabouts but because I sensed myself wandering, eyes wide open, right into paradise. Her words were like honeydew, molten lava, the water of life. I had only to push her a little closer to the edge before she would explode like dynamite and blow my body and my mind into a million tiny shiny pieces.

'Tell me, Charlotte. I cannot be held responsible for my actions – or those of my servant or, should I say, Lady Melcombe Regis.'

Emma had unloosened her belt and, expecting a beating, I closed my eyes, lay back and waited for the blows to land. But they never materialised and I jumped with a start as Emma's long blue-blooded talons eased their way through my petticoats and, whilst Lady P held me tight, prodded and poked until my lamentations indicated she had found her treasure trove.

I think, in retrospect, I might have preferred abject pain to the insufferable pleasure she inflicted upon me. She tugged and teased until I was sore but still I begged her not to stop. With sublime dexterity she dragged me closer and closer to the abyss but each and every time I stood staring into that blessed eternity she withdrew her damp fingers and left me gasping for more. She stirred me into a frenzy, submitted me to the most prolonged, excruciating and exquisite torture I am certain I shall ever experience, brought me relentlessly to the point of orgasm before withdrawing her delving fingertips. She stroked and scoured, examined every moist declivity, engaged upon a quest for the answer to the ultimate question until I passed out of the known universe into the bounds of infinity. I could take no more, conceded defeat. 'She's in the walled garden,' I cried, at which point Emma finally dragged me into delirium and granted me relief. I screamed and passed out.

When I regained consciousness I found myself lying beside Miss Fitzpiers, both of us naked and drenched in aromatic oils, before a roaring fire. An ethereal mist had settled over the grounds of Chilcombe Lacey, mixing with smoke to form a thick impenetrable curtain that shut us off from the rest of the world. In our lost little corner of rural England, under the shadow of the chase, the Society of Sin had become that which, since its very inception, it had sought to be. A tribe of archaic and antediluvian women dedicated to the realms of the senses.

Lady P and María Inés de la Cruz were hunched together over the flames: the former holding a large wooden spoon with which she was stirring a thick steaming broth; the latter letting drop into it a succession of small berries, dark red, bloodlike.

'Tlaxochimaco, the Scarlet Papaya. I do not believe such a plant exists in England, perhaps that is just as well.' María was lovingly examining the last berry. "'So enticing, so perfect, demanding to be eaten. But so lethal, too. I have often wanted . . . just to try it, maybe. Like forbidden fruit.' She opened her mouth and placed the bulbous fruit on her lips. For a moment I honestly thought she was going to imbibe but instead she tossed it high into the air, towards Lady P. 'I do not trust myself to handle them, Percy. I am almost jealous of your dear Charlotte.'

The scent of freshly peeled papaya filtered across the lawn, mingled with the scent of fragrant labia, dripping with sweat, of my swollen clitoris upon which Miss Fitzpiers had so recently sucked hard.

The scent of scarlet papaya. Its pungent aroma brought back to me those heady days of summer when barely a day passed by without my having to lie back on my bed and relieve myself. I thought I had seen everything, Lady P made me think again.

The Society of Sin had gathered round once more, hemmed us both in. The liquor was poured into a golden chalice which Lady P raised high and passed around the congregation for their blessing. I watched each slender hand take the cup, trembling, as if it were aflame, then hand it on quickly to her neighbour until it was finally returned to the high priestess.

'If thy mistress some rich anger shows, emprison her soft hand, and let her rave, and feed deep, deep upon her peerless eyes.'

Her eyes were closed, she repeated from memory but with such intensity that they ceased to be the words of a poet and belonged to her alone. She offered me the chalice and with it one last chance to reprieve myself. 'If you are able to resist the potion,' she whispered, 'your life will be spared and Miss Fitzpiers shall walk free.'

It was a hollow gesture. Both Lady P and I knew full well that to drink would bring upon us indescribable ecstasy followed by almost certain death. But she goaded me on:

She dwells with Beauty--Beauty that must die;
And Joy, whose hand is ever at his lips
Bidding adieu; and aching Pleasure nigh,
Turning to poison while the bee-mouth sips:
Ay, in the very temple of Delight
Veil'd Melancholy has her sovran shrine,
Though seen of none save she whose strenuous tongue
Can burst Joy's grape against her palate fine;
Her soul shalt taste the sadness of her might,
And be among her cloudy trophies hung.

The broth bubbled beneath my twitching nostrils; I drank. The delicate juices went straight to my head, fired my heart and set the earth alight beneath my feet. I twisted and spun like a dervish, picked a barb from the blackthorn and thrust it deep into my flesh, an arrow of desire. The blood flowed and flooded the forest, bringing love, light and life, where there was once only death and decay.

My last memory, etched forever in my mind: Lady P advancing, bearing down upon my naked body, whilst Grace Fitzpiers clutched my hand, cursing, demanding she leave us be. But my mistress was wielding the glowing brand and my uncovered flesh was drawn to it like a magnet. She held it for a while immediately under my gaze and watched the whites of my eyes widen and fill with fear. She tested me, taunted me, questioning my mettle, accusing me of being as weak as my chaperone. I could wait no longer. 'I am ready,' I cried then felt the sizzling relief of fire scorching my skin.

And so she crowned me, her sovereign queen, the last ever member of the Society of Sin.

Visit the Black Lace website at
www.blacklace-books.co.uk

FIND OUT THE LATEST INFORMATION AND TAKE
ADVANTAGE OF OUR FANTASTIC FREE BOOK OFFER!
ALSO VISIT THE SITE FOR . . .

- All Black Lace titles currently available
  and how to order online
- Great new offers
- Writers' guidelines
- Author interviews
- An erotica newsletter
- Features
- Cool links

BLACK LACE — THE LEADING IMPRINT
OF WOMEN'S SEXY FICTION

TAKING YOUR EROTIC READING
PLEASURE TO NEW HORIZONS

LOOK OUT FOR THE ALL-NEW BLACK LACE BOOKS – AVAILABLE NOW!

All books priced £7.99 in the UK. Please note publication dates apply to the UK only. For other territories, please contact your retailer.

CONTINUUM
Portia Da Costa
ISBN 0 352 33120 8

When Joanna Darrell agrees to take a break from an office job that has begun to bore her, she takes her first step into a new continuum of strange experiences. She is introduced to people whose way of life revolves around the giving and receiving of enjoyable punishment, and she becomes intrigued enough to experiment. Drawn in by a chain of coincidences, like Alice in a decadent wonderland, she enters a parallel world of perversity and unusual pleasure.

Coming in January 2007

BURNING BRIGHT
Janine Ashbless
ISBN 978 0 352 34085 6

Two lovers, brought together by a forbidden passion, are on the run from their pasts. Veraine was once a commander in the Imperial army: Myrna was the divine priestess he seduced and stole from her desert temple. But, travelling through a jungle kingdom, they fall prey to slavers and are separated. Veraine is left for dead. Myrna is taken as a slave to the city of the Tiger Lords: inhuman tyrants with a taste for human flesh. There she must learn the tricks of survival in a cruel and exotic court where erotic desire is not the only animal passion.

Myrna still has faith that Veraine will find her. But Veraine, badly injured, has forgotten everything: his past, his lover, and even his own identity. As he undertakes a journey through a fevered landscape of lush promise and supernatural danger, he knows only one thing – that he must somehow find the unknown woman who holds the key to his soul.

STELLA DOES HOLLYWOOD
Stella Black
ISBN 978 0 352 33588 3

Stella Black has a 1969 Pontiac Firebird, a leopard-skin bra and a lot of attitude. Partying her way around Hollywood, she is discovered by Leon Lubrisky, the billionaire mogul of Pleasure Dome Inc. He persuades her to work for him and she soon becomes one of the most famous adult stars in America. Invited on chat shows, dating pop stars and hanging out with the Beverly Hills A-list. But dark forces are gathering and a political party is outraged and determined to destroy Stella any which way they can. Soon she finds herself in dangerous – and highly sexually charged – situations, where no one can rescue her.

Coming in February 2007

THE BOSS
Monica Belle
ISBN 978 0 352 34088 7

Felicity is a girl with two different sides to her character, each leading two very separate lives. There's Fizz – wild child, drummer in a retro punk band and car thief. And then there's Felicity – a quiet, polite, and ultra-efficient office worker. But, as her attractive, controlling boss takes an interest in her, she finds it hard to keep the two parts of her life separate.

Will being with Stephen mean choosing between personas and sacrificing so much of her life? But then, it also appears that Stephen has some very peculiar and addictive ideas about sex.

GOTHIC BLUE
Portia Da Costa
ISBN 978 0 352 33075 8

At an archduke's reception, a handsome young nobleman falls under the spell of a malevolent but irresistible sorceress. Two hundred years later, Belinda Seward also falls prey to sensual forces she can neither understand nor control. Stranded by a thunderstorm at a remote Gothic priory, Belinda and her boyfriend are drawn into an enclosed world of luxurious decadence and sexual alchemy. Their host is the courteous but melancholic André von Kastel; a beautiful aristocrat who mourns his lost love. He has plans for Belinda – plans that will take her into the realms of obsessive love and the erotic paranormal.

Black Lace Booklist

Information is correct at time of printing. To avoid disappointment, check availability before ordering. Go to www.blacklace-books.co.uk. All books are priced £6.99 unless another price is given.

BLACK LACE BOOKS WITH A CONTEMPORARY SETTING

☐ ON THE EDGE Laura Hamilton	ISBN 0 352 33534 3	£5.99
☐ THE TRANSFORMATION Natasha Rostova	ISBN 0 352 33311 1	
☐ SIN.NET Helena Ravenscroft	ISBN 0 352 33598 X	
☐ TWO WEEKS IN TANGIER Annabel Lee	ISBN 0 352 33599 8	
☐ SYMPHONY X Jasmine Stone	ISBN 0 352 33629 3	
☐ A SECRET PLACE Ella Broussard	ISBN 0 352 33307 3	
☐ GOING TOO FAR Laura Hamilton	ISBN 0 352 33657 9	
☐ RELEASE ME Suki Cunningham	ISBN 0 352 33671 4	
☐ SLAVE TO SUCCESS Kimberley Raines	ISBN 0 352 33687 0	
☐ SHADOWPLAY Portia Da Costa	ISBN 0 352 33313 8	
☐ ARIA APPASSIONATA Julie Hastings	ISBN 0 352 33056 2	
☐ A MULTITUDE OF SINS Kit Mason	ISBN 0 352 33737 0	
☐ COMING ROUND THE MOUNTAIN Tabitha Flyte	ISBN 0 352 33873 3	
☐ FEMININE WILES Karina Moore	ISBN 0 352 33235 2	
☐ MIXED SIGNALS Anna Clare	ISBN 0 352 33889 X	
☐ BLACK LIPSTICK KISSES Monica Belle	ISBN 0 352 33885 7	
☐ GOING DEEP Kimberly Dean	ISBN 0 352 33876 8	
☐ PACKING HEAT Karina Moore	ISBN 0 352 33356 1	
☐ MIXED DOUBLES Zoe le Verdier	ISBN 0 352 33312 X	
☐ UP TO NO GOOD Karen S. Smith	ISBN 0 352 33589 0	
☐ CLUB CRÈME Primula Bond	ISBN 0 352 33907 1	
☐ BONDED Fleur Reynolds	ISBN 0 352 33192 5	
☐ SWITCHING HANDS Alaine Hood	ISBN 0 352 33896 2	
☐ EDEN'S FLESH Robyn Russell	ISBN 0 352 33923 3	
☐ PEEP SHOW Mathilde Madden	ISBN 0 352 33924 1	£7.99
☐ RISKY BUSINESS Lisette Allen	ISBN 0 352 33280 8	£7.99
☐ CAMPAIGN HEAT Gabrielle Marcola	ISBN 0 352 33941 1	£7.99
☐ MS BEHAVIOUR Mini Lee	ISBN 0 352 33962 4	£7.99

BLACK LACE BOOKS WITH AN HISTORICAL SETTING

BLACK LACE ANTHOLOGIES

To find out the latest information about Black Lace titles, check out the website: www.blacklace-books.co.uk or send for a booklist with complete synopses by writing to:

> Black Lace Booklist, Virgin Books Ltd
> Thames Wharf Studios
> Rainville Road
> London W6 9HA

Please include an SAE of decent size. Please note only British stamps are valid.

Our privacy policy

We will not disclose information you supply us to any other parties. We will not disclose any information which identifies you personally to any person without your express consent.

From time to time we may send out information about Black Lace books and special offers. Please tick here if you do <u>not</u> wish to receive Black Lace information.   ❑

Please send me the books I have ticked above.

Name ....

Address ....

....

....

....

Post Code ....

Send to: Virgin Books Cash Sales, Thames Wharf Studios, Rainville Road, London W6 9HA.

US customers: for prices and details of how to order books for delivery by mail, call 888-330-8477.

Please enclose a cheque or postal order, made payable to Virgin Books Ltd, to the value of the books you have ordered plus postage and packing costs as follows:

UK and BFPO – £1.00 for the first book, 50p for each subsequent book.

Overseas (including Republic of Ireland) – £2.00 for the first book, £1.00 for each subsequent book.

If you would prefer to pay by VISA, ACCESS/MASTERCARD, DINERS CLUB, AMEX or SWITCH, please write your card number and expiry date here:

....

Signature ....

Please allow up to 28 days for delivery.